# And You Call Yourself a Christian:

*Still Divas Series Book One*

# And You Call Yourself a Christian:

## *Still Divas Series Book One*

*E.N. Joy*

*www.urbanbooks.net*

Urban Books, LLC
97 N 18th Street
Wyandanch, NY 11798

And You Call Yourself a Christian: Still Divas Series
Book One Copyright © 2012 E.N. Joy

ISBN 13: 978-1-62286-750-9
ISBN 10: 1-62286-750-5

First Mass Market Printing October 2016
First Trade Paperback Printing March 2012
Printed in the United States of America

10 9 8 7 6 5 4 3 2 1

*This is a work of fiction. Any references or similar-
ities to actual events, real people, living or dead, or
to real locales are intended to give the novel a sense
of reality. Any similarity in other names, characters,
places, and incidents is entirely coincidental.*

Distributed by Kensington Publishing Corp.
Submit Orders to:
Customer Service
400 Hahn Road
Westminster, MD 21157-4627
Phone: 1-800-733-3000
Fax: 1-800-659-2436

# Other Books by E.N. Joy

*Me, Myself and Him*

*She Who Finds A Husband*

*Been There, Prayed That*

*Love, Honor or Stray*

*Trying to Stay Saved*

*I Can Do Better All By Myself*

*Ordained by the Streets*

*Even Sinners Have Souls*
(Edited by E.N. Joy)

*Even Sinners Have Souls Too*
(Edited by E.N. Joy)

*Even Sinners Still Have Souls*
(Edited by E.N. Joy)

*The Secret Olivia Told Me*
(Children's book written under the name N. Joy)

# Dedication

Why, of course, this book is dedicated to you. Yeah, that's right; I'm talking to you. You with this book in your hand reading this very dedication. If it were not for you, what would be my purpose to even write? If it were not for you supporting what I do, I wouldn't even be able to continue to write. If it were not for you telling any and everybody about me and my work, this book might not have even been possible. Your support is what drives me. Knowing that you deemed my work worthy to invest time, which is priceless, to read it means more than you will ever know. These are two very, very small words to show the enormous gratitude I have for you, but here it goes anyway: Thank You. You are the wind beneath my literary wings. Now, turn the page and come fly with me . . .

# Acknowledgments

&middot; God, we did it again. There is nothing in this world I can even almost do without you.

My husband and four children, I can't thank you enough for dealing with me during my creative craziness. I owe you all so much for supporting and believing in me. Jesus, I hope this really pays off . . . It just has to.

# Prologue

It had to be the hottest day of the year in Malvonia, Ohio. It wasn't even noon yet, so Unique could only imagine how much hotter it was going to get throughout the day. As Unique drove her sister's car through the hood, she became even more motivated to earn that pink Cadillac every Mary Kay cosmetic representative dreamed about. She needed her own car; one with air . . . one with automatic windows. And the fact that as a result of pushing cosmetics, skin, and facial care products she could have one for free only sweetened the pot.

"Phew." All Unique could do right now was thank God that she wasn't still pregnant with the twins. Otherwise, this summer heat might have been unbearable.

She rubbed her hand across her forehead and looked in the backseat at her three sons. Her oldest, catching her glance at them in the rearview mirror, gave his mother a smile, and then went back to looking out of the window.

Her boys, ages five, six, and seven, squinted their eyes as the wind roared through the car. It looked as if they could hardly breathe from the pressure of every single window in the car being rolled down. But they didn't have any choice. Although the breeze was nothing but a hot wind, it was the best they had.

*I've got to do better for my boys*, Unique thought to herself, steering her eyes back on the road. Her entire purpose for not keeping her twin girls to raise was so that she'd have an opportunity to do better for her three boys. That's exactly what she was determined to do; better. That's why she'd been pushing Mary Kay products like dope boys pushed crack rocks. She was tired of living with her sister and her sister's two kids. She was appreciative of all her sister was doing for her, but it was fine time she began to do things for herself; by herself.

"Be who you want your kids to be," were words the pastor of New Day Temple of Faith had once preached during a sermon. As a matter of fact, the pastor had declared June 1 as "Be Who You Want Your Kids to Be Day." Unique, in celebrating the holiday, pledged, along with parents across the world, "Today, I, as a parent, commit to doing, saying, typing, texting, wearing, and thinking only things I would want my children to. I will not do, say, type, text, wear, or think things that I would not want my children to do. Today, I am going to be who I want my children to be. Today, my children will see me love, smile, read, help a complete stranger, and turn the other cheek. Today, my children will see me be who I want them to be."

Those words were embedded in Unique's mind. She was determined to be who she wanted her children to be. And what she didn't want them to be was teenage parents with a bunch of babies by a bunch of different babies' mamas.

That's who Unique had been; a project chick with a bunch of babies all with different daddies. That's who she was. She did not want that life for her children. Heck, she didn't want that life for herself.

After getting saved and joining New Day, she set out to be a changed woman. She did it for herself as much as she'd done it for the sake of her children. But being saved hadn't been all that she thought it would be. Once she got saved, she didn't instantaneously stop doing those things she'd done while in the world. She still kicked it every now and then with her girls. She still got her drink on and took a hit from a blunt every now and then. Under the influence, she even fornicated. And even though she'd engaged in those things after being saved, she was proud to say that she hadn't done those things for some time now; not since getting pregnant with the twins.

The twins; those two adorable little girls who were now being raised by another woman. It wasn't just any woman, though. It was Lorain, Unique's mother. Although Lorain wasn't the mother that had raised Unique, she was, in fact, her biological mother. This is something the two women had found out by fate only a couple of years ago.

Initially angry with Lorain for abandoning her like trash when she was just a newborn infant, Unique grew to accept the fact that having her biological mother in her life was a blessing. It was double the blessing considering when Unique popped up pregnant with what was her fourth and fifth child, Lorain didn't hesitate to offer raising the girls.

Unique's intentions had been to give the babies up for adoption to a complete stranger. She knew it would have been a hard thing to do, but she really didn't have a choice. She didn't have a place for the babies to stay. There were already seven people living in her sister's leased three-bedroom house with a finished basement. Of course, the basement was Unique and her boys' quarters. There was no way she could squeeze in room for two more. There was no way she was going to give birth to two newborn babies and have them living in somebody's basement.

Not only did she not have a roof to put over the babies' heads, she didn't have a car to drive them in either. She barely had transportation to get to and from the doctor's office for prenatal care herself, let alone having to take the babies to the doctors once they were born. If it wasn't for Lorain running her back and forth to her appointments, the twins might not have turned out as healthy as they did.

Not only did all those material things play a part in Unique's decision to give the babies up for adoption, but the fact that she wouldn't even be thirty years old yet with five babies played a part as well. How crazy would that look?

See, before she was saved, she wouldn't have thought that it looked crazy at all. Where she came from, it was the norm. Her mama had a bunch of babies with all different fathers. Her sisters too, along with every other chick who lived back at their old projects in Columbus, Ohio. But now that she was saved, in the church with those good old saints of God, there was no way she could continue such a pattern. That's why when Lorain came up with idea to not only adopt the twins herself, but to tell people that Unique was doing her a favor by carrying the children for her, Unique jumped on it.

"A surrogate," Unique had said approvingly. It didn't sound too believable at first to Unique. Did black women do that; have babies for each other? But at the end of the day, Unique concluded that being referred to as a surrogate was far better than being referred to as a ho any day.

That little white lie between Unique and Lorain kept a lot of the chatter down at the church about Unique's pregnancy; at first it did anyway. That was because everybody just thought that Unique and Lorain were close friends who had served as leaders of the Singles' Ministry together. But then, thanks to the church secretary's eavesdropping on Pastor's counseling sessions, the entire church eventually found out the two women's secret; that they were mother and daughter. Those New Day divas had no idea that Unique wasn't carrying Lorain's seed, but that she'd backslid and fornicated with one of her son's fathers. The result was her being knocked up.

"I can hear those church hens now," Unique had told Lorain as she began mocking some of the things they might have said about her at the church had they known the entire truth. "She got three babies already with three different baby daddies. She's livin' up in her sister's house on welfare with no car. Now she's about to have two more babies out of wedlock, no husband . . . And she calls herself a Christian. Humph."

No way; that last insult was like nails down a chalkboard to any Christian. No Christian took kindly to their Christianity being questioned. Thank God for Lorain, because Unique had not had to deal with that type of criticism from the church. Unique could also thank Lorain for hipping her to that Mary Kay stuff as well. A former representative herself, Lorain had invested in a start-up kit for Unique and had trained her on everything she'd learned over the years. Unique had gained quite the clientele, as Lorain had even turned over her client list to her.

Once again, Unique looked in the rearview mirror at her boys. She then mumbled under her breath, "Don't you worry, boys. Momma's going to be driving y'all around in that Cadillac before you know it."

Turning down a numbered street in the Linden area of Columbus, Ohio, Unique spotted the house she was looking for. Unfortunately, there were several cars parked directly in front of the house, so she had to park about three houses down.

"Where we at, Mommy?" Unique's youngest son asked her.

"Where are we at?" her oldest son corrected him.

"Yes, that's what I meant," the youngest son replied. "Where are we at?"

Unique looked over her shoulder and nodded toward her oldest son. "We're at your brother's daddy's job." Next, she looked at the olive-green double family home that sat in between a yellow and a pink one.

"His daddy works in a house?" the middle son asked with a puzzled look on his face. He chuckled and looked at his brother. "Man, yo' daddy work in a house. I thought people was just 'pose to live in a house."

"Yeah, well, some people have gotta do what they gotta do, son," Unique replied. She knew that better than anybody. Unique sighed as her eyes left the house, and she turned back around. "Yep. That's where he works all right." That's pretty much where all of her babies' daddies worked. Not all in that same house, but in ones similar to it. Unique knew that it was some Section 8 house that a young mother, like herself, was renting out to the neighborhood dope boys to sell dope out of. Her oldest son's father just happened to be one of those dope boys.

Refraining from correcting both his younger brother's and his mother's use of bad English, the oldest boy asked, "Oooh, then, can I go with you to see him?"

"Uh, no, baby," Unique stammered. The last thing she wanted to do was to take her son to some drug spot. The last thing she wanted to do was be there her own self. Her son's father hadn't answered or returned her phone calls all week, and he hadn't thrown her any cash toward the well-being of his son in a month. Unique was not having that. She needed every dime she could get to help with the care of her boys.

After finding herself pregnant a fourth time, she made a vow to do everything within her will to be an example to her children. There was no more blowing money on just any old thing. She was now saving her money. She had almost twenty-five hundred dollars tucked under her mattress that she refused to touch. All that was the money she'd made from her Mary Kay sells. Prior to selling Mary Kay, Unique had worked a short period of time for a catering company one of the women who used to go to her church owned. She spent that money on clothes for her and her kids, a couple pieces of jewelry for herself, and on eating out. She'd made a nice chunk of change too, with nothing to show for but "stuff." Like the prodigal son who spent up all of his inheritance, she was not going to make that same mistake twice. She was going to have something to show for her labor this time, and that something was going to be a house. Not a subsidized apartment somewhere or a Section 8 house, but a house with a mortgage note. That's what she wanted for her children. And one day, as part of her and Lorain's agreement, once the twins learned that she was their real mother, they'd have a nice place to come over and visit and play with their brothers.

That's why hunting her baby daddy down for his contribution in taking care of the life he contributed in making was so important now more than ever. Never mind she was about to clown and be the stereotypical ghetto girl. The baby mama from hell. Making sure the fathers of her children paid up and helped to support them used to be a nonchalant thing for Unique. She used to be cool with them throwing her a little somethin'-somethin' every now and then whenever they could or whenever they felt like it. A conversation with Lorain, though, helped her realize that that wasn't fair for the boys. They deserved better from both her and their daddy, and Unique was on a mission to make sure they got better.

Perhaps she was about to embarrass herself by clownin', if that is, in fact, what she had to do in order to get her oldest son's father to give her some child support money. Perhaps she was even about to embarrass him in front of his boys. None of that kept Unique from throwing that car in park and getting out of the car to head toward that dope house though. This was for her boys; it was all for them. That's what she kept reminding herself with every step she took. Anything that this resulted in would be all worth it. That's what Unique thought when she got out of the car anyway. *Better . . . I gotta do better for my boys.* But, oh, God, how things would take such a horrific turn for the worse. Would any of this have seemed worth it several hours later when Unique would hear the words, "I'm sorry, ma'am, but your sons are dead."

# Chapter One

"Church cost too much money," Unique's friend, Joelle, spat. "It's cheaper for me to go to the club. I mean, after all, all I gotta do is pay my cover charge to get up in the club. Heck, if it's ladies' night, and if I get there before eleven o'clock, I don't even have to do that. On top of that, as long as I'm looking fly, I dang sure won't have to worry about buying any drinks. You know them ballers up in there got me on that."

Unique shook her head as she chuckled. "Joe, you a mess."

"Don't even act like you don't know what I'm talking about. After all, you roped you three ballers. You had babies for 'em on top of that. I know dem fools be breaking you off something real properlike. The same way when they knocked you up you were eating for two, now dem dudes got to pay for two." Joe sounded so matter of fact, like Unique had run game on her sons' fathers and it was now paying off big time. That could have been the furthest thing from the truth.

"You wish it was all like that," Unique huffed. "Huh, who am I kidding? *I* wish it was all like that. But trust, sweetheart, if it was all like that, would I be living up in my sister's crib? Would I be at the bus stop whenever I have to go somewhere?"

Joelle thought for a moment. "Dang, I guess I never really looked at it that way." The enthusiasm and certainty that was initially in Joelle's voice faded. "But I know you got paid for real a couple months ago when you had them babies for that woman."

"It wasn't even like that," Unique told her friend from back in the day. Unique and Joelle had grown up in the same project in Columbus, Ohio. Joelle had always been Unique's partner in crime. Once Unique got saved, she didn't hang out with Joelle as much. But every now and then, Joelle would call her up and talk her into going out with her. And every now and then, Unique would give in to the pressure and temptation and go. She hadn't given in, in quite some time though. She hadn't given in since the time she ended up going to the club with Joelle, but leaving with her oldest son's father. That's also the time she ended up pregnant. That experience alone kept her far from the temptation of running the streets. It didn't matter how hard Joelle begged her, Unique had not accepted Joelle's invitations. But now the tables were turned as the two women talked on the phone. This time, it was Unique extending an invitation to Joelle, but not to go to the club.

"Anyway," Unique said, exasperation lacing her tone, "it's Friends and Family Day this Sunday at my church. Girl, just come on."

"No, thanks. Like I said, church costs too much. At the church my mother used to go to, we had to pay for everything. We had to pay on Sunday morning to get the Word. We had to pay at Bible Study. We had to pay at Vacation Bible School. That collection basket went around at every single church function. I mean, I understand about tithes and offerings, but do churches have to pass the collection plate around for every single function they have? Sometimes that's why I never went. On days I was broke, I was scared they were going to pass that collection plate around and I wouldn't have anything to put in it.

"Them preachers always talking about the church doors are always open, but so are their pockets. I mean, on Sunday I expect to have to break the Lord off something, but I gotta pay for Bible Study too? I gotta pay for Vacation Bible School? Really? Come, on, 'Nique, you know you have to admit yourself that that becomes too much."

"I know that's how it is at some churches, but not at New Day Temple of Faith, I promise you," Unique assured her friend. "Pastor only passes the plate around once, and that's on Sunday morning after you've been fed the Word. We don't take up collection at Bible Study or anything like that. There is, though, a tithe and offering box in the back of the church that people can give to anytime they want. But usually just the saints who are more mature in Christ utilize that; those who know what giving truly is about."

"So what you trying to say? That I'm not a giver?" Before Unique could answer, Joelle continued. "Because you *know* I have never had a problem paying your way into the club on the times we had to pay."

"Yeah, that's because you were the one who always made us run late so that we didn't get there until after eleven when there was a five-dollar cover charge."

Joelle paused for a minute. "Oooh, I guess you are right about that," she laughed.

"Yeah, I know I am," Unique chuckled. "But anyway, I'm not going to keep pressuring you about going to church with me. Just know that the invitation is open for any Sunday; not just Family and Friend's Day, okay?"

"All right, Momma. But let me get ready to get off this phone. I have to go get my ponytail sown in. DJ Dizzle My Nizzle is going to be on the turn tables tonight. You know all he play are rappers from the South, so it's gonna be gettin' crunked up in there. I can't even think about wearing my short bob. I'll sweat it out so bad and walk up out of that club looking like a Treasure Troll."

Both Unique and Joelle laughed so hard before Unique decided she needed to get off the phone too. "All right, girl, let me let you go. I told the boys I'd take them to see the twins today."

"Awww, y'all going to see Tiny and Toya," Joelle joked, knowing darn well that wasn't the babies' names.

"It's Victoria and Heaven," Unique said.

"I know, I know. I'm just messing with you, girl. Give them a kiss from their would-have-been godmother, okay?"

"Okay, crazy woman. Be safe out there tonight."

"I will, Momma. Love you. Deuces."

Unique hung up the phone and shook her head with a smile on her face while staring at it. Talking with Joelle always reminded her how far God had brought her and where He'd brought her from. Next, Unique looked up. "Lord, I know that by no means am I where I need to be in you. But by God, I thank you that I'm not where I used to be. A mighty long way, God; that's where you've brought me from; a mighty long way."

"Are you talking to God again?" Unique's middle son asked as he climbed up on the sofa bed she and her youngest son slept on. Her other two sons slept on an air mattress.

"Yes, baby," Unique replied, her eyes lighting up like they always did when she looked at her boys.

"You always talking to Him. Does He ever talk back?" He played with the button on his Spider-Man pajamas.

"As a matter of fact, He does, and right now, He's saying . . ." Unique changed her voice to a deep monotone, ". . . Unique, if those boys of yours don't hurry up and wash their face, brush their teeth, and get dressed, I want you to . . . I want you to . . ."

Unique's son sat there looking at her with the most serious look on his face ever. He was on the edge of his seat waiting to hear God's instructions to his mother.

"I want you to . . ." Unique began wriggling her fingers. ". . . tickle them to death." She began tickling her son so hard that tears formed in his eyes.

"Mommy, stop," he pleaded in between laughs. "Stop or you gonna make me pee on myself. Stop, Mommy. For real."

Unique gave in to her son's pleas. The last thing she wanted to do was to have to give him a bath and change her bedding.

After her son settled down from all his laughing he asked, "Mommy, did God really say that?"

"Say what?" her oldest son asked, entering the room with his youngest brother beside him. They were in their pajamas as well.

Both Unique and her middle son looked at each other knowingly. "Should we tell him?" Unique asked her middle son.

With a little giggle he said, "Uh-huh. Tell 'em what God said, Mommy."

By this time all three boys were sitting on the sofa bed. Unique looked at them and said, "God said . . ." She changed her voice again. "'Unique, if those boys of yours don't hurry up and wash their face, brush their teeth, and get dressed, I want you to . . ." Once again Unique began wriggling her fingers. "I want you to tickle them to death."

For the next few minutes Unique took turns tickling her sons until one actually did wet himself. Before she had gotten saved and had learned to control her temper through the direction of the Holy Spirit, Unique probably would have raised sand, fussed, and cursed for all the extra work her son's wetting on himself was about to cause her. She would have said some things that might have broken her boys' spirits and ruined their entire day. But now they all just made a task out of changing the bedding together. She even let the boys work the buttons on the washing machine, where they placed all the soiled laundry.

God had certainly helped to turn Unique's life around. The devil was waiting in the wings, though, to turn her life upside down.

# Chapter Two

"So even though our mommy had them in her belly," Unique's youngest son said to Lorain as he, his brothers, Unique, and Lorain stood in between the two cribs admiring the sleeping babies, "they are your babies now?"

"That's exactly right," Lorain said, bending down and kissing her grandson on the nose.

"And they are going to call you Mommy?"

"They already do," Lorain smiled. "Well, they say, 'Ma-Ma.'"

Staring from one baby to the next he then said, "So those little things are our aunties, and we're older than them?"

Both Unique and Lorain laughed.

"Enough with all the questions, son," Unique told him, rubbing him on top of his head. "Besides, we go through this every time you see the twins."

"I know." A sad look covered his face. "I guess I just wanted sisters and not aunties."

Unique sighed and looked up at Lorain.

"In due time," Lorain mouthed, referencing the fact that she and Unique agreed that they'd tell the boys the truth about the twins really being their sisters once they got old enough to understand the entire situation.

"Since the twins are asleep, can we go have ice cream now?" the middle boy asked.

"Sure," Lorain answered. "I just bought a brand-new bucket on sale at Kroger. Let's go."

After giving the babies another once-over, everyone left the nursery and headed to the kitchen. Before quite making it into the kitchen, the ringing doorbell stopped everyone's trek.

"Hold on, boys. Let me get the door real quick," Lorain said. She walked over to the door, and then looked out of the peephole to see who it was. Little hearts danced in her eyes as she opened the door. "Well, hello. You're early." She looked down at her watch. "About two hours early to be exact."

"I know," Nicholas said as he stood on the porch. "But when you said that Unique and the kids would be stopping by for a spell, I couldn't miss seeing those boys of mine."

Dr. Nicholas Wright was truly heaven-sent into Lorain's life, and no one could tell her otherwise. She'd met him at the hospital emergency room the day Unique was experiencing abnormal cramping. She was pregnant with what she thought was just one baby at the time. It was Dr. Wright who informed them that one baby had been covering the other and that Unique was carrying twins. That day, Lorain walked out of the hospital with not only the news that she would be raising two babies, but with a new man in her life as well.

"Mr. Nick, is that you?" the oldest boy called out.

Lorain opened the door wide so that the boys could get full view of the visitor standing on the doorstep.

"Mr. Nick!" all three boys cheered, and then rushed Nicholas. They practically knocked him down as arms flung around his legs and waist.

"Can you play me in a video game?" one called out.

"No, let's play some catch," another one suggested.

"Hey," Lorain pouted, slinging her hands on her hips. "I thought you wanted to have ice cream with Granny Lorain."

"That was before Mr. Nick showed up," the oldest boy told her.

"Yeah, we like Mr. Nick better than ice cream," another confirmed.

"Oh, boys," Nicholas said, almost speechless. "How about we go wear ourselves out throwing the football back and forth, and then we come in for some of that ice cream with Granny Lorain?" He looked up at Lorain and winked his eye at her.

She couldn't help but blush. There was something about those soft brown eyes of his that were on the verge of being hazel but not quite, that made her feel like . . . like . . . she hadn't been able to put those feelings in words. But it was a good feeling. That much she knew.

"Once again, Mr. Nick steals the show," Unique smiled.

"Hey there, Unique," Nicholas said to her. He reached out to hug her like he normally would have done, but the boys were still clinging to him.

"Will y'all get off of him and let the man breathe?" Unique said to the boys, who immediately obeyed.

"The football is right there by the door," Lorain pointed. "You boys take it easy on Mr. Nick, y'all hear me?"

"Yes, Granny Lorain," the boys chimed before grabbing the football and dragging Nicholas out the door.

"Yeah, boys, don't wear Mr. Nick out or anything," Unique said, even though they were no longer within earshot. She looked over at a beaming Lorain. "Leave that for Granny Lorain to do."

Realizing the comment Unique had just made, Lorain shooed her hand in Unique's direction. "Cut it out. You know darn well Granny Lorain is a Christian for real. The only thing wearing Mr. Nick out is his work schedule."

"Oh, come on, Mama Lorain." Unique had started calling Lorain Mama Lorain for the boys' sake. Sometimes in general conversation she would refer to both the woman who raised her as Mama, which confused the boys as to exactly who she was talking about. So she just started adding their names after the word "Mama" for clarity. "You mean to tell me that you have absolutely no idea about just how hot Doctor McHottie really is?"

"If my daughter is standing here asking me if my boyfriend and I have a sexual relationship going on, the answer is no," Lorain clarified as she sat down on the couch.

"Come on, you can tell me the truth." Unique plopped down next to Lorain in anticipation of getting the scoop. "I mean, you two have been seeing each other for well over a year. And you said yourself that he's not a practicing Christian like you."

"But he's getting there, and with no pressure from me, might I add," Lorain said proudly. "I've only invited him to church once; just to let him know that he was always welcome to come worship at New Day. It wasn't until three months after that that he actually took me up on the offer. And since then, he's visited New Day at least a dozen times. He'd probably come more regular if it wasn't for his work schedule. So like I said, Nicholas's work schedule might be wearing him out, but it certainly ain't me."

Unique stared at Lorain for a minute. "You are dead serious, aren't you? You haven't even thought about backsliding, have you?"

"Now, let's not go *that* far."

"Uh-huh, I *knew* it," Unique said with a look of victory on her face. "Ain't no fine doctor like Doctor Nicholas going to hang around all this time without having at least an appetizer."

Lorain put her hand up. "Now, let's not go *that* far either. We've done some kissing, a little rubbing, but that's about it. That was enough. As a matter of fact, that was too much." Lorain snapped her neck back and sucked her teeth. "And by the way, could somebody please tell me why I'm having this conversation with my twenty-five-year-old daughter?"

"Who would you rather be having this conversation with? Your sixty-something-year-old mother?" Unique laughed.

"Hmm. I guess you're right. But come to think of it, I'd rather not be having this conversation at all."

"Not even with Nicholas?"

"Obviously Nick and I have had the conversation by now. He knows I'm saving myself until marriage."

"Speaking of marriage, are you going to marry him? You said yourself when you two got together that he was looking for a wife, not a girlfriend. Well, you've been his girlfriend for quite some time now. So what's the deal? Tell that cat to put his money where his mouth is and bring on the ring."

Lorain remained peculiarly quiet. She fumbled around for something until she set her sights on the remote. She quickly picked it up and turned the television on.

After a moment of glaring at Lorain flick through channels like a man, Unique kindly took the remote from Lorain's hand, turned the television off, and set the remote back down. Folding her arms and making a huffing sound, Unique finally spoke. "You turned the man down, didn't you? He's asked you to marry him already, but you've turned him down," Unique figured out. "You turned the man down *and* his ring?"

Lorain remained silent without making eye contact with Unique. The next thing Lorain knew, one of her throw pillows was being tossed upside her head. She shockingly looked toward Unique. "No, you didn't!"

"Yes, I did . . . And yes, you should have, yes, you should have said yes." Unique tossed another pillow at Lorain. This time, Lorain saw it coming and caught it.

"Hey, watch it. You've only known me to be your mama for almost two years, but I still am your mama," Lorain reminded her. "Never mind I'm only thirteen years your senior, but I still got thirteen years experience of butt whipping on you, so watch yourself."

"I can't believe you are depriving me of a daddy and the boys of a granddaddy. What's your problem?" Unique was a little frustrated with Lorain.

Lorain knew Unique was not going to leave this subject matter alone until she got answers. Lorain threw her head back against the couch and exhaled. "Well, when he first asked me, it was after the twins had just been born. To me, I felt like I owed all of my time to the twins and not to planning a wedding, you know."

"Okay, you said when he *first* asked you. So that means there was another time. So when was the next time?"

"On the twins' first birthday, after everyone went home after the party."

"And your excuse then was . . ."

"Unique, I'm not making excuses. It's just that . . . it's just that . . ."

"It's just that it all seems too good to be true, doesn't it?" Unique related. "You don't even feel deserving of someone like Nicholas, do you? You don't feel like you pray enough, praise God enough, thank Him enough, worship Him enough for Him to turn around and do something so wonderful for you, do you?"

Lorain nodded.

Unique nodded as her eyes watered. "I get that. Because that's how I feel every time I look at my boys." Unique then shook her head. "I have no idea why God chose me," she poked her finger at her chest, "chose me to be blessed with such beautiful boys. But He did, and I receive it." She closed her eyes, still shaking her head. "My God, do I deserve those three blessings running around out there?" She opened her eyes. "And those two blessings sleeping in their crib? And this blessing sitting right here in front of me?"

The two women smiled at each other. Lorain put her hands on top of Unique's.

"All I can say, Mama Lorain, is that if Nicholas is that blessing from God, and you know that in your heart of hearts, then you better receive it. Because the man has made his intentions clear from the beginning. How much longer do you think he's going to hang around if your intentions don't line up?"

Lorain thought for a moment. "Not much longer," she said. "Not much longer at all."

# Chapter Three

"Ladies, I thank you all for coming out this evening," Unique said to the group of seven women who sat around the kitchen table of one of her Mary Kay clients. "And thank you for allowing me to introduce some of you to my products." Unique pointed to the items she had displayed on the table. She then looked at the woman who had hosted the Mary Kay party. "And a special thanks to Brooklyn for opening up her home and allowing me to present my products." All of the women clapped their hands.

Once the applause had ceased, the host looked to Unique. "Thank you for coming out, Unique. I appreciate you, girl. You the bestest." She then looked at her guests. "Now, order up, ladies, so I can earn me some free products for having you tramps over here eating up my food and drinking up my wine." Once again, the ladies giggled.

Unique simply smiled at her host's comment. Once one to cuss and drink herself, she was not about to judge these women. But there was something that she could do. "Brooklyn, I'm so blessed to be here, that if you don't mind, I'd really just like to say a quick prayer."

The room went dead silent as Brooklyn, not a churchgoer or a practicing Christian, thought about it. "Well, uh, sure . . . I guess," she concluded. "Pray that these B's buy enough products so that I earn my Satin Hands set for free . . . the big one." There were only a couple laughs this time as several of the women had prepared themselves to go into prayer.

Unique stood, closing her eyes. "Father God," she started, as the seven women followed suit by standing and closing their eyes, "I thank you so much for these beautiful sisters who stand before me. I thank you that each and every one of them got here safe, sound, and free from harm. I thank you in advance that they return to their dwellings, families, and mates safe as well. God, you must love me so much to allow me to be in the presence of such strong, honorable women. I wish nothing but blessings and favor in their lives for whatever their endeavors, dreams, and goals are."

"Thank you, Jesus," one woman whispered.

A couple of eyes shot open in the direction of the woman. She'd been the one cursing the most all evening and telling dirty jokes. Some of the things that had come out of this woman's mouth Unique knew a sailor, not even a construction worker, would say. But now she was calling on the name of Jesus.

"Thank you, God, for making these women the head and not the tail. The lender and not the borrower. Thank you, God, for making these women beautiful already, in the image of you, Father God. But I thank you, God, for sending me here tonight to remind them just how beautiful they are. No, God, they don't need makeup to be beautiful; they already are. But Father, we should maintain and upkeep what you have blessed us with, so I thank you for using me to help them do so. God, I rebuke any word curses dating back to their youth in which anyone told them they were anything but beautiful."

"Yes, God," another woman said, wiping a tear from her eye. "I'm beautiful."

The woman standing next to her grabbed her hand and squeezed it for comfort.

"That's right, sister, you claim it. Say it again!" Unique ordered.

"I'm beautiful," the woman sniffled.

"Like you mean it. Like you believe it," Unique shouted.

"I'm beautiful," the woman repeated. "I'm beautiful!" This time she said it even louder.

A few seconds later, every woman in the room was declaring that they were beautiful. Once the declarations died down, Unique closed out the prayer. "So, God, again, I humbly thank you in Jesus' name. Amen."

"Amen," the women said, wiping tears and hugging each other.

Unique felt so good that the Holy Spirit had used her instantaneously and without planning ahead to speak life into those women's lives; to remind them that they were women; beautiful women. After an hour or so of skin care and makeup applications, Unique was certain that a transformation had taken place. It was a transformation other than a makeover. It had been a spiritual transformation for some of these women. And all Unique could do was give God the glory.

"It's getting late, so I guess I better go ahead and take you ladies' orders," Unique said, sitting back down after applying makeup to the last woman's face. "So what's it going to be, ladies?"

The women, some still hugging, looked at each other. Next they looked at Unique and almost simultaneously replied, "We'll take one of everything," before they all burst out laughing.

It took Unique an hour to get all of the women's orders in. Selling over eight hundred dollars worth of products, she couldn't do anything but thank God as she packed all of her things away and prepared to leave the house.

"Thank you again for hosting the party," Unique told Brooklyn. "It truly was a blessing."

"Girl, you the one who blessed us," Brooklyn stated, looking at the remaining two guests in her home that were also preparing to leave.

"You sure did, sista girlfriend," one of them cosigned. "I think I'm gonna call my uncle and take him up on his offer to come visit his church this Sunday. He's only been asking me for ten years," she chuckled, "ever since he became senior pastor."

"I'll meet you there," the other woman said.

"To God be the glory," was all Unique could fix her lips to say, because that's exactly what He'd done; shined His glory on her beyond measure. "When I follow-up with you guys about your products, let me know how service was, okay?"

"Will do," one of the women said, grabbing her purse. "Come on, chick," she said to the other woman.

The other woman grabbed her purse and said to the driver, "I know we said that we were going to go by The Lobby for a minute after we left here, but I think I'ma pass tonight."

"Me too," the woman driving agreed after digging her keys out of her purse. "Smooches, Brook." She gave Brooklyn a kiss on her cheek, and then headed out of the door with her passenger in tow.

"Okay, Miss Brooklyn, I'll talk to you soon. And thanks again for everything," Unique said, double-checking that she had everything before walking out of the house.

"No problem, girly. Take care." Brooklyn closed the door after watching the last three women to leave her home step down the walkway.

Unique was carrying two cases of products. Thank goodness the women had practically bought her out. At least they weren't as heavy going as they had been coming. Having to catch two city buses to get from her house to Brooklyn's, Unique had broken a sweat hauling the cases. Even though it was nine o'clock at night now, the summer heat had not tucked itself in for the night. It was live and active. With the bus stop only being four blocks away, Unique prayed she wouldn't break a sweat.

It was times like this when she wanted to dig into her stash of money and buy a car, but that money was for a house for her and her boys. Besides, she didn't want to waste her money on some hooptie that would break down on the side of the road every other month. She had plans; buy a house, earn a car. She believed it could be done, so she was going to stick to the plan at all costs.

"Where are you parked?" Unique heard someone call out to her.

She looked back over her shoulder to see a woman standing up at the driver's side of her car with the door open. It was one of the women from the Mary Kay party; the one who said she was going to take her uncle up on his invitation for her to visit his church.

"Oh, I'm, uh, just headed to the bus stop down the street," Unique replied.

"Do you need a ride? It doesn't seem safe being out here this late at night," the woman said.

"Oh, I'll be fine," Unique assured her. "I'm a child of the King." She looked up and pointed upward. "He's got me covered. He's not going to let anything happen to me."

"Where do you live?" the woman asked, as if she was going to offer Unique a ride anyway.

"I live in Malvonia," Unique replied. The woman's face dropped, and Unique understood why. Here they were on the north side of Columbus. Unique's house was about a forty-minute drive in the car; the city bus, with all those stops, not to mention its scenic route, was another story. "So don't worry about it, I'm good," she smiled, letting the woman off the hook. "But thanks anyway, and God bless you." Unique continued her trek to the bus stop.

A few seconds later Unique could hear a car coming up behind her. It was the two women from the party in the car. As they passed her they smiled awkwardly, then proceeded to the stop sign a few feet away from Unique.

"I guess God ain't been that good to her. He got her walking down the street at night with no car," Unique heard the woman in the passenger seat say.

"Child of the King, my foot," the driver spat. "Christian folks kill me, always talking about they are a child of the King; an heir to throne."

"Okayyy," the passenger said. "You mean to tell me that this great God you serve can't even hook you up with a car? Then you ain't no better off than me," she chuckled, and the driver joined in as they pulled off and their rear end lights soon faded, but not before Unique heard one say, "Girl, let's go on to The Lobby. I need a drink."

Unique felt like a big joke as she fought like mad to keep the tears that filled her eyes from falling. Just a moment ago her insides were doing backflips for the Lord, but in just a few seconds, the devil had used those two women to try to steal her joy.

"Get thee behind me, Satan," Unique spat as she continued her walk to the bus stop. "There is nothing you can say, there is nothing you can do to keep me from loving my God, from giving Him all the honor, all the glory, and all the praise. So He hasn't blessed me with a car yet or a place of my own; so what, devil! He will. I know He will. The God I serve is going to provide me above and beyond anything I could have ever hoped, dreamed, or prayed for."

Unique stomped down that street like she was stepping on the devil. She ranted and spat off at the devil, not caring what the cars driving past her thought. Once she arrived at the bus stop, she began to praise God like never before. When the bus finally arrived about ten minutes later, she sat on the bus more excited and pumped up than she had been in a long time.

She was a child of the King. She was an heir to His throne, and she was going to get every single blessing God had for her. But she knew in order to do so, she couldn't just sit around and wait on God. She had to do her part in it as well. She was going to make a way for her children and herself at all costs, and she wasn't going to do it alone. Yes, she had the Lord by her side. But there were some other people that played a role in this thing as well; her children's fathers.

Unique had let them get away long enough with her just getting by on whatever money they could throw her way whenever they could to help her support her kids. Heck, her oldest son's father hadn't shot anything her way in a good while. She'd been trying to get in touch with him for the past week, but that sucker had the nerve to not take her calls. She could see him now just sitting there allowing her calls to go to voice mail. Well, he was going to be the first one she hit up on her list of deadbeat dads. He and those other two baby daddies should prepare themselves for the wrath of Unique Emerald Gray. Tomorrow would be the first day of the rest of her life.

Unfortunately, though, it would be the last day for the people who mattered most to her in life.

# Chapter Four

"Oooh, flowers," the temp serving as the office receptionist said to Lorain as she stood at the receptionist desk sniffing the colorful array of mixed flowers. "What's the occasion? Birthday? Anniversary? 'I'm sorry,'" the young brunette probed.

"Nope," Lorain smiled, walking away, still sniffing the flowers. "Just because it's Monday."

Back when she and Nicholas had first met, he'd told her all the things he wanted to do for her. He'd told her all the things he wanted to be for her; her husband was one of them, and a man who sends her flowers just because it's Monday was another. Well, at least he'd been one out of the two. By now, he could have been two out of two if it weren't for Lorain rejecting his marriage proposals. She'd stared at that three-point-five carat diamond he'd purchased for her for so long now that a vision of it was embedded in her head. She would often imagine what it looked like on her finger. Unfortunately, the little ring had never made it out of the box and onto her finger. She had possession of the ring, per Nicholas's request, but she just didn't wear the ring.

"Here, you keep it and just think about it," Nicholas had told her the last time he proposed and she declined. "When you're finally ready, I'll know."

"How will you know?" Lorain had asked.

"Because I'll look down at your finger one day and you'll be wearing it," he replied, staring into her eyes and tucking the box in her hand. "But don't let that day be too far off, Lorain."

For Lorain, his last comment sounded more like a warning; like a threat. But like Unique had even asked her, how much longer did she think Nicholas was going to hang around if her intentions didn't eventually line up with his?

Throwing out last Monday's flowers and re-placing them with this morning's, Lorain sat down in her chair as thoughts fluttered through her mind. One thought was how she could possibly turn down a marriage proposal from a man like Nicholas. He was truly every woman's dream. Well, maybe not every woman's, but hers and more than likely, a handful of others anyway. She just never imagined in a million years that that dream would come true; that God would really do it for her.

"But why wouldn't He?" Lorain mumbled to herself. "Why wouldn't God give me a man like Nicholas?" A huge grin stretched across her lips. "A doctor; an attentive, kind, loving man who is exactly who he says he is," she questioned.

*But if he was from God,* her subconscious mind interrupted her personal conversation with herself, *wouldn't he have been a Christian? Why would God give me someone who I have to invite to church, or who goes to church whenever he feels like it? And on top of that, someone who smokes cigarettes?*

Nicholas wasn't a chain-smoker or anything. He just smoked after a long surgery or something. He said it helped to calm his nerves. He never smoked around Lorain, and he never smoked in a closed-in place like a car, lounge, or his apartment. He always smoked outside in the open air. As a matter of fact, Lorain never even knew he smoked until three months into their relationship. They'd gone into a gas station. While she strolled the snack aisle, he paid for gas and asked the attendant for a pack of cigarettes. She was surprised, to say the least. She'd been so concerned about his purchasing a pack of smokes, that over dinner, she picked at her food. It wasn't until Nicholas detected that something was bothering her and called her on it that she mentioned him purchasing cigarettes. He explained his use of them, and though she wasn't keen on being in a relationship with a smoker, she really liked this man and wasn't going to let a pack of Newports come between them.

But Nicholas, being a smoker, played no part in her decision not to marry him just yet. It was that subconscious mind of hers that kept rearing its ugly head that did. It kept reminding her of her past; all the ugly things she'd done when it came to men, and all the ugly things they had done to her. She thought about all the other women's husbands she'd slept with and feared that God couldn't wait to pay her back by allowing another woman to sleep with hers. She wouldn't be able to stand the heartache.

Then there was the fact that perhaps Nicholas was just too good to be true. What if it turned out that he wasn't all that he seemed? What if he wasn't this cool, calm, and collected gentleman that he'd been displaying himself as all of this time? How could she be so sure? What signs could be there that she could have overlooked?

She thought about her church sister, Paige. She thought about Sister Nita as well. Both women had married men who turned out to be abusers. Each of them thought they were marrying the perfect man, but they'd missed the signs. What if Lorain, too, was missing the signs?

Lorain buried her head in her hands and shook her head. She was trying to shake all those crazy thoughts out. They wouldn't go away though. She had to do something, and she had to do something fast about all these feelings and fears she was having regarding Nicholas.

Sometimes Lorain's thoughts and fears got so bad to the point where she'd actually called Nicholas's voice mail, left him a breakup message, but then deleted the message before it could be delivered. That's just how serious this thing had become.

Now, leaned back in her chair feeling mentally exhausted, Lorain decided that today would be the day she confronted her fears. She couldn't keep them bottled up inside any longer. There was someone who could perhaps help her overcome this thing, because if she didn't, she felt that in her heart of hearts, she'd lose Nicholas.

Lorain pulled her chair in front of her computer and clicked onto the Internet. After going to the New Day Temple of Faith Web site, and then clicking on the church member e-mail directory, she was one step closer to conquering her fears.

"Thank you for replying to my e-mail so quickly," Lorain said through the phone receiver. "And thank you so much for taking the time to talk to me on the phone."

"Well, if you don't mind me saying, your e-mail came across pretty desperate," Paige chuckled.

"I guess it did," Lorain agreed. She had to admit, though, she was desperate.

"So, the man you were talking about in your e-mail, Nicholas, he's the one who visits church with you sometimes?"

"Yes, that's him," Lorain blushed. "He's the man that I, like every other single woman in the church feels when she meets a man, believes God sent me."

Paige let out a laugh. "Girl, you ain't never lied there. I've heard that a million times from some of the women I speak with when I go to different places and give my testimony. That's exactly how I felt when I met my ex. Nobody could tell me that man wasn't missing a rib and I was, in fact, that rib."

Lorain sighed. "That's exactly how I feel." She thought for a minute. "Well, kinda. I mean, like I said in my e-mail, he's not a practicing Christian. He even smokes. But on the flip side, Sister Paige, he is such a wonderful man. He works hard. He works hard at his profession, which is a doctor. He works hard at being attentive toward me, even though we don't have lots of time together due to him always being on call. He even works hard at being a good role model to my grandsons. And with their deadbeat daddies, you know that's priceless. And Unique likes him. My mom likes him . . ."

"What about you?" Paige asked. "How do you feel about him?"

Without even hesitating Lorain replied, "I love him. I love everything about him. He is the man God has made him to be right now; that's how I feel in my heart. We as people always have room to grow. We are always changing. Yes, we get set in our ways, but God will always ultimately have His way. So if that means He has to change some things about us, then so be it."

"I hear you, but what if Nicholas stays the same forever? What if God makes changes in you?"

"I . . . I . . . don't understand." Lorain was confused.

"Listen, Sister Lorain, I know what it is you want me to do," Paige said. "You want me to tell you how I went from thinking I was married to the man of my dreams to trying to wake up from a nightmare. You want me to tell you what signs to look for in Nicholas that were there with Blake. I can't do that, Sister Lorain. I can give you some signs of what to look for in an abuser. As a matter of fact, there are pamphlets laid out in the church lobby that list some signs. Sister Nita is head of the Swatc Ministry, so you might even want to talk to her."

"Sheltered Woman and Their Children, yeah, I remember attending the meeting that one time."

"Yes, so you know some of the things we discussed regarding signs of an abuser. But that's not your real concern. You are not concerned with whether Nicholas is going to turn into a different person once you marry him. You are more so worried that *you* are going to turn into a different person once you marry *him*."

That darn Sister Paige had hit it right on the money, Lorain had thought to herself. "You are absolutely right," Lorain agreed. "When it really comes down to it, I'm so afraid that I'm not going to be the woman he desires now. What if I'm not everything he thinks I'm

going to be as a wife? I'm not perfect, Sister
Paige, but when I look at myself in his eyes . . .
Really, when I see the way he looks at me, it's
as if I am perfect; that I'm everything he could
ever want, and more, in a woman. How can I
ever live up to that? And then once he realizes
that I'm not really that woman, what if he just
ups and leaves me? What if he's like Sister
Tamarra's ex-husband? What if he has a baby
by another woman while we're married? What
if he's like how Sister Deborah's baby's father
was? Or Mother Doreen's late husband or . . ."
Lorain stopped her thoughts.

"Or like Blake, my ex-husband?" Paige finished for her. "Go ahead, you can say it. After
all, out of all the folks listed in the church
directory, you picked me to contact because
my marriage woes were the most recently
public. I get it, Sister Lorain, but sister, if you
don't get it, you just might lose a man who really loves you. Now I might not be telling you
what you want to hear. Who knows; after you
hang up with me, you might have another list
of women from church you are going to call
up. Let me tell you something; don't let the
church have you end up being a single, lonely
woman for the rest of your life. Because if you
are going to base your life, your relationship

with your man on what other women in the church have gone through, then that's exactly how you are going to end up."

Lorain remained silent as a tear fell from her eye. It wasn't a tear of sadness, nor could it really be deemed as a tear of joy. It was a tear of revelation, of confirmation that Lorain needed to start living her life . . . her life . . . not fearing she'd end up living the life of other women. "Thank you, Sister Paige. Thank you so much. You have no idea of the release I just received from your words. I thank you for letting God use you."

"No need to thank me. All God did was use me to confirm what He's already told you . . . or what He's been trying to tell you anyway. You just wouldn't listen until now."

"And you are so right about that," Lorain agreed. "Thanks, again, Sister Paige. See you in church Sunday."

"Bye-bye," Paige said before the women ended the call.

"Yes!" Lorain shouted out, nearly scaring to death one of her coworkers that was walking by.

"Lorain, are you okay?" the woman asked.

"Yes!" Lorain stood up and grabbed the woman by the shoulders with excitement. "Yes, I'm okay, and yes . . . I'm going to marry him!"

# Chapter Five

Lorain could barely make it through her work-day. Initially, she was going to skip lunch so she could leave an hour early, but she decided to skip work entirely, working only a half day. It would have been impossible for her to wait it out. In just that little bit of time she'd had to continuously pump herself up so that she wouldn't talk herself out of what she was about to do. She figured if she didn't leave now, by noon she would have chickened out.

Obedience was better than sacrifice, so she obeyed the traffic laws as she drove from her job to her house. Finally arriving, she pulled up in front of her place and jumped out of her car, not even closing the door. She knew she'd only be in her house for a second. All she needed to do was grab something really quick.

Once inside her house, she was moving so fast to her bedroom that it felt like only a half a second. So excited was she that she tripped over her own feet and fell at the foot of her bed before making it over to her dresser drawer.

"Girl, relax yourself," she told herself with a chuckle, getting up off the floor and dusting herself off.

Once back up on her feet, she made her way over to her dresser and opened up the jewelry box she'd had ever since she was a little girl. Her mother had given it to her to keep her first pair of diamond earrings in that her father had bought her.

"Gosh, my mother!" Lorain exclaimed. The gift from her mother reminded her of her mother and the fact that she had the twins. She needed to call her to tell her she might be late picking them up. If things went as planned, she and Nicholas would be doing some major celebrating. But first things first.

Lorain grabbed the small box that held the engagement ring that Nicholas had proposed to her with . . . twice. She opened the box and pulled out the ring. She didn't know what was brighter; the sparkle in her eyes or the sparkle in that huge, beautiful diamond. "Well, here goes." She took the ring out of the box and placed it on her finger. "Perfect fit," she smiled . . . and cried. She'd never, until now, even placed the ring on her finger. "Of course it's a perfect fit. Why wouldn't it be? Nicholas and I are a perfect fit."

She looked up. "He's perfect for me, God, and I know—that I know—that I know he's from you." She paused before saying, "Thank you, God."

She looked around the room and spotted the phone. "I gotta call Mom and tell her I might be late picking up the girls," Lorain said aloud, and that's exactly what she did. She dialed Eleanor's phone. After answering on the first ring, Lorain quickly blurted into the receiver that there was a chance she would be picking up the twins late. She didn't want her mother to worry just in case she was late.

"Why? Is everything okay?" a concerned Eleanor asked.

"Yes, Mother, everything is just fine. As a matter of fact, things couldn't be more perfect. I'm going to marry Nicholas!"

"What? When? How? Who? Oh my God, baby, that's wonderful!" Eleanor's joy could be heard and felt by her daughter through the phone receiver. "Congratulations." Now Eleanor could be heard sniffing.

"Thanks, Mom," Lorain, told her, "but I gotta go, 'kay?"

"But I wanna be there. Why didn't you tell me?" Eleanor began to question. "Are you eloping? Y'all going downtown? But I wanted to throw you a big wedding." Eleanor's voice went from happy to irritated. "Now I really like that Nicholas, and I know he's a busy man and all, but if he can't find the time to marry my daughter with a proper—"

"Mom," Lorain said, making her way to the front door. "I don't mean we're getting married right now. I mean that I'm going to tell him that I will marry him."

Now Eleanor sounded concerned. "Hmm, I know Nicholas is a good man and all, but I just don't think it's right for a gal to be asking her beau for his hand in marriage. Isn't it supposed to be the other way around? Doesn't the Bible say that he who finds a wife—"

"Oh, Mom, there you go talking like you're from the South again. Gal? Since when am I a gal? I thought I told you to cut that out once before. Besides, it's not what it seems. Nicholas proposed to me, down on one knee, ring and all. It's just that at the time I declined. I was confused. I . . . I . . ." Lorain sighed and went on to explain a little bit more about the situation and how she was about to show up at the hospital with the ring on her finger. "Look, Mother, I'll tell you everything; I promise. But right now, I have to get to the hospital and find my husband."

"That's fine, dear, as long as he found you first," Eleanor said, giving her blessing. "Because the

Word says, 'He who findeth a wife'—not 'she who findeth a husband.' So I just had to be sure everything was in order according to the Word."

"Yes, Mother, now, please, I have to go. Kiss my girls for me and let them know that they are about to have a daddy." Lorain hung up the phone and left her house. She jumped into the driver's side of her car that awaited her with an open door and drove straight to the hospital.

Arriving at the hospital, Lorain parked in the visitor's lot and headed to the ER unit. Most of the staff there was familiar with who Lorain was. Nicholas had introduced her to some of them on the days they shared lunch in the hospital cafeteria. She'd met others the time he'd given her a tour of the hospital, while she'd met the majority of them at the hospital's Memorial Day picnic just that year. He'd invited her, and she'd brought the boys along. The twins had stayed with Eleanor. The boys had had the time of their lives there.

"Well, hello . . . Lorain, right?" a nurse stopped Lorain and asked before she could get to the nurses' unit.

"Yes," Lorain replied, looking at the nurse's face, trying to recall the name by face and not the name tag the nurse was wearing. "Jim, right?"

"That's right," he said. "Looking for Dr. Wright?"

Lorain had to chuckle inside. She was looking for Doctor Wright all right, never even realizing that God had made it plain and clear by sending her a man with the last name of Wright. Sure, it was a play on words, but God had a sense of humor; oh yes, He did. "As a matter of fact, I am looking for Doctor Wright," Lorain confirmed.

"You're in luck. He just got out of a surgery, so he headed outside to—"

"Take a smoke break?" Lorain finished the nurse's sentence.

"Well, yes. I guess you know the good doctor very well."

"Yes, I know all about the good doctor's nasty little habit."

The nurse leaned in and whispered in Lorain's' ear. "Try working on that with him, would you? Doctor Wright is an excellent doctor. I can see him having his own practice one day, and me working for him. But that's not going to happen if the poor man dies of lung cancer. So try to get him to kick the habit, all right? My future and his are at stake." The nurse stood up straight and winked at Lorain.

"I'll do my best," Lorain assured him.

"Good. You know where the lawn is?" The nurse pointed down the hallway. "Down the hall, go right, second door on your left."

"Thank you, Jim," Lorain said, then followed the directions he had given her to find Nicholas.

When Lorain walked outside, she spotted Nicholas standing beside a picnic table where a few members of the hospital staff sat. He was exhaling a puff of smoke. As she walked in his direction, he took one last puff, put the cigarette out, then threw the butt away, all without even noticing that Lorain had approached him.

"Boo," Lorain said, surprising Nicholas.

"Lorain, honey, what are you doing here?" he asked, hugging her.

Lorain hugged him back, but only with one arm. Her left arm was unavailable, as her left hand was hidden in the pocket of her sky-blue dress slacks. She didn't want Nicholas to spot the ring just yet. She wanted to tease him a little first.

"Is everything okay?" Although Nicholas was smiling, there was a worried expression some-what hidden in the background.

"Everything is fine, sweetheart," Lorain smiled. "I just . . . I just decided to drop by to kill some time. Mom is keeping the kids a little longer today."

"Oh, okay, well, what a surprise. I don't have much time, maybe five minutes or so—"

"That's all I need," Lorain smiled.

Nicholas gave Lorain a peculiar look. "Babe, are you *sure* there's not something else going on? You haven't stopped smiling since you saw me."

"I guess you just have that affect on me, Dr. Wright. Imagine if I could wake up every morning with a smile on my face."

"Yea, imagine that," Nicholas agreed, still not catching on to Lorain's subtle hint.

Knowing that Nicholas's time was limited, Lorain decided to just swoop in for the kill. She slowly began removing her hand from her pocket and rested it on Nicholas's shoulder. "I have been imagining it—me waking up with a smile on my face every morning—and keep it there—all day long. And that's why—"

"Dr. Wright! Dr. Wright!" a voice yelled from the doorway that Lorain had exited from to meet Nicholas on the lawn.

Every head turned to see Jim with a frantic look on his face. Just then, it was as if everyone's pagers who were outside began to beep. As they began checking them, the hospital staff scurried inside like their lives depended on it. Obviously, someone's life did depend on it.

"I'm sorry, baby, I gotta go," was all Nicholas had time to say to Lorain as he rushed off with the rest of the medical staff.

"I'll wait for you in the lobby," Lorain shouted to him.

"Okay," he yelled back. "I don't know how long I'll be though. We've got to go prepare for three patients that were just called in by the EMTs. They are on their way to the hospital now. I don't know what's going on or how long I'm going to be."

"I'll wait as long as I have to," Lorain assured him before he disappeared behind the door. Just like that, every ounce of excitement Lorain had felt vanished. And just like that, doubt had managed to creep back into her mind.

She looked up. "God, was that you or the devil who interrupted my moment?" she asked. She looked down at the ring and let out a disappointed breath. Lorain figured that either one of two things was going on here; the devil was testing her to see if she would give up, or God was testing her to see if she would give up. Either way it went, as Lorain headed back inside the hospital and went to wait in the ER lobby, she was bound and determined to pass either test. She would not give up.

# Chapter Six

"Will you please listen to me?" Unique yelled to the questioning detective that stood over her. "I don't sell dope." She looked around the small white room that had one table and three chairs. She'd seen this room before; not in person, but on that show, *The First 48* that she'd watched a million times. But never, not ever in her lifetime, did she imagine that she would be one of the people being questioned and interrogated.

*Could this really be happening? Is this a dream, or worse, a nightmare?* These were the questions that kept attacking Unique's mind ever since she woke up in a jail cell wearing handcuffs.

For the life of her, she could not recall how she'd gotten there. The last thing she could clearly recall was earlier that morning, her walking up to the crack house where her oldest son's father hustled. Although it was only around 10:00 a.m., it was never too early for a hustler to hustle.

She'd knocked on the door and Two-Step, her baby daddy's flunky, had answered the door. Ironically, he'd been given the name Two-Step because he always remained two-steps behind her baby's daddy. Unique knew of some pastors who didn't even have armor bearers that were on the job as well as Two-Step.

"Girl, what you doing up in here?" Two-Step had asked Unique.

"You know exactly what I'm doing here." Unique looked over Two-Step's shoulder while scanning the inside of the house. "And so does that no-good baby daddy of mine."

Two-Step flashed a crooked-tooth, gold-cap-wearing grin. "Which one?" That was his attempt at a low blow.

"Ask your momma. He's her baby daddy too," Unique shot back.

That comment turned his grin into a frown. "And you call yourself a Christian," Two-Step replied, turning his lips up. "You go to church every Sunday and you talking like that."

Unique put her hands on her hips. "Uh-huh, so if you think this is bad, imagine how bad I'd be if I *didn't* go to church every Sunday."

Two-Step just rolled his eyes while saying, "Wait right here." He closed the door in Unique's face but then five seconds later, it opened again and there stood Unique's baby daddy.

"What's up?" were the only words he had to say to her as he sucked on a toothpick and tugged on the brim of his Yankee cap.

"Fool, you know exactly what's up, some money to take care of your son is what's up." Unique got loud.

Her oldest son's father looked over his shoulder at his crew that was busting dominos, playing spades, smoking weed, and drinking alcohol behind him. "Look, don't be coming up to my place of business trying to cut the fool, Unique."

"Seriously?" Unique replied. "Your place of business?" She let out a laugh. "This ain't nothing but a Columbus Metropolitan Housing Unit that some dumb broad and her six children probably live at, that you and your boys pay her to run drugs up out of here and probably run a train on her every now and then too." Unique knew some awful things were coming out of her mouth, but being back in the hood, being in this atmosphere, being out of her element was starting to get to her. Her baby's daddy lack of responsibility was starting to get to her.

"Girl, are you crazy talking all loud like that?" he snapped, grabbing her by the arm, and then pulling her into the house. He slammed the door closed with an attitude. "Wait your tail right here. Let me go see what I can do."

"Yeah, go see what you can do," Unique spat while pointing to his back as he walked away.

He went into the kitchen. She peeked her head around and watched him open the fridge. The next thing she knew, he walked back over to her with a plastic Kroger bag.

"Here, take this." He handed the bag to Unique.

She felt it, and it was hard as a rock. It was freezing cold where she could barely hold the bag. "Ice . . . You think a block of ice is going to put food in your child's stomach and clothes on his back? I'll tell you what—"

"Police!" Unique remembered hearing before she could even get the rest of her words out. "Police!" She heard it a second time, then looked over her shoulder to see a swarm of men dressed in black with caps and masks and bullet shields storming the place. With her being right there in front of the door, she received the complete wrath of what felt like a human tidal wave.

The rushing bodies pushed her to the floor where her head slammed on the edge of a cheap, wooden coffee table. After that, Unique was in and out of consciousness. It was dark one minute, then light for a second, then dark again. She was alone one minute, then the next, she remembered being surrounded by a bunch of dudes in handcuffs in the back of a van or something. She was riding one minute, then the next, she was sitting in a room behind bars. Now, two hours later, she was here, in a tiny questioning space, being accused of being a dope runner.

"You don't sell dope, huh?" the officer said with disbelief all throughout his tone. "Then why is it when we busted in the place, you were standing there with a bag full of dope?" The officer stood up. "You can sit here and lie all you want, but my men know what they saw, and they know what they confiscated from you, which was enough dope to get you at least ten years locked up."

Unique felt as if the wind had just been knocked out of her, or that someone was playing a very cruel joke on her. This could not be happening to her. This could not be real. She began to massage her temples with her hands. "Look, Officer, I don't know who your men saw, or what they think they saw this person with, but it wasn't me because I don't do drugs, nor do I sell drugs."

"Okay, so you don't do drugs, nor do you sell drugs, Ms. Gray, but yet, you were in a well-known drug spot?"

"Yes, I was there, but—"

"Come on, Ms. Gray, let's not play games. I got a wife and a kid at home who are expecting me to take them to a baseball game tonight. And you know what? I'll make it if you stop jerking me around and just tell me the truth." He slammed his fist on the table angrily. He slammed it so hard that Unique thought it was going to break; his table and his hand.

"Officer Givens," a female officer called out from the doorway. "You want to take a break?" she asked. She now walked into the room to take over for the officer.

Once again, Unique had seen this song and dance on *The First 48* and every other cop show out there. They were doing their "good cop-bad cop" routine.

"Look, Miss," Unique said desperately, "you two don't have to play good cop-bad cop with me. I'm going to tell you just like I told him, I don't sell drugs. I was only at that house to see about child support for one of my sons."

"So your son's father is the one who sells dope?" the female officer asked.

"Yes, I mean, no, I mean, I don't know," Unique stammered. She might not have lived in the hood anymore, but the code of the streets traveled with a person no matter where they lived. She wasn't about to throw her baby daddy, Two-Step, or anyone else up under the bus. But at the same time, she couldn't see herself going to jail for this mess either.

"So which is it, Ms. Gray?" Officer Givens asked. "Either your son's father does or he doesn't sell dope out of that house."

"I . . . I've never actually seen him selling dope out of the house, but . . ." Unique's words trailed off. She couldn't think of what to say fast enough without incriminating anyone.

Officer Givens stood up from the chair he'd been sitting in across from Unique. "Like, I said, I don't have time for your games, Ms. Gray." He looked at his partner. "Let's just book her for possession with intent to sell. Let her serve her ten years in prison so I can get home to my family."

"No!" Unique yelled out as the officer headed to the door. "You can't leave me here. You have to believe me. I was just stopping by to get child support for one of my sons. I have three sons. It was my oldest son's father who I was there to see."

"Okay, so did you see him?" Officer Givens asked, turning to face Unique again. Now he was showing some interest in what Unique had to say as if she were about to tell him exactly what he wanted to hear.

"Yes, I saw him," Unique recalled as best she could. "We argued for a minute, but then he told me to hold on. He went into the kitchen, got something out of the freezer, then came over and handed it to me."

Officer Givens slowly walked back over to Unique. "So do you want me to believe that you thought your son's father was giving you a box of popsicles for your son and that you were going to go on your merry way?" Before Unique could even reply, he spat off, "That's it; you're done, Ms. Gray. I've had enough of you playing with me." Officer Givens made his way back over to the door and through gritted teeth told the female officer, "Come on; let's not waste any more time with this one. I'm going to go find and question the so-called baby daddy. She's just accused him of providing her the dope." A mischievous grin covered his face as he glared at Unique. "He'll be in jail until your son makes him a granddaddy."

"No! Wait!" Unique cried out, but her plea fell on deaf ears as Officer Givens closed the door behind him. "Oh my God, what have I done?" Unique was more so asking herself and not the female officer that remained in the questioning room with her. "What have I done?" Unique looked up and hollered out, "Jesus, help me!" She could only hope that that plea didn't fall on deaf ears as well.

# Chapter Seven

Lorain sat in the hospital emergency room lobby twisting the engagement ring around and around her finger. The longer she sat there, the more antsy she got. Not only that, but the battle going on between her heart and her mind was starting to physically exhaust her as if she'd been in a boxing match.

She looked down at her watch. "Geez," she said after realizing she'd only been waiting a whole five minutes. "Jesus, give me strength," she began whispering to herself until her whispers were drowned out by a loud voice.

"We've got three African American males coming in now," a nurse said as she dashed through the lobby to the huge double doors. She was followed by about five or six other staff members. Lorain couldn't be exact on the count. They were all going by so fast it was like one big blur. "They said the boys look to be around the ages of six, seven, and eight . . . five, six, or seven even. It looks like they're victims of heat stroke, and they're not breathing," was the last thing Lorain heard before the hospital staff was outside of the double doors.

"Oh my," Lorain said. She then felt guilty that she was sitting in the ER stressing herself out over nothing but pure obedience to God, while there was a family being traumatized by something much bigger and much more serious than what she was going through. She looked around the ER room at mothers with sick babies. There were mothers that were sick. Mothers are the glue that keeps the household together and running properly. So when Mama was sick, down, and out, that was a big deal.

There was a grown man sitting in the ER moaning and clutching his stomach. He wore a thick, heavy brown work uniform. He was probably a father; the head of the household. It was probably his duty to bring home the money necessary for the family's livelihood and essentials. Yet all that was about to be jeopardized because he was sick in the ER.

Coming to that realization, instead of sitting in that ER and allowing her mind to drift into doubt, Lorain began to pray for others. She began to pray for the mothers, the babies, the fathers, and their loved ones. She'd barely got two sentences out when the same staff that had exited the hospital doors came zooming back in. This time they were joined by several paramedics helping them wheel in three stretchers with tiny, little bodies on them.

Closing her eyes, Lorain extended her hands toward the hospital doors and began to pray harder. First, she prayed in English, and then she began to pray in unknown tongues.

"They're not breathing," someone yelled frantically. "None of them are breathing." That voice faded as it cut across Lorain's path. This only made her begin to pray even that much harder.

"Where's the mother? Where's the father? Is anyone here with them? Did anyone ride in either of the ambulances with them?" a male voice asked.

"I don't think so," another male voice replied. "They were alone. They were all alone."

Within seconds, the tornado that had just spun through the ER lobby was gone, but little did Lorain know, it would leave more destruction in its path than she could have ever imagined.


"I know those kids. I know those boys," Jim said as each stretcher was whizzed by him, headed toward its designated room.

"Well, good, that's all the more reason for you to help save them," a woman, appearing to be the head nurse in charge, replied. "Don't just stand there," the nurse spat off to Jim. "Jump in and help."

Jim turned to the nurse's aide that was standing beside him, ready to assist in any way needed. "What room is Wright in?" he asked her. Not even giving her a second to answer, he yelled, "What room is Dr. Wright in?"

"There," she pointed nervously. "Where they just took one of the boys."

Jim's eyes followed where the aide's index finger was pointing. He then ran into the room. When he arrived, Nicholas was at the sink finishing up scrubbing and drying his hands. When he turned around, there was a nurse on each side of him with a rubber glove in hand. Each woman eagerly, and with precision, placed a glove on each of Nicholas's hands.

"What do we got?" Nicholas asked, walking toward the motionless body lying in the middle of the room.

"Dr. Wright," Jim tried to warn, but it was too late. The two nurses that had just assisted Nicholas in putting on the gloves had to assist him in standing. For just one second, two seconds tops, Nicholas felt as though his knees were going to hit the ground. Upon seeing the

tiny, little body before him, his knees had buckled.

This was the part about being in the medical
field that most medical professionals detested;
a sick child . . . a helpless, sick child. Something
about their innocent little selves made a medical staff member work just that much harder.
It made them research just that much more to
find cures, solutions, and antidotes. Nicholas
had his own personal viewpoint about why God
would send a child into the ER with a serious
condition every now and then. He felt it was
just to remind him why he was doing what he
was doing.

"Dr. Wright, are you okay?" he heard a voice
ask him. It was so faint, like it was in the background.

"Yes, yes. I'm just fine," Nicholas assured his
comrades. "What do we have?" Nicholas immediately went into 100-percent doctor mode.

"Male, African American boy who has suffered
from . . ." a nurse began to rattle off as everyone
began to move in sync to do whatever needed to
be done to save the boy's life. This was the exact
scene in two other rooms in the ER. And the
results, in each room, would be the same.

After working for over forty-five minutes
nonstop on the little boy, Nicholas was relent-
less. He was giving the child mouth-to-mouth.

He was trying to pump life back into the little boy with his hands; his hands that were placed on the little boy's chest going up and down. He was trying to breathe life back into the little boy with his mouth; his mouth placed over the little boy's exhaling. All this had more than likely been done in the ambulance, Nicholas knew. It had been the EMTs' first resort, but now it was Nicholas's last.

When the boys had been brought into the ER, none of them were breathing. Breathing tubes had been tried. Nicholas had placed paddles on the boy's chest, hopeful the shock would have jump-started his heart. He'd closed his eyes and instead of the boy lying underneath him, he pictured his old Toyota he'd driven throughout the better part of medical school. He remembered how it would always lose its juice, but after a jump start, it never let him down. It always came back to life. This little boy had not come back to life.

"Come on, God. Do it," Nicholas said in between the pumping and the breathing. "I know you can do it, God. I've seen you do it before." Nicholas knew the chances of his act getting the boy breathing again was small, but God was big. He could use any method. He'd seen God do some unexplainable things before in that ER. "Do it now, God!"

Nicholas pumped some more. Nicholas breathed some more. Yet, the child remained lifeless. Nicholas pumped some more, and then breathed some more, realizing he was now the only one in the room doing anything to try to save the boy. The nurses just looked from one to another, knowing in their hearts that Nicholas's efforts were in vain—that he was just going through the motions out of pure desperation. They'd already tried everything medically possible to get the boy breathing. His heart was dead. His brain was dead due to the long period of time it had gone without oxygen.

"Why are you all just standing there?" he yelled at the top of his lungs at his staff that appeared to be standing in the background allowing him to do all the work. "Help me! Help me!" he ordered. "Help me!" Nicholas repeated to his staff, but in essence, he was really talking to God.

The staff looked at each other, but nobody moved.

"Did you all hear what I said?" Nicholas yelled before an expletive jumped off of his tongue.

"Dr. Wright. Dr. Wright." Jim solemnly walked over to Nicholas and put his hand on his shoulder.

"Get off of me, man," Nicholas spat. "It's him that needs help. It's the boy that needs help, not me."

Jim, once again, and carefully, placed his hand on Nicholas's shoulder. "Dr. Wright? Dr. Wright?"

Nicholas looked over at Jim with blood-shot eyes. Jim didn't say a word at first, he just shook his head. Finally he spoke. "He's gone, Dr. Wright. He's gone." Jim was right. The little boy was gone. Technically, he was gone the minute they wheeled him into the hospital. He was already gone when Nicholas and his staff had begun their efforts to try to revive him; all efforts were in vain.

Nicholas turned his attention from Jim and back to the little boy. Everything in him wanted to break down right there in the middle of that room. It was the hardest thing for Nicholas to stand there and keep his composure and remain professional. Swallowing the lump in his throat, he looked at Jim and said, "Take me to the other two." He felt as though there were still a chance he could help save the other two.

Maybe he couldn't save that one, but that didn't mean he had to give up on the others. That wasn't God's mentality, and neither was it Nicholas's.

Not waiting for Jim to lead the way, Nicholas brushed past him and out of the room. In the hallway he was greeted by a thick sheet of grief. His eyes met those of his comrades who had exited the rooms of the other two little boys just minutes before. By the look on their faces, Nicholas knew they'd had the same result with their boys as he'd had with the one assigned to him.

"The boys," Nicholas started, "did either of them make it?"

When he saw the head nurse wiping a tear and then rushing off before anyone else would notice, he knew the answer. It was when someone verbalized it by saying, "No, neither of them made it," that Nicholas's knees, once again, buckled. This time there was no nurse at either of his side to catch him from falling. Fortunately for him, though, just like when Jesus had died on the cross, God was there. God was there.

# Chapter Eight

"Just calm down, Ms. Gray," the female officer said to a hysterical Unique. "Would you like something to drink?"

Unique shook her head as tears fell from her eyes. "No. I just want to go home. I want to go home, and I'm pissed that your partner is trying to play with my mind. He's trying to get me to admit to something that I didn't do. Since I won't tell him what he wants to hear, he's going after my son's father. This is crazy. I mean, what's his deal? Why is he being such a jerk?" Unique wiped her tears away with her cuffed hands.

"Oh, don't pay him no never mind." The female officer shooed her hand at the door as if Officer Givens was still standing there. "He's really a big softie."

"Oh yeah?" The sarcasm in Unique's voice could be well detected.

"Yes. It's just that he gets tired . . . We get tired of seeing young ladies like you taking the rap for their boyfriends. I mean, you wouldn't believe how many women choose to do the time for their man, rather than just tell the truth."

"But I *am* telling the truth. I promise to God I am. Why won't you believe me?"

"I believe you." The female officer reached out and grabbed Unique's hand. "I really do, and I want to help you, Ms. Gray. In order for me to help you, though, you are going to have to help me." She leaned in closer and began to whisper, as if there weren't three officers watching the entire thing going down on a television camera in the next room. "We really don't want any of the worker bees in the game. We want the queen bee. Well, in this case, the king bee, if you know what I mean."

"I know exactly what you mean, and if I had a name to give you, I would, but I don't. I'm telling you, I'm not into the dope game. Yeah, I hit a joint once in every blue moon, but not since I've been saved. I try to do right by my kids."

The officer stared at Unique without saying a word. It was as if she almost wanted to believe her. It was as if she almost felt . . . felt . . . felt sorry for the young, single mother. "So you said you have three sons, huh?"

"Yes, three beautiful sons who I'd never jeopardize being away from, especially by getting caught selling drugs." Unique sucked her teeth. "You think I don't know that a drug dealer gets jail time? Please. I'd never risk being away from my boys."

"Speaking of being away from your boys, while you were supposedly seeing about child support from your baby daddy, where were your three boys?"

"They were with my . . ." Unique's words trailed off. She wasn't quite clear if she'd left them at home with her sister, if they were at Lorain's, or what. That bump on the head had mixed her up a little bit, but not enough to sit there and let someone accuse her of being a dope dealer. A dope dealer she was not; that much she knew.

After thinking for a moment, Unique jumped up so fast from the table that the officer drew her gun and aimed it directly at Unique.

"Freeze!" the officer warned Unique. Not two seconds later, the door flung open and two other officers stood with their guns drawn.

Unique didn't freeze though. She hadn't even comprehended the officer's direct order. Her good sense had left that room and went back to the last time she'd seen her boys' faces.

*"Y'all stay out here. I'm not going to be but a second,"* Unique had ordered her children after parking her car a few houses down from the one her son's father hustled out of.

*"But it's hot out here, and I want to see my daddy,"* her oldest son had countered.

Wiping the sweat from her forehead, Unique had to agree that it was indeed hot outside. *"The windows are down, and I won't be but a second, I promise you."* Unique got out of the car and closed the door. No sooner had she done that than some young thug came down from the porch of the house she had parked in front of.

*"What you need?"* the Li'l Wayne wannabe asked her.

*"Excuse me,"* Unique replied.

*"Man, she don't want nothing,"* another young guy from the porch called out to the young thug.

He sucked his teeth and rolled his eyes at Unique. Then he turned around and walked back to the porch while mumbling, *"Witch, made me walk all the way down here for nothing. I oughtta . . ."* he looked back over his shoulder at Unique with a crooked lip and threatening look in his eyes, but then kept it moving back to his spot on the porch.

*"On second thought," Unique said to herself, quickly going back to the car and rolling up the windows, "I'll only be a half a second," she promised the boys, locking the door, and then hurrying to the house her baby daddy was at. She didn't want that young thug retaliating against her by using her boys. She didn't want anyone having access to her boys in that neighborhood.*

Making a split-second decision, Unique had weighed whether it would have been better to take the boys to the crack house with her or leave them in the car. Having no idea the police would have raided the place, she was glad she hadn't had her boys in the house caught up in that drama. Besides, the police would have probably attacked them too. And by now, they'd been down at Franklin County Children's Services scared to death. But as she stood there with three guns pointed at her, she was willing to take all the bullets they could fire off to find out just where her sons were.

"But my sons, my babies . . ." Despite the orders the female officer had shouted out to her, and despite the three guns pointed at her, Unique charged at the door. "I have to go back and get my sons. My boys. They're at the house. They're still back at that house."

"Ms. Gray, settle down," the female officer ordered. "I gave you a direct order to freeze. Don't make me have to use this weapon, Ms. Gray." She nodded to her two fellow officers. "Don't make any of us."

"Go ahead, shoot me, but I'm going to get my boys. My boys!"

One of the officers tucked away his weapon and decided to physically restrain Unique. She was in cuffs. He knew he could take her.

"Please, please, let me go." Unique kicked and screamed until the second officer who had entered the room assisted in restraining her as well.

The female officer put her gun away. "Ms. Gray, we searched that house. We turned it upside down. Your boys are not there. No one is there. Anyone in that house was arrested along with you, so trust me, your boys are not at that house."

"The car," Unique cried as her body, weak from fighting the officers, went limp. "I left them in car while I went to the house. I was only going to be a second. I told them I would be right back. So you see, I have to go back. I have to go back to get them. I have to go back to get my boys. I promised them I'd be right back. I promised them."

Unique began to weep uncontrollably. It was no good. Every ounce of strength she might have had just ten seconds ago was now depleted.

"Officer Crouse, can I talk to you for a second." The voice came from Officer Givens who appeared in the doorway.

"Sure," the female officer replied to Officer Givens. She then addressed the other two officers as she exited the room. "Keep an eye on her. I'll be right back."

"Bring my boys back with you, please," Unique cried. "Please bring my boys back to me. They're probably scared. I told them I would be right back. I told them I would be right back."

With a sick feeling in the pit of her stomach, Unique lay on the floor thinking that her boys being down at Franklin County Children's Services might not have been so bad after all.

# Chapter Nine

Lorain had no idea how much time had gone by when Nicholas finally entered the ER waiting room. She'd been way too busy praying and trying to figure out how to make her shining moment that had been interrupted by a casting of darkness, shine again.

Before Nicholas was pulled away from their conversation outside, Lorain had known exactly how she was going to tell Nicholas that she would finally marry him. Well, she wasn't exactly going to tell him; more like show him. The flashing of the engagement ring on her finger would have said it all. It would have let him know that she was ready. She was finally ready.

Standing up to greet Nicholas as he walked over to her, Lorain was afraid her little plan wasn't going to pan out so well. Whatever emergency it was that had pulled Nicholas away from her earlier must not have panned out so well either. That was evident by the dreadful look on his face. Still, Lorain slipped her hand back in her pant pocket for an attempt to play this thing out all over again; successfully this time.

"Nicholas, is everything okay?" Lorain didn't know why she asked that. It was apparent that everything wasn't okay. Still, she had to ask.

Nicholas didn't speak. He opened his mouth, but he didn't speak. He clasped his hands together and stared at Lorain. "Uh, come on, let's go somewhere else to talk," he suggested.

"Okay. That's fine," Lorain agreed. Actually, she'd rather they did go somewhere else. Telling the man she loved that she was ready to marry him in the ER room with all those ailing people just didn't seem right. She'd be smiling, happy, crying tears of joy while others were in pain and misery.

Nicholas turned on his heels and led Lorain through a door she'd seen patients go behind after the nurse had called their names. As Lorain followed Nicholas down a hall, she had the strangest feeling that everyone was watching her. She spotted Jim. When she caught him watching her, he quickly shifted his eyes from her direction. Something was going on. Lorain didn't know exactly what it was, but something was certainly going on.

"In here will be fine." Nicholas opened the door to the staff lounge area. He moved aside so that Lorain could enter first. That's when he noticed the head nurse startled by his and Lorain's arrival.

"Oh, I'm sorry, Dr. Wright. Let me excuse myself," the nurse said, gathering her composure and whisking by Nicholas and Lorain to exit the lounge.

Lorain looked at the nurse's back for a moment as she walked away, and then she turned to Nicholas. "Was she okay? It looked like she'd been crying or something. Does it have something to do with the patients you all got called away to handle?"

Nicholas felt sick to his stomach. What he was about to do—what he was about to say—he'd said and done on several occasions before in his five years of being a doctor. This wasn't his first. For some reason, though, this time it was far more difficult than any other time. Not for some reason; the reason being, it had never hit so close to home before.

"Nicholas, what's going on?" Lorain was no doctor, but it wasn't that hard to diagnose that something was not kosher up in that place. Especially with the way everyone in the hospital was acting. "You're not acting like yourself. Jim was a little weird acting compared to how upbeat he'd been earlier. And then that nurse . . ."

"Have you talked to Unique?" That's all Nicholas could think to say.

"Unique?" Lorain shook her head, puzzled at Nicholas's line of questioning. "No."

Nicholas tried to think of something else to say, but his mind was blank.

"Okay, now you're scaring me. You're just standing there like some zombie. You need to start talking."

Nicholas agreed; he needed to start talking. He just needed to say it. Just say it. If Nike could just do it, surely he could just say it. "That emergency; it was three children. It was three little boys."

"Oh no. I can only imagine how it is when you guys have to deal with sick children. I mean, not that taking care of sick or injured adults isn't just as important. There's just something about seeing a child go through . . ." Lorain shook her head. "Then I guess that explains everyone's mood around here." Walking over to Nicholas, Lorain took his hands. "Do you want me to pray?"

Nicholas gently shook Lorain's hands. "No, hon. Why don't I pray?"

Lorain couldn't hide the complete look of shock that displayed itself on her face. Besides a grace over his food here and there, she had never heard Nicholas pray before.

"Sure, by all means you can pray," Lorain replied.

Even after Nicholas bowed his head and closed his eyes, Lorain still stood there in shock. At first she couldn't believe this was happening. She honestly couldn't believe Nicholas was actually leading the two of them in prayer. She was ashamed that she was jumping for joy on the inside. She wasn't ashamed that her soul was giving God glory for showing her a sign in the eleventh hour that He was doing a great work in her life and in her relationship with Nicholas. She was ashamed, though, that it had taken three sick children for the manifestation.

"Heavenly, Father, I . . . I just want to thank you, first and foremost, for all you have enabled me to do," Nicholas prayed. "For all the miracles you have allowed me to witness right here in this hospital. I thank you, Lord." He paused and then continued. "Father, I've seen you take a heart that has stopped beating and make it beat again. Lord, I've seen you take a brain that couldn't function, that hadn't functioned for years, and restore it whole."

"Praise God," Lorain spoke. Her eyes were now closed, and she was fully engulfed in Nicholas's prayer to God.

"What I thank you for most, God, though, is the strength and comfort you provide daily in this place to families who don't always get to experience your earthly miracles with the saving of their loved one's life. Today is one of those days, Lord." He gently shook Lorain's hands. "Today, Lord, I need you to send your comforter like never before to saturate this place. For today we lost not one, but three souls, God. Three young souls." Nicholas's voice began to crack. "And, God, I don't know how I'm going to tell the boys' family. They were so special. So kind and loving. If I didn't know any better, Lord, I'd say they were angels right here on earth. They were so loved; so very loved, and they will be missed." Taking a deep breath, Nicholas closed out his prayer. "So, God, I ask you to give me the strength to say the words that I need to say. In Jesus' mighty name; Amen."

"Amen." Lorain, so moved by a praying man, a praying man that was her man . . . her soon-to-be husband, pulled her hands from Nicholas's and threw them around his neck. "Nicholas, that was beautiful."

Nicholas put his arms around Lorain and squeezed her tightly. He didn't want to let her go, because he knew that when he did, he'd have to say those dreaded words to her.

Sensing a presence behind them, Lorain pulled away from Nicholas and looked behind her. In the process, she wiped away the tear that had fallen from her eye. "Oh, hi, Jim," she said with a sniffle.

"Oh God, Lorain, I'm so sorry." Jim walked over to Lorain and extended his hands to her. Although slightly caught off guard, Lorain extended hers to Jim. "They were such fine boys. I know I've only met them once, at the picnic, but they were like little angels, those grandsons of yours. I know you are going to miss them. But please know that you have my deepest condolences."

"Jim . . . wha . . . what are you talking . . ." Now it was as if the pit had jumped from Nicholas's stomach to Lorain's. She looked back over her shoulder at Nicholas. "Nicholas, what is . . . What is Jim talking about?"

All Nicholas could do was exhale.

That was Jim's sign that he'd spoken too soon; sooner than Nicholas had spoken. "Oh my, Dr. Wright, I'm sorry," Jim apologized. "I thought you'd told her. When I walked in and saw you two . . ." he looked at Lorain. "And her crying . . . and I just thought . . ."

"Tell me . . . Tell me what?" Lorain asked Jim. When Jim didn't reply, Lorain snatched her hands from his and sharply turned to Nicholas. "Tell me what, Nicholas?"

"Lorain . . ." Nicholas tried to speak, but he still couldn't get the words out.

"Look, somebody better tell me something before I go straight Mel Gibson up in here," Lorain warned.

Nicholas looked over at Jim. "Uh, Jim, could you please excuse us?"

"Sure, Dr. Wright." Those words were music to Jim's ears as he hurried up out of that room as quickly as he could, closing the door behind him.

Once Jim was gone, Nicholas addressed Lorain. "Baby, you might want to sit down."

"Why, Nick? Sit down for what? I'm telling you, if you don't stop playing with me, man . . ." Lorain's voice hit high pitches and cracked like Usher's did when he was going through puberty and experiencing a voice change earlier in his career.

By now, reality was starting to kick in with Lorain. Before, she'd been so fixated on the entire engagement thing and whatnot, that she wasn't really listening and putting the pieces together of Nick's prayer. But now, after Jim's premature condolences and the way Nicholas was acting, it was all starting to come together.

"Oh my God . . . those boys. The three boys you keep talking about. And then you asked me if I'd talked to Unique. Are you trying to say that . . . are you trying to tell me that . . ." Lorain began to breathe in and out as if a Lamaze coach had taught her breathing techniques. She placed her hand over her rapidly beating heart. Her hands began to take on a life of their own as they went to her eyes, then clinched in fist, then back to her heart.

"Lorain, calm down." Nicholas put his arm around Lorain for support and guided her over to one of the couches in the lounge.

"No. Get off of me!" Lorain removed herself from Nicholas's arm. "I don't want to sit down. I just want you to tell me if those are my grandsons you're talking about. Because in your prayer you said . . . you said . . ." Before Lorain knew it she was down on the couch anyway.

"I'm sorry. I'm so sorry, Lorain," Nicholas said as he put his arms around Lorain and hugged her.

Lorain's insides were screaming—crying out, but a sound never released from her mouth. Her mouth assumed the position for a loud roar of denial, that feeling she was feeling inside, to come out. But nothing ever came out. Let her tell it, air wasn't even coming out of her nose. She didn't know how she was even breathing. She could only remember being in this position one other time. She'd done something to upset her mother. The next thing she knew, Eleanor had knocked her upside her head so hard that she felt as if the world were coming to an end. It had hurt so badly that Lorain's body was in shock. It hurt so badly that her brain couldn't believe her body had absorbed such pain. Her brain was in so much denial of the pain that it had a delayed reaction. It was like it took forever for the cry that had built up in her little body to come out. Eventually it did though. And just like now, in the hospital lounge, in Nicholas's arms, the cry that had built up in her body would come out. It came out, but not even the closed door could keep it from ricocheting down the hospital halls.

# Chapter Ten

Maybe the female officer was a good cop, or maybe she was just a mother. Whatever the case was, right now she was the only comfort Unique had. The Holy Spirit couldn't even be felt in the room by Unique.

When the female officer had returned back to the questioning room after being summoned by Officer Givens, the grim look on her face had said it all.

"My boys!" Unique cried from the floor, witnessing the look on the woman's face. "My babies! Oh God, my babies! God, nooo. God, nooo." At this point, Unique really was talking to God. She was screaming at the top of her lungs up at heaven. "This better not be happening, God. This better not be happening." She looked back at the female officer. "Did you tell my boys Mommy is okay, that she didn't lie, and that she is coming back for them?" Unique was in complete denial. She put her face down as tears poured out like a water faucet. "My boys; where are they? Please." Still in denial, she began rocking back and forth in an attempt to comfort herself.

Swallowing hard, the female officer walked over to Unique and kneeled down. "I'm sorry, ma'am, but your sons are dead."

*Ma'am* is what the woman had called Unique; not Ms. Gray. No, that would have been far too personal. She had to disconnect herself from Unique at all costs. She was there to do a job, not be a friend, and definitely not for Unique's support. She was there to lock this drug-trafficking woman up and throw away the key. She was there to use her female advantage to fake a bond with Unique and get her to roll over on the big dawgs. But when Unique threw her cuffed arms around the female officer's neck and shook with tears . . . with pain, somehow, right then and there everything changed.

Before the female officer knew it, she was down on the ground with Unique and her arms had somehow managed to wrap themselves around Unique. Next, one of her hands had the nerve to move itself up and down Unique's back. And before she could stop them, words came out of her mouth. "It's okay. It's okay. I'm here. Everything is going to be all right."

The female officer signaled for the other officers in the room to leave them alone. "I got this," she worded to them. She dug for her keys to the handcuffs to remove them from Unique's wrists.

One of the officers shot her an "Are you sure?" look. She replied with a nod and the officers exited quietly.

"My boys," Unique moaned over and over. She herself was now cuddled up like a baby on the floor against the officer.

After about twenty minutes of consoling Unique, the female officer was able to get Unique off the floor and back into a chair. Too weak to sit up, Unique's upper body was sprawled out over the table. Eventually, Officer Givens returned to the room. He walked over to his fellow officer and whispered something in her ear. The brown caramel color flushed from her face.

"Ms. Gray." Officer Givens's baritone voice caused Unique to lift her head. "I'm sorry about all of this, I really am. I can only imagine how devastating this must be for you. Still, we need to talk to you about why you are here."

"I know, I know." Unique managed to sit up. "Just take me to jail. Charge me with whatever. Lock me up and throw away the key. Throw me away with the key. Don't worry; I've been thrown away before. Charge me with selling drugs, using drugs, being a dope kingpin, whatever you want. I have nothing to live for out there anyway. I have nothing to live for now."

Officer Givens looked at his female counterpart. He was a tough cop. He'd been on the force for over seventeen years, but his job never got any easier. Immune to pretty much everything to a certain degree, still, the things he had to do sometimes never got any easier.

"I'll do it," the female officer told him. Sitting across the table from Unique, she stood up. Hesitating at first, she walked over to Unique and rested her hand on her shoulder.

Just the warm, comforting touch caused Unique to break down all over again, crying out for her boys. Again, the officer assured Unique that everything was going to be all right as she patted Unique's shoulder.

Was this all part of the officer's good cop act? Whether it was or wasn't didn't matter to Unique at the moment. She needed someone there to tell her that everything was going to be all right, even though she knew that "all right" was a long ways away. Right now, everything was "all wrong." Things couldn't have been more wrong as far as Unique was concerned. But they were about to be. Boy, oh boy, were they about to be.

"Ms. Gray, I hate to do this, I really do," the officer told her, "but you're being arrested."

"I don't care. Arrest me! Arrest me!" Unique demanded. "I don't care if I die in jail. My boys are dead. My boys are dead. Can't you see, I might as well be dead too? So do you think I care about some trumped-up drug charges? No! So, here, take me to jail." Unique stood up and extended her hands to the officer to return the cuffs to her wrists.

The officer took a deep breath, then looked over her shoulder back at Officer Givens. He cast his eyes away from her. He'd allowed her to do a dirty part of his job. Here he was this tough, bad cop, and yet he couldn't have mumbled out the words to Unique that the female officer was about to.

Turning back around to face Unique, the female officer slowly pulled the cuffs back out. "Turn around." Before Unique's hands had been cuffed in front of her, but now, the officer was going to cuff them behind her back.

Slowly, Unique turned around. She stood staring at the little camera up in the corner of the ceiling that she was noticing for the first time. A tear fell from each of her eyes. She closed them when she heard the jingling of the metal bracelets. The coldness from the rings making contact with her wrists caused her to flinch. The sound of the cuffs locking around her wrists sounded more like thunder in a huge storm, making it only seem normal for Unique to feel as if lightning were ripping through her when she heard the officer say, "Unique Emerald Gray, you are under arrest. You are being charged for the death of your sons."

# Chapter Eleven

"Oh my God! I have to get to Unique. I have to get to my baby!" Lorain became frantic as she removed herself from Nicholas's embrace and darted for the door to exit the hospital lounge.

"Wait a minute." Nicholas stood and caught up with her before she could leave. "I really don't think it's a good idea that you drive in this condition, Lorain. I don't want you to end up back here in the ER as a patient."

"I have to go. I have to see about Unique."

"And I understand that, but you're a mess right now. Just wait here a little while longer. I'm sure Unique is probably even on her way here to the hospital to see . . . to . . ." Not wanting to say the wrong thing, Nicholas just said nothing at all. There'd been many a-time that family members insisted on saying final good-byes to their loved ones after they'd passed in the hospital. Then there were the families who insisted on having their last memories of their loved ones of when they were alive. He didn't know which Unique would choose, but he knew as a mother, she'd still come up to the hospital to get details.

The thought never even crossed Lorain's mind that nine times out of ten Unique was probably on her way to the hospital. She wondered if Unique even knew that her sons had passed; that they couldn't be saved by the doctors and nurses. Lorain thought for a quick second of the emotions her daughter must be going through right now if she, in fact, did know the boys were dead. Lorain, herself, nearly collapsed just thinking about it. How they died she hadn't even thought to ask. She had to get over the sheer shock of them being dead first.

"Oh, God!" Hunched over as if she had a belly ache, Lorain began to weep.

"See, that's it. I'm sorry, honey, but I can't let you leave from here like this." Nicholas led Lorain back over to the couch and sat her down. "Just calm down and let's call Unique, okay?"

Lorain nodded.

"Where's your cell phone?" By the time he asked, Nicholas was already digging in Lorain's purse for the phone. A few seconds later he pulled it out. "Here it is."

With a trembling hand, Lorain accepted the phone. She didn't dial or anything; just looked

down at the phone. Shaking her head and sniffing she said, "I . . . I don't even know what to say
to her." She looked up at Nicholas. "What do I
say to her, Nick? What do I say?"

Nicholas was at a loss for words. Yes, he'd
had to tell many families that their loved
ones had passed on to glory. After that, though,
there had always been someone else there
to comfort them. There had always been
someone else there who just knew what to
say. He'd never had to be that person, not
until now anyway.

Although Nicholas wasn't a practicing
Christian, he knew God was real. He knew of
all God's miracles and power. He'd witnessed
them and given God credit for them every day he
worked with patients. As far as he was concerned,
to some degree, he was more of a believer than
some Christians he knew. That was the reason
why even though every member of his immediate
family was a practicing Christian and member of
a church, he just couldn't follow suit. He felt his
place to worship God was right there at the hospital. That's where he felt his strongest connection
to God and saw Him at work in lives every day;
not just Sunday.

He'd seen the reactions on so-called
Christians' faces when he'd told a story of how

a person who'd been pronounced dead, no vital signs whatsoever, was brought back to life simply because God breathed on them. He'd seen their faces when he'd told stories of how a person who had been diagnosed with HIV, had been sick from it, eating pills daily just to survive the next day, had come in, and all of a sudden, tested negative for the deadly disease. Cancers not simply gone in remission, but cured . . . gone forever; all this simply because God chose to do it.

What really baffled Nicholas were the ones who had prayed at their loved one's bedside endlessly for days at a time. They'd prayed and fasted, fasted and prayed. Then when God did what they'd been asking Him to do, they couldn't really believe He'd done it. He could see the question marks on their faces. "Did God *really* do that?" Sometimes they'd give him as the doctor more honor, glory, praises, hugs, kisses, and flowers than they would the God they claimed to serve.

No. Nicholas could not be a part of that. Lately, though, he had found himself attending church more often than he had in the past. That was mostly because of Lorain though. He'd watched her, and she wasn't like some of the other Christians he'd encountered. That's why, oddly enough, he'd been attending New

Day versus the church his own family had been members of for years; the church he used to drop in on every now and then. It wasn't that there weren't these types of Christians at New Day just like at his family's church. There were just less of those types. The reason being because New Day was smaller than his family's church. In addition to that, Nicholas was just learning, after all these years, to close his eyes to man and open his heart to Jesus. But right now, his heart seemed to be aching with pain for the woman he loved so dearly. How could he sit there and tell her what to say to Unique, when he barely knew what to say to her? It was only by the direction of the Holy Spirit that he'd managed thus far.

"Baby, just tell her that you love her." The words fell out of Nicholas's mouth like they'd been sitting on his tongue all along. "Tell her that you are here for her. Tell her that God is going to make everything okay." Nicholas grabbed Lorain by the shoulders tenderly and looked into her eyes. "You do believe that, right? You do believe that God has this?"

Lorain nodded. "I do, Nicholas. I do." It was at that moment that a wind of strength trickled through Lorain's body. Until just that moment when Nicholas reminded her, she really had forgotten that God would make this thing okay.

That God would take care of Unique as well as herself. "Yes, God is going to make everything okay. That's exactly what I'm going to tell her." Lorain's shoulders lifted. Her head lifted. It was as if she was a transformer about to go into action.

Nicholas smiled. "That's it. That's right. That's my girl . . . That's my strong woman of God."

Lorain smiled, something she thought she would never do for a long time. "Yes . . . a strong woman in the Lord. I'm going to use that strength to get through this. I'm going to use the strength of Christ Jesus to help Unique get through this. Yes, that's exactly what I'm going to do." Lorain dialed Unique's cell phone and hit the button for the call to go through. She looked over at Nicholas while the phone rang.

Nicholas's smile broadened as he took her hand. He was so thankful that God had showed up and orchestrated his communication with Lorain. He'd kept his eyes off of the situation and on Jesus. Even now his eyes were still on Jesus as Lorain made that call to Unique. His eyes were so much so on Jesus that even though Lorain's hand rested in his, not once did he notice she was wearing the ring.

# Chapter Twelve

Unique lost count a long time ago of how many times she'd been up in the club doing the electric slide, the Detroit Hustle and even the booty call . . . sometimes literally doing a booty call. She never thought, though, in her wildest dreams she'd ever be in a situation in which she would be doing the perp walk. Yet, here she was dressed in jailhouse garb, hand-cuffed, being escorted out of the county jail to a van that would take her to her next destination. The past twelve hours had been unbelievable. Everything was happening so fast—just like in a movie. Only this was real time.

She wanted to cry, but this moment was too surreal for her to cry. This wasn't happening. It wasn't real. It was all in her head. It was a test from God to see if she could endure. It was a nightmare. It was all of those things, is what Unique hoped. It was anything but real. She could think about the situation any way she wanted to, but it was real all right; as real as it gets. And it was happening in real time as she trailed last in line behind five other women dressed and cuffed just like her.

Unique wanted to ask where she was going and why. Why was she being transported to another location so soon? What was so special about her circumstances where they felt she couldn't stay at county in general population? She was too stunned about the entire situation though. She couldn't even put her words together in order to ask the question, but it would soon be answered—just how *special* her circumstances were.

As all the women in line before her exited the building, Unique followed suit.

"You," a guard's voice shot at Unique. "You wait right here."

As if on cue, another guard walked over carrying some type of vest in his arms. While he prepared to put the vest on Unique, another guard removed the cuffs from her wrists so that she could put her arms through the openings in the vest.

"What's this? What's going on?" Unique was visually confused as the jacket was put on her and tightened. "I said what's going on?" Unique repeated after none of the guards had replied to her first query.

"It's a bulletproof vest." The guard who had taken her handcuffs off now locked them tightly back around her wrists.

"Ouch." Unique wondered if the guard was mad at her for asking a simple question and was trying to punish her by stopping her blood flow with the handcuffs. "Why . . . Why are you putting a bulletproof vest on me?" Worry was written on Unique's face.

The guard laughed. "Do you know how many people would love to get their hands on a mother who leaves her kids locked up in a car in the hot sun to die while she goes in a drug house to get some crack?" He laughed again. "A bulletproof vest; my friend, you need the National Guard." He looked at Unique and shook his head. "There's already been a bomb threat made. Why you think we getting you outta here quick fast and in a hurry?" He shook his head at Unique's ignorance. "Come on, let's go."

As if her feet were cemented to the ground, Unique couldn't move. Even when the guard pulled at her, her feet stayed planted where they stood.

"Did you hear me? I said, let's go." This time the guard, along with another guard, snatched her up and practically pulled her out of the building.

As a girl in the projects, Unique had lay across her dirty mattress on the floor many a time just imagining the day she'd walk out of a restaurant or something and see cameras flashing. She'd be donning a gown by one of the world's top fashion designers. She'd have bodyguards protecting her from the public. Everyone would be trying to get a picture of her to sell to newspapers and magazines. People would be calling out questions to her, and she'd reply with a pearly white grin and perfect teeth. From there she'd be ushered into a waiting limo with a driver who would take her anywhere in the world that she wanted to go.

What she never imagined is that she'd be escorted by prison guards and not bodyguards. That she'd be escorted from one jail to the next, not wearing an expensive designer gown, but instead, prison clothes and a bulletproof vest. She never imagined that all the cameras flashing would be owned by criminal news reporters and not paparazzi. It was late. The sun was going down, so the reporters would miss getting Unique's story on the five o'clock news, but she was sure come eleven o'clock, her face would be plastered on every channel.

Instead of questions like, "Ms. Gray, who are you wearing, what is your next project, and who are you dating?" Unique heard questions like, "Ms. Gray, did you leave your sons in the car in a hundred-degree weather while you went into a crack house to get high off drugs? Ms. Gray, is it true you are dating one of the cities most notorious drug lords? Ms. Gray, is it true you're a female hustler?"

Unique thought she was going to hyperventilate at the scene taking place around her. She felt as if she were outside of herself. It was as if she were nothing more than a shell already on the van along with the other prisoners, watching herself. A shell just waiting for her body to join her.

She never said a word as she made her way to the van. The people yelling out questions to her were all just blurry faces as Unique fought back tears of fear.

*Do not walk in fear. God will work this out,* she kept telling herself over and over again. *Do not walk in fear.*

Well, she was no longer walking in fear. Now positioned on a seat at the front of the van, she was sitting in fear. The ride to wherever it was that Unique was going started off on the smooth I-71 Interstate, but after about forty minutes, it became bumpy. Unique hadn't even realized they were no longer on the highway. They were now riding through some dirt roads with no signs of community living within miles.

After a few moments, the van pulled up in front of a very tall iron gate. A female guard exited a little booth and approached the driver's window. A man on the van handed the guard a piece of paper or a card or something; Unique couldn't quite make it out. The guard read over it, then nodded as she handed it back to the driver. Next, she walked around and opened the van doors. She gazed over the occupants as her lips moved, but no words came out. Unique surmised she was taking count. After doing so, she nodded at the other guard who had ridden along for the entire ride in the van. After the guard exited the van and walked across the front of the van and back over to her post, the gate opened and the van moved through it.

Unique's stomach began preparing for the Olympics by doing all sorts of crazy backflips and somersaults. She pressed her tongue against the roof of her mouth and put her cuffed hands over her mouth. She thought she might puke any minute.

*Jesus,* she repeated over and over in her head. *Jesus.*

When the van finally came to a stop, the guard stood up and opened the van doors. Several guards on the prison grounds, armed with guns, surrounded the van.

"All right, ladies,—" the guard started. He then looked over at a big, butchy-looking broad. "—and gentleman." He let out a chuckle. "You're home sweet home. Stand up and follow the instructions of your new mothers and fathers."

Everyone followed instructions, everyone, that is, except for Unique. She couldn't. If she moved she was liable to barf.

"Hey, that includes you," the guard snapped at Unique. "And let's get something straight. See those men and women out there with those nice, pretty guns?" He didn't wait for Unique to respond. "They don't really tell you things twice, if you know what I mean."

Unique looked out of the van at the gun-toting guards.

"So get your black tail up and get the heck off of my van." The guard looked up. "That goes for all of you convicts; get to moving."

Unique stood, and with a queasy stomach and queasy legs to match, she became the designated line leader, leading the other women from the van. Once all the women were off the van, a guard began to call out further instructions about where they were to go, different rules, regulations, etc. . . .

After awhile, for Unique, the words began to sound scrambled and eventually faded. By the time things became clear, she was inside a building and the guard was still howling off instructions.

"So come on, you're first." The guard was looking directly at Unique. Unique felt a tug on her arm, and then realized that the guard had been talking to her. "Hurry up, hold your hands out before I make you try to undress with the cuffs on." Initially, there had been a male officer guiding the inmates into the building. Somehow it was now a female officer doing all the instructing. Where had Unique's mind gone?

Unique held her hands out, and the guard removed the cuffs.

"Now go in there and take it off." The guard nodded to the open doorway behind her.

Unique slowly walked through the entryway and stood still.

"Like I said, through the door and to your right," the guard shouted to Unique once she saw that she was idle.

Unique looked to the right before she stepped to the right. There were several female guards lined up, each of their hands covered in rubber gloves.

At first, Unique didn't know if they were doctors or what, but then reality set in, and she realized exactly what was about to go down.

"Come on over here, sweetness, and let's see what you've got—or hopefully what you don't got," a female guard joked, holding her gloved hands up. "Get over here and take off every thing."

"Everything?" Unique questioned.

"You heard me, honey. This ain't your annual gynecology exam where you can take everything off but your socks. Those need to go too."

This nightmare of a dream just kept getting worse for Unique as she walked over and stood in front of the guard. She slowly removed her clothing.

"Now bend over," the guard instructed.

Humiliated, Unique had stripped off her clothes. As if standing there without any clothes on wasn't bad enough, the guard began poking, prodding, and lifting parts of Unique's body that made her sick to her stomach; so sick that this time, the puke she'd been holding back for the past hour or so spilled from her mouth and down the front of her body.

"Jesus!" Thank goodness the guard had been standing behind her. "Darsey!" the guard called out, then the female guard who had removed

Unique's handcuffs appeared in the doorway. "Get somebody to clean this crap up."

The guard that had been summoned looked at Unique in disgust, shook her head, then exited the room.

"I'm . . . I'm sorry," Unique apologized.

"Yeah, you're sorry, you and every other piece of poop criminal in this place," the guard replied. "Head on back to showers and clean yourself up."

Unique looked around through another opening where she saw showers. "Through there?" she questioned.

"You got a problem listening or something?" The guard stood erect and poked her chest out as if she was calling Unique out. "Didn't you hear the instructions Officer Darsey gave you out there?"

Without replying, Unique just turned and headed through the doorway and straight to the showers.

"Geez, you stink," she heard a voice say, then turned to see an armed officer standing in the front left corner of the room. "You need to hurry up for real and get in that shower." Her nose was turned up.

Unique took a couple more steps toward the shower, then she paused and looked over at the correctional officer. "Is there any soap?"

"Sure, there is." Unique was relieved until the officer added, "But not for baby killers. Now get in that shower before I change my mind and leave you with your dinner all over you so that the rats can feast on you."

*Baby killer*. Those words had stung Unique. Obviously everyone was expecting and knew what the so-called baby killer looked like.

Fear removed itself from Unique and allowed for rage to take its place. Hearing that officer refer to her as a baby killer made her want to go back to the hood of things like when she lived in the projects. She had to remind herself that she now lived in the Kingdom though. So with that she just walked on over to the shower, turned it on, and prayed that the water would wash away her anger and would wash away any remnants of fear.

During that shower was when it really set in Unique's mind that perhaps that guard was right. Maybe she was nothing more than a baby killer. Her boys were dead. Who else could have killed them? Who else left them in that car to die in that heat? No, she hadn't done it on purpose, but she had done it nonetheless.

"I'm a killer," Unique proclaimed softly to herself. "I've committed the ultimate sin." It was a sin that she knew that the running shower water could not wash away. Nope, only the blood of Jesus could do that. But Unique felt what had happened was so heinous that she doubted whether even Jesus' blood could wash that one away. She deserved to be where she was. She deserved to spend the rest of her life in that place. And that's exactly what she planned on telling the judge when she had her day in court. But hopefully, someone would stop her before it got to that point; otherwise, Unique would be digging her own grave.

# Chapter Thirteen

When Lorain couldn't get a hold of Unique, she drove over to her sister's house where she and the boys had lived the last few years. She would have called the house, but they didn't have a land line. A lot of people were doing that lately; choosing cell phones over land lines. Lorain understood the fact that they wanted to save money, and if adults were just living in the house, that was fine. But most of the time, adults carried their cell phones on their persons. With children in the home, what if one of the children needed to make an emergency phone call? Having access to a land line seemed like a must when children were in the home.

Unique's sister had two children of her own. Lorain never really knew their ages, but from the looks of the little girl who'd answered the door, one of them was around nine or ten. Lorain was surprised to see that the child was still up considering how late in the evening it was, but then again, it was summer break.

"Hi, honey, is your mother home?" Lorain tried her best to maintain her composure. Although Nicholas had forced her to sit in the hospital lobby for a few more minutes while she pulled herself together, there was no way she'd be completely okay. No, that was going to take some time. But still, she'd managed to calm down enough to make the drive to Unique's, crying the entire time.

"She in there mad," the girl pointed over her shoulder, "trying to get a hold of Auntie Uni—"

"Is that her?" Lorain heard the agitated voice of a grown woman crawling up behind the young child.

"No, Mama. It's the lady who be picking up Auntie Unique sometimes," the little girl informed her mother.

"Oh." The woman was visually disappointed. "Hi, Lorain."

"Renee," was all Lorain mumbled out.

"If you're here to see Unique, I have no idea where that child is with my car." And that was the beginning of the sibling's rant. "I let her borrow my car way earlier this morning. She said she was just supposed to be going to pick up some money from one of her son's fathers, but she ain't back yet. It's almost eleven o'clock at night. I've been calling her back to back but the phone keeps—"

"Going to voice mail," Lorain finished. "Yeah, I know. I've been trying to get a hold of her too. That's why I came on over." It was apparent to Lorain that Unique's sister had no idea about the boys; otherwise, her concerns wouldn't have been of a material thing; her automobile. "Listen, Renee, can I come in for a minute?"

"Why not?" She let out a heated wind and allowed her arms to flail, and then drop to her sides. "I already had to call my boss and let her know that I wouldn't be able to make it in to work because I was having 'car trouble.'" She used her fingers to make quotation marks in the air.

Unique's sister led Lorain over to the couch. "You can have a seat."

Lorain accepted the offer and sat on the worn but pretty decent sofa.

Picking up the remote from the table and handing it to Lorain, the young woman about five or six years Unique's senior sat down as well. "The kids been watching *Nickelodeon* all day. It keeps them off my nerves. But you can turn to something you'd like if you want to."

"No, thank you." Lorain kindly shook her head as Sponge Bob's theme music filled the air.

"Oh, I can't take that song no more," Renee spat, turning to one of the local channels. Placing the remote on the table, she sat and waited for Lorain to speak.

Gathering the exact words she needed to tell this woman that her nephews were dead, Lorain remained silent. Like Nicholas, she didn't want to say the wrong thing.

Before Lorain could speak, Unique's sister did. "You know, I think that's cool what you and Unique did for each other."

"Pardon me?" Lorain didn't know what she was talking about.

"You know with the twins and all, her having them for you and you raising them and all that other stuff. Because when that child first told me she was pregnant, I was about to tell her that she had to pack her stuff and keep it moving. There's no way we had room in this place for two more. So how are those babies anyway? The boys just love 'em. They can't stop talking about their aunties. As far as they are concerned, them girls are their sisters."

"The twins?" Lorain remembered that her mother was watching them. She'd forgotten to call her and let her know what was going on. She was surprised her mother hadn't called her first. But then again, Lorain had told her she might be late and not to worry. Lorain figured her mother probably didn't want to interrupt her and Nicholas's moment; the moment that never happened. Lorain figured she'd go ahead and call Eleanor now, but she couldn't do it in front of Unique's sister, especially with her not knowing yet. "My mother has the twins. Do you mind if I step out and call to check on them?" Lorain stood.

"No, I don't mind at all." Unique's sister wondered why Lorain felt it necessary to have to leave the house just to talk on the phone, but she didn't want to be nosy and question her.

Lorain excused herself and went on the porch and dialed her mother's phone number.

"Lorain, I was just about to call you," Eleanor said after picking up on the first ring. "Did you see it? It's on right now! Did you see it on the news? About Unique and her boys?"

"It's on the news?" Lorain asked.

"Yes. Dear God, how's Unique doing?" Eleanor asked. "Have you talked to her? My God, baby, how are you doing? Here I am thinking I'm letting you be to enjoy your engagement, and you've been dealing with this. I can't believe what I'm seeing on this television."

"Television?" Lorain mumbled to herself. "Mom, let me call you back, please. I promise I'll call you right back." Lorain hung up the phone and darted back into the house. She found Unique's sister standing with her hands over her mouth staring at the television.

"Did you know? Is that why you're here?" Unique's sister stared at Lorain waiting for an answer. "I was wondering why you showed up at the house so late." She turned her attention back to the television. "They, they just said Unique's boys are dead. See, watch." She nervously fumbled with the remote and pressed a button that would rewind live television like it was a movie in a DVD player.

Lorain watched as a reporter covered the story. "Police say they had no idea children were even in the car; nobody did. Apparently the boys were hiding down on the floor of the car where no one could see them. They'd probably been frightened by all the action and noise of the raid on the crack house their mother was in."

The reporter looked down at a piece of paper she had in her hand. "Reports say that while the three boys were locked in the car on the hottest day of the year, their mother was inside copping drugs, they believe, with the intent to sell based on the quantity. No telling how long their mother might have intended on staying inside, but when the house was suddenly raided, whatever her intentions were no longer mattered. Hauled off to jail, police say the mother never said a word to them about her children having been left in the car. They were only discovered when, after the raid, some of the landlords in the neighborhood came by to sort of 'clean house.' One landlord in particular was having cars towed that were parked in front of his houses that didn't belong to his tenants."

Next, the news showed a picture of a near toothless old man. "I knocked on the doors of my tenants to see if the car belonged to any one of them. Nobody claimed it. I even went and knocked on a couple houses across the street. Again, nobody claimed it. I figured it belonged to somebody who had something to do with that big drug bust, so I called the police to have it towed from in front of my property. They the ones found them boys down inside the car." The man's voice began to crack. "They say they was huddled together on their knees, like they'd been praying or some—" The man couldn't finish. He broke down and signaled the camera man to cut him off.

And just like the man, both Lorain and Renee broke down as well.

"Oh my God. Oh my God!" was all Unique's sister could say as she fell to the couch. "This isn't real . . . my nephews . . . no . . . this can't be . . . no. God, Unique, what were you thinking?"

Hearing Unique's name, Lorain turned her attention back to the television screen where she saw footage of Unique being escorted into a van. Seeing her child in jail-issued clothes and a bulletproof vest, Lorain was done. There was no more time for breaking down and falling out. It was time for warfare. Lorain knew her daughter. She knew Unique well enough to know that what these reporters were saying was not true. So if the police thought for one minute they were going to charge her daughter with the death of her own sons, drug possession, or anything else, they had another think coming.

"Where are you going?" Renee asked Lorain when she saw her hightailing it out of the living room to the front door.

"I'm going to the jail to see about Unique."

"They're not going to let you do that. It's too late."

"Oh yes, they will. I'm her mother, and they are going to let me see my baby." On that note, Lorain charged out of the house and into her car. Putting the pedal to the metal, she took off to go see about her daughter, but unbeknownst to her, she wasn't the only one. It looked as though the police weren't going to be the only somebody Lorain would have to deal with when it came to seeing Unique.

# Chapter Fourteen

It was so late by the time Lorain got home in the wee hours of the night-morning-whichever that she just left the twins with her mother. This morning she'd already called into her job, informing her boss what was going on and that she'd need a few days off work. After doing so, she jumped in the shower, got dressed, and headed out of the door on her way to see Unique.

Last night had been a failed attempt. She'd gone to the county jail only to find out that Unique had been transported elsewhere. Lorain didn't know much about jail procedure, but she found it odd that Unique would be moved before any type of court appearance.

"It was for her own safety," a deputy had told Lorain after she questioned why Unique had been transported without even having been arraigned. *Special circumstances* were the words the deputy had used to further explain the situation.

Lorain had made a couple of phone calls to find out exactly what was going on with Unique; if she was going to be arraigned today or not. The answer was "not." Today she was being assigned a public defender who would read over the police reports and interview Unique.

Having a public defender defend Unique didn't sit well with Lorain. So when the pastor of New Day Temple of Faith phoned her this morning and suggested the church raise funds to at least be able to afford the retainer for a good private attorney, Lorain was relieved. "Let's just do what we can for now," her pastor had said. "We'll trust God for the rest."

A lot of trust in God was going to be needed to get them through this ordeal. Lorain could just feel it. She could also feel the bumps all over the secluded, dirt road she was driving starting to shake up her empty belly. She hadn't eaten in almost an entire day now, and she wasn't going to until she saw her daughter.

Parking and entering the jail, Lorain made her way over to the visitor sign-in window. Fourth in line, after about fifteen minutes, it was finally her turn.

"Hi, my name is Viola Lorain Watson." She knew she had to give her full government name that appeared on her ID. "I'm here to see Unique Emerald Gray. I'm her mother."

The woman on the other side of the window looked up at Lorain knowingly. She obviously knew exactly who Unique was; not personally, but the reason why she was in jail. Lorain could tell the woman knew Unique's story and was probably wondering just who had given birth to the evil woman the media was portraying Unique to be.

Lorain knew in her heart something wasn't right about that story. It wasn't the entire story. The Unique she knew loved her boys and would never put them in harm's way. She wouldn't do it for crack cocaine or anything else, for that matter. Besides, Unique didn't even do drugs, and she darn sure didn't sell them. Had she been a drug dealer, she would have had a pimped-out ride and a blinged-out cross necklace around her neck. Maybe a gold tooth or two . . . maybe. At least that's the stereotypical drug dealer Lorain had seen on television shows . . . or were those the rappers she'd seen on awards shows? Who knows. Perhaps drug dealers didn't look like that. Perhaps they did look like Unique. Perhaps they were just regular-looking people who felt as though they couldn't feed their families just any ol' regular way. Who really knew? Because all Lorain knew was that whatever a drug dealer was supposed to look like, and whatever their reasons for selling drugs, Unique was not one of them; no way, no how. And Lorain would testify to that to a million juries if she had to.

"*You're* her mother, huh?" There was something about the way the woman behind the window said it that made Lorain feel strange.

"Yes. Yes, I am. Unique Emerald Gray is my daughter," Lorain said with a hint of arrogance. She was not about to stand there and let this woman make her feel belittled because of who she was. She was Unique's mother, and she would shout it out on a mountaintop to the world if she had to.

The woman shook her head and had a menacing grin on her face. "Okay, whatever." She scribbled something down on a log sheet in front of her, and then pushed it to Lorain through a small opening at the bottom of the window. "Fill this out."

Lorain nervously took the log sheet and the pen the woman offered.

"You never done this before? You never visited anybody in lockup before?" the woman asked Lorain, taking note of her demeanor.

Lorain replied with the shaking of her head.

"Okay, well, here's the deal. I'm going to need to see some ID. You're going to have to go through a search . . ." The woman proceeded to rattle off all kinds of information. "Right now, she's back visiting with her counsel, but just as soon as—"

Lorain cut the woman off. "But I'm going to . . . my church . . . Unique's and my church, we're going to hire her a private attorney."

"That's all good, but for now, your *daughter* needs representation, honey. Do you want her to just sit here and rot while you find her an attorney? If that's the case, you should have found an attorney first and brought him up here with you."

Maybe the woman was right, but she could have been a little bit more diplomatic in expressing it. Lorain made a mental note to stop by the church after she left the jail. Not only would she need to further discuss with her pastor the funds for hiring an attorney for Unique, but she'd need to discuss funeral arrangements for the boys as well. She wanted to see to it that her grandsons had a proper burial.

"Anyway, *Unique's mother*, you can take a seat and someone will call you when you can go back and start the visiting process."

"Thank you," Lorain said before adding, "God bless you." She turned and headed to a seat in the waiting area, not knowing if she really wanted God to bless that woman or not, or if that was just her sarcastic way of letting that woman know that she needed Jesus. She needed Jesus in her life to give her an attitude adjustment.

Finding a seat in the middle of the waiting room, Lorain sat down. And she sat, and she sat, and she sat. She felt bad about the fact that this public defender was spending so much time discussing Unique's case with her when soon, and very soon, his or her services would no longer be needed. She didn't know just how much money the church would donate or raise, but she was willing to borrow from her 401(k) retirement plan if she had to in order to make sure Unique had decent representation.

At least an hour had gone by and Lorain still sat in the waiting room. Her legs were bouncing as a sign of her anxiety. She'd tried taking out the miniature Bible she carried around in her purse and reading it, but her mind couldn't stay focused on the scriptures before her. Just when she thought she was going to lose her mind, she heard a deputy say, "Unique Emerald Gray. Unique Emerald Gray's mother, please." The deputy then looked over his shoulder at the woman behind the window who had checked Lorain in. They shot each other a smirk.

Lorain wasn't about to let their little antics get the best of her. She let their taunting slide as she clutched her purse and stood up to go see about her daughter. As Lorain walked toward the deputy, she could feel someone else walking behind her. She looked over her shoulder and realized that it was a woman who'd been sitting in the waiting room even before Lorain herself had gotten there. Figuring the woman was heading back over to the window to ask what the holdup was on her own visit, Lorain turned her attention back to the path in front of her.

Stopping a couple feet in front of the deputy, Lorain informed him of who she was by stating, "I'm Unique Emerald Gray's mother." But it was like she had an echo as a voice beside her had said the exact same words.

"I'm Unique Emerald Gray's mother," the woman standing next to Lorain had said simultaneously with Lorain. It was the same woman Lorain had thought was heading over to the sign-in window.

Both women looked at each other strangely. This was simultaneous with the deputy and the woman behind the window looking at each other and smiling.

"Well, well, looks like we have a matter of confusion before us," the deputy said, holding back a chuckle and a smile. "Ms. Gray is back there waiting to see her mother, and I got two women standing in front of me claiming to be that person. Hmmm." The deputy scratched his head. "Now which one of you women is the inmate's mother?"

"I am." Once again both women spat out the words together. Once again, they both shot each other a strange look.

"Look, Officer, it's complicated," Lorain said in their defense from looking like two imposters.

"Well, it can't be too complicated. A person has only got one momma, and I need to know which one of you that is."

"Me," both women shouted.

"I'm Korica Sherod," the woman said to the deputy, and then shot her next words over at Lorain, "the woman who raised Unique. I'm the woman Unique calls Mommy."

With hands on hips, Lorain shot back, "I'm Lorain Watson, the woman who gave birth to Unique."

"Humph," the woman said under her breath, "and threw her away."

The deputy looked over at the woman in the window. They were getting a real good kick out of this. "Hmm. Looks like we're not going to get anywhere here. What do you say I go back and ask Ms. Gray who her real mother is and which one of you women claiming to be her mother she'd like to see?" The officer turned and went back through the door he had come from, leaving the two women standing there, staring each other down, knowing the only winner of this standoff would be the woman who Unique called back there to see first.

Which one of them would it be? Who, in Unique's most desperate time of need, would she call on? Who would she declare as her mother? Would it be the woman who gave birth to her or the woman who raised her?

# Chapter Fifteen

"Mommy!" Unique exclaimed when she saw Korica being escorted by the deputy over to her.

"Oh, my baby girl," Korica said. Korica was the woman who had raised Unique as her daughter, even though technically, or legally, she wasn't. She'd always treated Unique like she was blood. Nobody could tell her that Unique hadn't grown in her belly and she'd given birth to her herself. Unique even looked like her other four children, who somehow managed to look exactly like her, and like each other, even though they all had different fathers.

"They're dead, Mommy. The boys are dead," Unique began to cry. This was the first family member Unique had been afforded the opportunity of sharing the deaths of her sons with.

Korica went and flung her arms around Unique for an embrace. She couldn't hold her the way she wanted to, though, because of Unique's hands being cuffed in front of her.

Korica went on a cursing rage to get the cuffs taken off of Unique. "Can y'all at least take these things off of her while her momma is here to see her? Y'all got her chained up like she's an animal. My daughter is not an animal. She's a human being. She's a mother whose children just died yesterday, for Christ's sake."

"Ma'am, if you don't calm down, you're going to be chained up next," a deputy threatened Korica. "So I'd advise you to sit on down and take this visit."

After rattling off a couple more expletives under her breath, Korica followed the advice of the officer. The last thing she needed was for her kids to be trying to rustle up money to bail her out of jail.

Sitting down, tears streamed down Unique's face. "Mommy, I killed my boys. I left 'em in that car to die, Mommy."

"No no no, baby." Korica shook her head as she sat down in a chair next to Unique. "I know you. I know how much you love them boys. That would never happen. You would never do something like that. There's got to be a mistake or some explanation."

"There's no mistake. I let this happen; their mother, who was suppose to protect them. This is my fault, and for what? Some child support money?"

Korica placed her free hands on top of Unique's cuffed ones. "Baby girl, is that why you were in that house? Just to get child support money from one of them sorry behind baby's daddies?" Korica sounded relieved and expressed it with the hot wind she let loose from her mouth. "Thank God."

"Why else did you think I was in there, Mommy? Why else would I be up in a crack house?" Unique questioned.

"Well . . . I . . . the television said . . . and—"

"What? What is the television saying about me?" Unique was starting to get agitated in a bad way.

"Nothing, baby, nothing. Just calm down."

"No, Mommy, I need to know what the world is thinking. What these people are telling the world."

Giving in, Korica replied. "They just saying that you left the boys in the car while you went in to get some crack, that's all." Korica tried to downplay it as much as she could.

"That's all? That's all?" Unique was outraged. "But that's not what happened. You know I don't do drugs, Mommy."

"Yeah, I know, I know." Korica felt guilty for almost believing what the media was saying.

"Then why did you think—" Unique shooed her hand. ". . . never mind. It doesn't even matter anymore. It doesn't even matter why I was in that house. All that matters was that I left my babies in that car, and now they're dead." Unique broke down in tears. "I deserve to be in here. That's what I just told that attorney guy that was just in here. I told him that he doesn't even need to bother wasting the taxpayers' money on this one. It's my fault my boys are dead, and I deserved to be punished, even if it's being in here the rest of my life."

"Unique Emerald Gray, I will not listen to such trash talk," Korica spat. "You have to stop thinking like that, baby." Korica rubbed Unique's cheek. "What's that you're always telling me about if Jesus sets you free, then you are free indeed?"

"John, chapter eight, verse thirty-six," Unique mumbled.

"Then be free, baby girl. Because otherwise, whether you're in this here jail or not, you're not going to be free. You are going to be a prisoner in your own mind. A prisoner of guilt and shame and every other negative emotion. What you are going to do to yourself is going to be more confining than a jail cell could ever be." Straightening up, Korica concluded, "And I know that little skinny white boy with long hair with that piece of napkin stapled to him while hanging on a tree didn't go through all that for you to make yourself a prisoner, did he?"

Unique looked up to see Korica looking as serious as a heart attack. She'd acted like she had just recited the scene at Calvary straight from the Bible. Suddenly, Unique did something she hadn't done in a long time; her lips cracked a smile. She covered her mouth with her hands, but then the smile turned into a chuckle. Then she just all-out began to roar in laughter.

Although confused regarding what her daughter was laughing about, it became contagious nonetheless. Korica started chuckling too, in between asking Unique, "What? What's so funny?"

"Nothing, Mommy, just please . . . pretty please, if I'm out of here by the time we have Friends and Family Day again at church, will you please come with me?" Unique laughed harder. "Even if I'm not out, go without me, Mommy, please. Go to Bible Study or something."

Picking up on why Unique was laughing, Korica nodded and rolled her eyes in her head. "Okay, so I'm not the best at telling Bible stories, but you know what I was saying."

"Yes, Mommy, I know what you're saying." Even though Korica hadn't relayed the scene at Calvary as though she were some Bible scholar, Unique still got it. She got the fact that Jesus had died for her and had suffered for her. Unique thanked God that her mommy had been there to remind her of it. A few more hours and Unique might have given up completely, not just on herself, but perhaps on God. But she'd never know, because right now she had to focus on getting free, both mentally and physically free from rotting in that jail. Unique stared into her mother's eyes. "I'm free, Mommy; I'm free."

"Yes, you are, baby girl. Yes, you are," a teary-eyed Korica replied.

Unique let out a long breath as she sat looking as though she were a mountain climber about to tackle the climb of her largest mountain yet.

"What's the matter, baby?" Korica could see a look of defeat on her daughter's face already.

"Well, I may know that I'm free, but now all I have to do is get the penal system to jump on board." Unique shook her head. "That's not going to be easy, not with a case that involves the death of children. It's going to be a hard mountain to climb."

"Hmmm." Korica thought for a minute. "Yeah, you're right, but I got another idea on how you can bypass that."

"Really?" Unique lit up, sounding hopeful again.

"Yes, I do," Korica said like she was some know-it-all.

"What is it, Mommy? Tell me what I've got to do and I'll do it."

"Okay, first, you stand up. You stand up straight like the judge, the jury, the news media aka that mountain is standing right in front of you." Korica stood up to demonstrate for Unique. Unique followed suit. "Okay, then, you close your eyes. You concentrate real hard on that mountain, and then you open your mouth and say, 'Move, Mountain!' And if you really believe that your words have the power that the Bible says they do, then when you open your eyes, that mountain will be moved. Now it might not be gone, but at least it will be moved so it will make it a little easier to get around it, you know what I'm saying?"

Once again, Unique started laughing.

"What?" Korica threw her hands on her hips. "What's so funny now?—because you the one who told me that story. You know I don't be reading no Bible. So unless you were lying to your poor mother about being able to say stuff and it happens and all that mess, then you should be able to do it."

"Yes, Mommy, you're right. I did say that, didn't I?"

"Yes, you did. Now put your money where your mouth is. You've been going to church for all these years, serving on ministries, paying tithes and whatnot. Were you doing all that for nothing? Were you doing it for show, or do you believe all that stuff?"

Unique thought for a minute. "I believe, Mommy. I really do believe." The expression on her face showed that she really did believe.

"Good, then do it," Korica ordered. "Stand there and do it."

With every ounce of faith, hope, and prayer Unique had in the world, she stood erect, shoulders up, head held high, and closed her eyes. She meditated for a few seconds, and then, with all the authority she had, yelled out, "Move, Mountain!" She yelled it over and over again, believing that once she opened her eyes, that mountain would indeed be moved.

# Chapter Sixteen

Lorain honestly didn't know how to feel as she sat out in the waiting area to see Unique. She didn't know if she should feel hurt that Unique opted to see Korica before seeing her. She didn't know if she should feel jealous that Unique felt Korica was more of her mother than she was, even though Lorain was the one who had given birth to Unique. Lorain may not have known exactly how she should feel about the situation, but she did know that the feeling she did have inside didn't feel good at all.

*It's not about me. It's not about how I feel,* Lorain kept telling herself as if she were doing some type of mental exercise. She had to be selfless for Unique's sake. Unique was the one locked up in jail while her boys lay in a hospital morgue dead. Lorain could only imagine. She didn't want to imagine. She brushed the visual of the three lifeless bodies out of her mind and tried to focus on being strong for Unique.

"Unique Emerald Gray's *other* mother." The deputy still had jokes. "You can come back and see her now."

Lorain stood up and walked over to the deputy who wore a smirk on his face. "I'm Unique's mother, but I think you know that already." Lorain's tone was sharp. She didn't care what those deputies thought about her or how funny they thought this entire thing was. It wasn't a laughing matter to Lorain. Through it all, she would stand her ground as Unique's mother. She didn't care who had raised her.

"Yeah, yeah, yeah, I get it," the deputy said, a sign that the joke was over and that he could get serious and take Lorain to see her daughter. "Come right this way."

After going through a search, Lorain was finally led into a room where Unique sat at a table waiting. The door to the room had a huge glass window block that Lorain could see through. She could see Unique even before they got to the door. She was surprised to see Unique sitting up, with almost a smile on her face. She was tapping her fingers on the table, waiting for her next visitor.

Lorain had to admit, this isn't the sight she expected to see from a mother who had just lost her three boys. She'd expected to see a more drained, worn-out, and defeated version. Distraught even. Lorain felt as though she herself had shown more emotion back at the hospital with Nicholas than

Unique was showing now. She knew that through the strength of Christ Jesus, Unique could stand strong through this trial and tribulation. But she had no idea she'd be standing so strong . . . and this soon. She hated the next thought that came into her mind; the thought that if this is how Unique displayed herself in the courtroom, she was doomed. What jury in their right mind would have sympathy for a grieving mother who didn't appear to be grieving at all?

"You've got fifteen minutes," the deputy said to Lorain before opening the door and allowing her inside.

"Thank you." Lorain walked inside the room. Her eyes met Unique's. No words were spoken. All of a sudden, Unique didn't look so much like the strong individual Lorain had peered at through the glass window. Now she looked like someone who was trying very hard to be strong on the outside, but on the inside, she could crumble at any minute.

"Ma, Lorain," Unique smiled with trembling lips and eyes that became moist.

"Hey, sweetheart." Lorain walked over and embraced Unique. She held her for a moment while rubbing her back. "You okay, baby? How are you holding up?"

"Better than I could have ever thought," Unique replied. "Thanks to Mommy. She helped me realize some things that I, as a Christian, should have never forgotten."

Lorain released Unique as a tinge of jealousy ran through her body. "Oh, is that so?" she questioned. What had this woman her daughter called Mommy told her? What words had she used to comfort Unique? Is that why Unique had chosen for her to come back and visit her first? She knew that she would do a better job at comforting her than her own natural mother? And why did Unique have to call her Mommy? That was such an endearing term. The word *Mommy* stood for so much. It stood for the woman who loved, cared for, and nurtured a child. It stood for the woman who was deserving of the best Mother's Day card on the shelf. It stood for the woman who cooked and cleaned for the child, who nursed the child back to health in times of sickness and so much more. Lorain wanted to be—Mommy.

While all these thoughts and emotions fluttered through Lorain's being, she managed to ask Unique, "So what did Mo—" She cleared her throat and started over. "What did your mother say?" Referring to someone else as Unique's mother was difficult for Lorain. Yes, she knew this woman had existed in Unique's life all along, but she'd never met her before. She'd never even been the topic of any of their conversations. The only thing Lorain had ever asked Unique about the woman was whether Unique had told her that she'd found her birth mother. Once Unique told her that she, in fact, had, Lorain then asked her how she handled it.

"She wasn't really fazed one way or the other," Unique had replied.

Lorain had left things at that. So far it had all worked out just fine. Lorain had never requested to meet Korica, and Korica never requested to meet Lorain. Why did the two women have the need to meet anyway? Their common denominator, Unique, was a grown woman. She didn't need the approval or representation by either one of the women. Anything Lorain needed to know about Unique, Unique was well and able to tell her herself. So as far as Lorain had been concerned, her getting together with the woman who raised her child was of no benefit . . . the woman who Unique so lovingly referred to as Mommy.

"Mommy reminded me of what Jesus did for me at Calvary."

*Is that it?* Lorain thought. *I could have done that.* "Oh well, that was nice. Good for her." Lorain sat down. "I didn't know she was a churchgoing woman. But then again, why would I? You never talk about her." Lorain let out a forced chuckle. "Heck, I forgot all about her until the guards called for your mother to come back and visit you and we both stood up."

"That must have been an awkward moment," Unique replied. "I'm sure the guards didn't know what to think."

"I don't think either myself or . . . your . . . uh . . . mother," Lorain stammered. "Korica, is it?"

"Yes, Korica Sherod."

"Sherod, that's right," Lorain recalled. "I remember you telling me that because it's the name of that huge hotel and suites over off of the 70 Exit, Sherod Hotel and Suites."

Unique nodded her confirmation.

"Anyway, baby, I'm not here to talk about her. How are you feeling?"

"Like I said, better than I thought I'd be. I mean, I'm really trying hard not to break down. The weight of guilt is so heavy," Unique admitted. "And you know what's so funny? I've never really known until now just how much of a toll the emotion of guilt can take on a person's body. I've never felt guilty, not like this, about anything I've ever done in life." Unique looked to Lorain. "You know me; if I done it, I done it . . . I meant to do it, and I'ma tell you I meant to do it." She shrugged. "Now, shame, well, that's another story . . . that's another emotion . . . one that I can deal with better. Shame seems much easier to shake off than this guilt thing."

"I know what you're saying. I walked around with guilt for years. And the funny thing about guilt is that it's buried so deep inside, that sometimes you forget exactly what caused the pain inside of you. But like you said, shame, on the other hand, huh, that's written all over a person's face, and it ain't so hard to fix up your facial expressions. It's darn hard to fix up what's inside though."

"So true," Unique agreed. "I'd trade guilt in for shame right about now."

There was a brief moment of silence. "So . . . What did happen? How did the boys end up, you know, in the car like that?"

Unique shook her head. "Because I'm stupid . . . so stupid. Had I just listened to you a long time ago when you told me that I needed to get regular child support for my babies, none of this would have happened. I would have been getting a check in the mail every month instead of hunting those fools down." Unique shook her head. "God, why didn't I listen to my mother?"

Lorain figured that Unique was referring to her, but now she couldn't be too sure. "It's okay. Never mind all that. You were doing something that you thought you had to do for your boys."

"Yes, and while I was in there, the cops just happen to run in and bust the place. It all happened so quickly," Unique recalled. "I remember hearing the cops yell, the door caving in, me being tackled to the ground, and that's about it. I blacked out. When the cops took me down, I hit my head on the table or something." Unique rubbed a spot on her head that was still a little tender.

"Oh, I know how that feels." Lorain was referring to the time she fell and hit her head, causing her temporary selective memory loss. "But the news said they found drugs on you."

"I know, it's crazy, right? I kept telling them that I don't do drugs. They said maybe not, but with as much drugs that they found on me, they know for a fact I sell drugs." Unique turned to Lorain with pleading eyes. "I don't sell drugs; you know that. Everybody who knows me knows that."

"Well, the guards said your attorney was here earlier. What does your attorney think?"

"He said, according to police statements from my son's father and Two-Step, my son's father's sidekick, that it was all just some crazy mishap. My attorney said that both drugs and money were found in that freezer. What happened was that my son's father probably thought he was taking a bag of money out of the freezer and handing it to me, but instead, he handed me a bag of drugs. Of course, with my pitiful timing, the police bust in and catch me red-handed with drugs."

"Okay, okay, then it sounds like we don't have much to worry about. That's a pretty clear-cut, convincing story. We just have to relay it to the judge."

"I'm glad you feel that way. My lawyer is already talking plea bargain."

Lorain banged her fist on the table. "I won't hear of such a thing. *Feeling* guilty is one thing, but actually *being* guilty is another. You are not responsible for my grandbabies' deaths, and we're not going to let some fresh-out-of-law-school kid make you admit to it. That's why pastor called me this morning and suggested the church retain a good lawyer for you."

"Really?" Unique had a look of surprise on her face. "Pastor . . . the church . . . They want to help me? But do they know what the media is saying? Isn't New Day afraid that if they support me that—"

"New Day Temple of Faith and its leaders do not walk in fear. So to answer your question, no, . . . No one is afraid." Lorain rested her hand upon Unique's shoulder. "And you shouldn't be either."

A tear fell from Unique's eye. Lorain pulled her into her shoulder and began comforting her. "It's okay, baby. It's okay. Let it out."

That tough exterior Unique had been draped in was starting to fall off. "They're gone. Oh, God, I can't believe they're gone. My boys are gone." Unique lifted her head and wiped her eyes. "Do you know the lawyer says I might not even get to go to the funeral? He said he's going to have to seek permission from the courts."

"Oh no," Lorain replied. "Speaking of the funeral, would you like me to go ahead and begin making the arrangements?"

Just hearing those words caused Unique to break down completely. "I have to bury my babies. Oh, God, I have to bury my babies. I can't believe this."

"It's all right. I'll take care of it. I'll take care of everything."

Eventually, Unique regained her composure and wore a serious look on her face. "I want them to wear all-white, like angels, because they were my little angels." Not able to hold it together, Unique broke down again.

"Don't worry, I'll do everything, anything you want."

Unique looked into Lorain's eyes. "Thanks, Mom. Thank you so much. I really appreciate it."

"No problem, honey." Lorain took Unique in her arms again and held her tightly, her chin resting atop Unique's head. Unique had called her "Mom." It still didn't mean as much as the word Mommy did though, but Lorain would keep working at it.

# Chapter Seventeen

It was the day of her boys' funeral, and Unique had spent the entire day balled up and crying in her cell. She felt as if the wind had been knocked out of her when her attorney told her that she didn't get granted permission to attend the funeral.

"But why?" Unique had asked her attorney over the phone. The coward hadn't even had enough courage and respect to show up and tell her to her face.

"The system just feels that with the severity of the crime, and you being the one actually held responsible for their deaths, that it wouldn't be a good idea for—"

"That's bull crap!" is what Unique, being a Christian and all, should have said. Unfortunately, something else besides the word "crap" slipped out of her mouth. After going back and forth with the attorney, with even more expletives flying out of her mouth, she slammed the phone down and was escorted back to her cell where she'd been ever since.

Her cell mate, Kiki, had made it her business to stay outside of their cell as much as she could to give Unique time to mourn. Being alone with her thoughts probably wasn't what Unique needed at the time, but it's all that she had. Everyone she knew was off paying their last respects to her boys. Her boys!

Wails began to escape from Unique's mouth. Other inmates walked by, but none of them seemed to have any empathy as she heard them mumble things like, "Serves her right. What killer shows up at the person's funeral that they killed?" A couple sputtered off threats to do her bodily harm, while some inmates even spat in her direction as they walked by. Not only had the media pronounced Unique guilty before being proven otherwise, even other criminals were doing the same thing to her. She didn't care though. She knew the truth, and the truth was that all she wanted right now was to be with her sons, to see them one last time before they were put back into the earth from which they came.

"God, I know they were yours before they ever were mine," Unique prayed. "But here on earth, you gave them to me, and I just wanted to be able to say good-bye. I just wanted to be able to say good-bye," she cried.

Unique cried for the next two hours straight before falling asleep. When she woke, she could feel that it was late. The funeral and the burial were probably over by now. Lorain had told her that they were going to have the repast at New Day. More than likely, Lorain was still at the church. Korica's phone was off right now because she hadn't paid the bill, so she couldn't call her. So she thought of someone she hadn't even talked to yet, but that she was sure had gone to the funeral and could tell her all about it.

Mustering up enough energy to stand, Unique made her way to where the phones were. There were only two phones and what seemed like a gazillion people waiting in line to use them. Unique didn't feel like she had the energy to stand in line that long, but she had to. She had to see about her boys' homecoming.

Before Unique knew it, she was next in line to use the phone. She had no idea how long she'd been in line. There was no sense of time in that place. The woman who was in front of her finished up her call. That was Unique's sign that it was finally her turn.

"God, let her phone be on," Unique pleaded as she dialed and requested the operator to put through the collect call. "And Jesus, don't let her have a block on her phone." People were good for having the service on their phones that blocked collect calls. She hoped to God her sister wasn't one of those people.

All Unique's prayers were answered as her sister accepted the call. "Unique?" Renee answered once the call was put through.

"Yeah, Renee, it's me," Unique replied. "I'm sorry I haven't called you before now. It's just been mad crazy."

"Yeah?"

"Yeah. So how was, you know, how was the boys' homecoming?"

"It was beautiful. Lorain and that church of yours laid it out. It was like a picture from heaven. The dance ministry danced and some heavyset, dark-skinned woman sang her tail off."

"Did she have dimples?"

"Yeah."

"Oh, that was probably Sister Paige."

"She be with some white dude?"

"Yeah, it was Paige."

"Well, Miss Thing can sing. And your pastor can preach to be a white woman, Lord have mercy. Like I said, it was beautiful. I heard they wouldn't let you come. That's jacked up, especially since they let your sorry baby daddy out of jail long enough to come."

"Gerald? Gerald was there, at my boys' funeral? They let him out of jail to go and not me?" Unique was fuming.

"Guess he got him one of them street lawyers that got some pull, you know what I'm saying?"

"I can't believe that crap." Unique, being a Christian, tried her best to be delivered from the cursing demon. Whew, there was something about those prison walls that were just pulling Unique slowly but surely back into some of her old ways. Man, oh, man, did she want a drink and a joint so bad right now she could taste it. She needed one or the other, or both, to calm her nerves.

"Yeah, I was surprised too. But don't worry, I checked his tail for you," Renee told her little sister.

"What do you mean?"

"Mommy told me how he's the one who supposedly gave you that dope they found on you. I know it wasn't cool, but while he was standing at the casket viewing the body, I walked up next to him and asked him why he played you like that; since when is a bag of dope child support? I mean, I thought that was his way of trying to put you to work to make you go earn the money for child support, but that wasn't the case."

"Why—how do you know that? What did he say?" Unique hadn't been able to correspond with her oldest son's father at all, so she had no idea why he'd given her that bag of dope from the freezer other than what her attorney had suspected. Unique didn't trust that coward, but her sister, she did trust.

"He said he thought he was handing you some loot. He must have grabbed the wrong bag. He feels real bad about it. He said he wanted to talk to you, but his attorney said that's not a good idea. Besides, I don't think they would let y'all talk anyway. They don't want y'all trying to get stories straight with each other and everything. He said he told his attorney, and his attorney supposedly told yours, but I don't how much good that's going to do you."

"Yeah, me either, but at least I know the real now from the horse's mouth," Unique said.

"Yeah, and like I said, he sounded sincere, so don't be too mad at him. On the other hand, I got a slight attitude with you."

"Oh yeah? Well, so does 90 percent of the people up in here. So join the club."

"No, but on the real, I been walking, taking the bus, and having to hitch rides to work. The police haven't released my car yet. I wish I'd never let you borrow it. Had I known you were going to drive it to a crack house I wouldn't have."

Once again, Unique started to fume. "My boys are dead, and they didn't even let me out of this place to go to their funeral, and you're worried about your old, funky hooptie?"

Renee copped an instant attitude. "Oh, really now? Well, if it was so old and funky, why were you always borrowing it? If it was so old and funky, then maybe you shouldn't have borrowed it. How about that? Humph, then maybe I wouldn't be having to walk, catch the bus, and bum rides. Then just maybe your boys would still be alive!"

A rage rose up in Unique like never before. The heat surrounding her was so hot she could barely breathe. Never, ever had she called her sister out of her name, but the B-word slipped from her tongue so quick, there was nothing Unique could do to reel it back in.

"I know you did *not* just call me that," Renee declared.

"You suppose to be my sister and you trippin' over your car being impounded and my boys are laid up in a casket dead. Really, Renee? Oh, trust me, I can think of some other names to call you." And as Unique thought of those words, she allowed them too to spill from her tongue.

Renee shot the F-word at Unique, followed by the word "you," and then slammed the phone down. But not before shooting the B-word back at her too.

"You stinking . . . son of a . . . black . . ." Unique spat as she pounded the phone receiver against the hook.

"Hey, if you break that phone before I get a chance to use it, I'ma break your freakin' neck." Of course, the word "freakin'" wasn't the actual word spit out by the inmate next in line behind Unique.

Unique was too fired up and hotheaded to even hear the threat, let alone take heed to it. She continued beating the hook with the receiver until finally someone grabbed her wrist.

"Cut it out! Are you crazy? You wanna mess with these broads' only means of communication to the outside world besides funky letters?" Shaking her head, Kiki, Unique's cell mate, added, "I don't think so." Kiki made an attempt to remove the receiver from Unique's hand.

"No! I'm 'bout to call that ho back and cuss her out," Unique yelled. She was so angry that tears fell from her eyes.

By now, a couple of guards were making their way toward Unique.

"Hey, it's okay. It's okay," Kiki said, trying to keep them at bay. "Her kids' funeral was today, and they didn't let her out to go. Give her a break. I got this. For real, she's good."

Convinced it was all good, the guards backed off.

Kiki yoked Unique up by her shirt and spoke through clenched teeth. "Calm down before you end up in solitary before you even go to trial. Then what is that gon' look like to the judge?"

"I don't care what things look like. I know people think my boys are dead because of me, but I didn't kill 'em. I didn't leave my boys for dead. Okay, so they found some dope on me; charge me for that, but don't charge me for the death of my boys," Unique yelled as snot ran from her nose.

"Are you crazy?" Kiki couldn't believe what was coming out of Unique's mouth.

"You'd rather go to jail for the drug rap than the charges against your boys?" She chuckled. "You a single black woman who they think covering for your baby daddy who is supposed to be some big drug kingpin." She chuckled again. "Girl, don't you know *that's* what you should be worrying about? If I were you, I'd rather go with the charges of killing my boys. Get the sympathy of the jury and you'll probably get less time."

Unique was lost. There was no way what Kiki was saying was logical. "You mean I could spend less time in jail for killing my boys than for selling crack? No way." Unique refused to believe a crack rock held more value than the life of a child.

"Hey, can you two go somewhere else and play Doctor Phil and Oprah? I need to make a call here," the woman next in line shouted.

Kiki shot the woman a menacing glare, causing her to fall back a little. She then turned her attention back to Unique. "Humph, so you don't believe me, do you? Come here." Kiki grabbed Unique by the arm and took her back to their cell. "Looky here."

Kiki pulled her thin mattress up and newspapers were layered under it. She dug around until she could find the one she was looking for. Picking up a paper, she scanned it momentarily. "Yep, this is the one I was looking for." She handed it to Unique. "Here, you take it and read that, then tell me what charge you're more willing to take." She headed out of the cell. "Now, I gotta go get my place back in the phone line. My chick is waiting on my call."

Unique looked down at the *Washington Post* newspaper Kiki had handed her. "How in the world did she get this?" She began to scan the article. The more she read, the more interesting it got; she got what Kiki had been trying to tell her. By the time she finished reading the article, she was convinced that she would rather admit to killing her boys than to selling drugs. She made up her mind what she was going to have to do.

# Chapter Eighteen

"I must advise you as my client, that I feel what you want to do is not in your best interest," the suited-up woman said to Unique as she sat across from her at the same table Unique had visited the attorney before her.

Unique's attorney nodded. The public defender that was initially assigned to her had been replaced by the woman sitting across from her. New Day had raised money to pay the retainer fee, but then after reading the case and talking to the former attorney, she decided the notoriety that would come from the case was worth more than anything they could have paid her. Besides that, and more important, she felt Unique was innocent, and that to some degree, she was a victim. Unique didn't care what the attorney's reasons were for taking over her case for no additional monies. She knew it was nothing but favor from God.

"Pleading guilty to causing the death of your boys could be the worst possible mistake you make in your life," her attorney told her.

"No, ma'am," Unique replied. "I think I've already made the worst possible mistake in my life when I left my boys in that car for what I thought was only going to be a couple of minutes."

There was a brief silence. Unique had her attorney on that one.

"Anyway," Unique continued, "the last attorney told me that the prosecuting attorney assigned to this case had already suggested the idea of a plea bargain. They said if I plead guilty to some charge, I can't remember what it was but it had something to do with indirectly causing the death of my boys, that they might possibly drop the drug charges." Unique sounded adamant that her mind had already been made up.

"Unique, statements from some of the other defendants who were busted in that crack house, including your son's father, indicate that was pretty much your first time ever even stepping foot inside that house." She flipped through the case file that the other attorney had turned over to her. "They all are saying the same thing; that you and . . . Gerald were arguing about money—child support."

"That's true. I told you that already. I've told everybody that already, but it doesn't seem to matter." Unique sounded exasperated. "That's why I'm just ready to cop this plea and be done with it. I'm tired."

Unique's lawyer got intense as she leaned in and looked Unique in the eyes. "From what you've told me, from what you've told the last attorney, your story has not wavered. What these other people are saying, even the woman who owns the house, most of them didn't even know you. I believe you, Unique. I believe your story. I believe that at the time, on that unimaginable day, you felt taking those boys inside the crack house was the worst of two evils. Your intentions were to go get what your son's father rightly owed you, and then get back to your boys as soon as possible. No mother in her worst nightmare could have foreseen such a horrific thing occurring. No mother!"

The attorney slammed her fist down, making Unique jump. She didn't know how much more of this table pounding her nerves could take.

"It sounds all good, but who's going to buy it? Who cares about the truth anymore? Certainly not the media." Unique rolled her eyes and pouted her lips.

"Forget about the media." Her attorney appeared to be thinking. "Let's work an angle that has always worked for me."

"And what angle is that?" Unique leaned in with anticipation and curiosity.

"The truth," her attorney said, plain and simple.

That was not what Unique wanted to hear. She thought her attorney was coming up with something much more creative than the truth. "I can't take that chance."

"What chance are you talking about? I'm still not understanding why you're hell-bent on spending the rest of your life having people think you are responsible for the death of your children versus being a dope dealer." Annoyance and confusion displayed itself on the attorney's face.

"Because of what I read in the *Washington Post*, that's why." Now Unique banged her fist against the table. If you can't beat 'em, join 'em.

"*Washington Post?* This story made *Washington Post* news?"

Unique could see the attorney about to get all Hollywood on her. "No, not my case." Unique rolled her eyes and sucked her teeth. "I read an article about the harsh penalties for crack cocaine that were introduced back in the '80s. I read that Congress approved the law back then to discourage all the crimes that were taking place as a result of the selling of crack. It said that if someone was caught with five grams of crack cocaine, they could get a mandatory minimum sentence of five years. That possession of fifty grams of crack got them ten years minimum. I mean, fifty grams, that's like what? The weight of a couple of pennies? Is that true?"

"Yes, those laws were specifically for crack cocaine, which is what was found in your possession. Had it been powder cocaine, then it would have been a different story," her attorney told her. "But all that is going to start changing, hopefully, with the latest Fair Sentencing Act."

"Yeah, I read about that too. That's the bill that eliminates a mandatory minimum sentence for simple possession. It said that an offender would have to be convicted of the possession of twenty-eight grams or more of crack for the five-year mandatory sentence and 208 grams or more for the ten-year prison term."

Once again, Unique's attorney nodded. She smiled, impressed with Unique's research.

"So how much was in that bag I had?"

Her attorney's smile faded. "About thirty grams."

"Oh, Jesus!" was all Unique could say. Nervousness took over as her hands began to tremble. "I'm hit. I'm done." Sounding more desperate than she ever had in her life, and feeling more desperate too, she said to her attorney, "Get me a plea. I don't care what you, my mama, sisters, brothers, or anybody else in this world thinks. I'm not about to let them throw the book at me. No way, no how. Now I'm done talking. Come back and see me when there's a deal on the table." Unique looked over her shoulder at the door with the window behind her. "Guard, this visit is over!" she shouted, stood up, and then walked over to the door.

Her attorney slammed the case file closed. "Okay, Ms. Gray, if you say so." The attorney stood. "I'll go get to wheeling and dealing on your behalf just as soon as I leave here." Sarcasm laced the attorney's voice as she gathered up her things and walked over to the door just as the guard opened it. Before exiting, the attorney stopped in front of Unique. "This is a first for me; a client doubtful of my abilities in the courtroom, forcing me to run out and make a deal with the devil." She looked Unique up and down. "Oh ye of little faith." She sucked her teeth and twisted up her lips. "And you call yourself a Christian." On that note, the attorney exited the room.

# Chapter Nineteen

"How are my little angels?" Lorain placed kisses all over her twin daughters' foreheads. With the death of her grandsons, she was not taking any given moment for granted. Tomorrow was not promised. Heck, not even tonight was promised.

"Your little angels just about ran their granny ragged." Eleanor wiped invisible sweat off of her forehead as she sat down on her couch. "Lord, it's so cute when they start walking, but I don't know about chasing they little behinds all over my house. And they get into everything." She looked at the chubby faces of her grandchildren, who were in all actuality her great-grandchildren.

At first, Eleanor was anything but pleased with the idea that her only child was expecting a baby; but not one that she would be giving birth to herself. Out of all the random women at New Day Temple of Faith Lorain could have asked to carry her child, she'd picked, according to Eleanor's standards, the most ghetto thing up in there. And besides, allowing another woman to carry her child for her just didn't seem natural in Eleanor's eyes.

As if that weren't enough to deal with, through a little church gossip, word got back to Eleanor that Unique wasn't some random woman at all; she was actually Lorain's child. She was the child Eleanor never knew her daughter had because she'd hid her teenage pregnancy. And when the baby was born, Lorain threw it in the trash can, leaving the baby for dead. As a matter of fact, for years Lorain had thought the baby had died, but she would learn otherwise.

To add salt to the wound, Eleanor had to deal with the fact that not only had Lorain gotten pregnant and had a child at the age of thirteen, but it had been by a grown man; a trusted school counselor. If *that* wasn't enough to handle, unbeknownst to Eleanor, the retired principal she'd just married was that man. Eleanor didn't find all of this out until her late husband's death, and it had been a hard pill to swallow. But now, as she looked at the twins, her grandchildren legally but her great-grandchildren biologically, nothing else mattered anymore.

"So, y'all been giving Granny Eleanor a hard time?" Lorain said to the twins in between kisses. "Did y'all?" She began tickling them. The smiles on each of their little faces were priceless.

Tears formed in Lorain's eyes as she squeezed the girls close to her. She was holding them so close, so tightly, that she squeezed the smiles right off their faces. The girls began fidgeting and clawing at Lorain.

"Lorain, honey, you're smothering them." Eleanor got back up off the couch and went over and rescued her grandchildren. Shooting Lorain a half-evil, half-concerned eye, Eleanor grabbed each twin by the hand and began escorting them into the kitchen. "Come on, Granny's babies. Let me go put y'all in y'all's highchair and give you another snack before Mommy whisks you away." Eleanor and the twins disappeared behind the kitchen door.

*Mommy. I'm somebody's Mommy*, Lorain thought. She sat there on the couch, picked up a throw pillow, and hugged it like it was a real person. She might have been somebody's Mommy, but Korica would always be there to remind her that she wasn't Unique's. Korica had even made that very clear at the funeral.

*"You didn't leave a stone unturned," Korica had said to Lorain after the burial, when*

*everyone else was making their way to their cars. Just the two of them stood over the triple graves.*

*"It's everything Unique wanted," Lorain sniffed, wiping her eyes with the handkerchief someone had slipped into her hand while at the viewing earlier that day.*

*"Everything she ever wanted, huh?" Korica never took her eyes off the boys' graves. She stared straight on, as if looking at the woman standing next to her was the last thing she wanted to do. "And you don't think it's a little too late for that; giving Unique everything she wants? After all, the girl will be twenty-six years old before we know it. She's not a baby anymore. You missed those years."*

*Korica seemed to have enjoyed saying that very last statement far too much. Too much for Lorain to do the Christian thing and let it slide.*

*"And from what I hear, so did you," Lorain shot back. "How old was she when you bought her? Or was she sold to you? I can't remember."*

*"Oh, so you want to go there, do you?" Korica bobbed her head up and down slowly as she allowed her tongue to make a popping noise against the roof of her mouth. "I guess the fact of whether I bought her or sold her is irrelevant. She would have never ended up in foster care*

*in the first place had you not thrown her away like she was garbage. Everything she wants included the love and the care of a mother, which is what I gave her."*

*"Yeah, you and the woman who sold her to you in the first place; or whatever arrangement it was the two of you schemed up."* Lorain put her index finger to her temple and began tapping, as if trying to recollect something. *"Oh yeah; I remember. The real foster mother and her husband moved away, only they didn't want to take Unique with them. Only they didn't want to give up the check the state was paying them either. So that's when you decided you'd keep Unique and the check. The system was so messed up that you got away with it. But I bet had that check stopped, you would have—"*

*"Thrown her away like her birth mother did?"* Korica snarled, this time staring right into Lorain's eyes. *"Never. You might have been able to live with yourself knowing that this,"* she pointed to one of the graves, *"that this right here could have been your baby . . . could have been my Unique, but I couldn't."* She looked Lorain up and down. *"And you call yourself a Christian. Well, maybe you and your mama should have asked what would Jesus do, because I'm sure He wouldn't have thrown out the baby for dead, like a murderer."*

"Stop it! Stop it right there!" Lorain yelled. Her pastor, who was quite a few feet away talking to the funeral director, looked Lorain's way momentarily, but then continued her conversation.

"You want me to stop?" Korica was using a whiny voice. "Oh, but baby, I'm just getting started. Trust me, the mommy lion's fangs are about to show."

"But why? I don't get it. Why are you so bitter toward me?"

"Why? The fact that you have to ask makes it even worse." Korica let out a tsk sound. "Aren't you Christians supposed to serve this all-knowing God?" She lifted her hands up to heaven in a mocking way. "Then ask Him."

"I'm choosing to ask the devil instead." Lorain glared at Korica so that there would be no doubt about whether she was being referred to as the devil. "So what's your deal?"

Korica appeared to be filled with so much anger as she turned her body to face Lorain. She began speaking through gritted teeth while pointing in Lorain's face. "My deal is you waltzing back into Unique's life like this born-again saint who can do no wrong." Korica looked over Lorain's shoulder at her pastor. "Does your reverend know your dirty little secret?"

"As a matter of fact, she does." Now what? was what the expression on Lorain's face read.

"Yeah, but I bet your entire church doesn't know. I bet you haven't gone down to the altar and testified." Korica threw her hands up and leaned back, faking being touched by the Holy Spirit.

"So is that what this is about? You want me to tell the entire world how it is that I'm . . ." Lorain pointed at herself in the chest, ". . . Unique's real mother?"

"Puhleeze. Real mother, my foot." Korica looked Lorain up and down as if she stank. "You might be the woman who spit her out from between your legs, but I'm her real mother. Need I remind you who she told the guards at the jail she wanted to see first?" Not that there was much space between Lorain and Korica, but Korica was surely closing in the little space there was. "I'm the one who all those years ago sacrificed being able to take care of my own flesh and blood so that I could take care of yours."

Korica was starting to become emotional, and she tried her best to fight it off. "We struggled, I mean, struggled. There were times I had no idea where our next meal would come from. And there were times I had to do the *unthinkable in order to make sure my kids had a meal. And when there wasn't enough for me to eat, I had to pretend I had a stomach ache or something and didn't want to eat anything. Then there was boosting and doing everything under the sun to get them school clothes so they wouldn't be teased and talked about. But a new pair of shoes and a couple outfits from the Ten Dollar Store can only go so far."*

The more Korica spoke, the angrier she got. Soon tears of anger erupted from her eyes. "And what's her real mother doing? Off living in some condo, getting the Holy Ghost every Sunday and pushing Mary Kay cosmetics like some white woman in the 'burbs." Korica, embarrassed that she'd been brought to tears, turned quickly back to face the graves and sharply wiped her tears away.

"You make it sound as if what I did didn't affect me either," Lorain told her. "Well, it did."

"Well, I can't tell. All I know is that I'll be darned if I just sit back and watch you take over the reins after all I've done to raise Unique and those boys." Now Korica broke down from grief after staring at the boys' small caskets.

"Look, I can't take back what I did. All I can do is—"

"Repent and ask God for forgiveness." Korica finished Lorain's sentence sarcastically. "Yeah, *that's what all you Christians do. Live a hellish life, then take a shower in Jesus' blood, and it all washes down the drain. Yeah, I get all that, but guess what? I ain't Jesus, and I ain't forgiving or forgetting about nothing. And neither is Unique. And if I have to keep reminding her who Mommy is, who the real mother who raised her is, then so be it."*

*"You do what you need to do," Lorain said nonchalantly. "But nothing you do will ever change the fact that I am the woman who carried Unique in her womb for nine months. I am the woman whose veins pump the same blood as Unique's." This time Lorain closed in the space between her and Korica. "I am the woman who, by law and any other definition, is Unique's mother. Point-blank . . . period. So if you can't get that through your head, then I don't know what else to say to you." And on that note, Lorain began to walk away.*

*"Thank you," Korica mumbled.*

*"What?" Lorain turned back around to see what else this woman had to say.*

*"Thank you." Korica turned and glared at Lorain with sadness in her eyes. "You could have said thank you. That would have been nice." Korica brushed by Lorain, leaving her with plenty to think about.* So much to think

about that that is exactly what was consuming Lorain's mind at this moment as she sat on her mother's couch.

Was she so hell-bent on making sure that the world knew she was Unique's mother that she never stopped for one minute to think about what life must have been like for the woman who stepped in and took care of Unique? Korica was right. It didn't matter how it came about that she would raise Unique as one of her own. The fact remains that she did it. And it was at that very moment that Lorain realized she did owe Korica a thank you. But her flesh also reminded her that for now, it would be a cold day in hell before she gave it to her.

# Chapter Twenty

The twins were down for the night, and Nicholas and Lorain were sitting on her living-room couch enjoying a movie. Well, Nicholas was enjoying the movie. Lorain's mind was a million miles away.

Nicholas burst out into laughter. "Oh, my goodness, that was hilarious, wasn't it?" Lorain didn't reply. "Wasn't it, baby?" He nudged her. "Wasn't that the most hilarious thing you've ever seen?"

Snapping out of her daze, Lorain replied. "Yeah, yeah, that was too much. That Tyler Perry is something else."

Nicholas twisted his lips in disbelief at the sincerity of Lorain's statement. "Really now?"

"Yeah." Lorain looked at the television, pointed, and feigned laughter. "See, there. Ha-ha. Whew."

There wasn't a trace of laughter anywhere on Nicholas's face. "Lorain, that scene was a serious funeral scene. So what did you find to be so funny about that?"

Busted, Lorain didn't know what to say.

Nicholas took the remote and turned the television off. "That's it. Spill it. What's on your mind?"

"Noth—"

"And don't say nothing. I'm tired of hearing that. It's obvious that something is weighing heavy on your mind, and I'd wish you'd stop lying to me. How do you expect us to build on this relationship if we can't even tell each other the truth about something as simple as what's going on in our lives?"

Taken aback, Lorain replied to Nicholas, "Did you just call me a liar?"

Nicholas thought for a moment. "No, I didn't exactly say that, but if the shoe fits . . . If lying is what you're doing to me . . ."

"For God's sake, Nicholas, my grandsons just died, and my daughter is locked up in jail being held responsible for their deaths. Not to mention the world thinks she's some crackhead or crack dealer or both. People look at me sideways on the job every day and whisper after I walk by. And you expect me to just sit here and enjoy a movie like all that isn't going on in my life?"

"No, I expect you to let me know all of what is going on in your life. That's why I'm here, baby. Didn't you believe me when I told you? I mean really, how many times do I have to say that I love you and that I want to spend the rest of my life with you? You're the one who can't seem to reciprocate here."

Lorain put her hands up. "Look, Nicholas, I'm not going to go there with you; not right now."

"Then when? Because I'm tired, Lorain."

"And what's *that* supposed to mean?"

"Just what it sounds like." Nicholas stood. "Look, I've told you from day one that I wasn't out to just date. I can date anybody. I wasn't getting in this thing for just dinner and a movie every now and then, and a couple of conversations on the phone. I was looking for a wife. And if you knew you couldn't fit the bill, then you shouldn't have allowed me to waste my time this long."

Lorain was appalled. "Waste your time? Is that what I am to you, Nick? A waste of time?"

"Don't try to play the victim, woman. I know you too well for that, and you, my dear, are nobody's victim." He looked her up and down. "Besides, it doesn't look good on you."

"So you think this is a game to me?" Lorain was now standing with one hand on her hip and the other laying at her side.

"I don't know what to think anymore."

"Me, neither, Nicholas. Me neither." Lorain couldn't believe how he was coming at her, and all because she wasn't paying attention to some movie. This was a side of Nicholas that she'd never seen before. He'd been so understanding thus far, and now, when she was dealing with so much in her life, he decided to flip the script.

At this very moment, Lorain couldn't help but to think divine intervention had taken place at the hospital on the day she was going to tell Nicholas that she was ready to marry him. Of course, she wished the situation that pulled him away from her hadn't been what it was. But it was what it was, and right now, it is what it is.

"Look, I think maybe we better—" Lorain honestly had no idea what the next words that were going to come out of her mouth were. The interruption of the ringing telephone kept Nicholas from knowing too. Lorain held her index finger up at Nicholas and went to answer her phone.

"Lorain, is that you?"

"Who else would it be, Ma?" Lorain hadn't meant to get out of the pocket with her mother.

"Excuse me?"

"I'm sorry, Ma. It's just that Nicholas is here and—"

"Oh, my goodness!" Eleanor exclaimed. "You know, with so much going on in the last couple of weeks, I haven't had a chance to talk to Nicholas. Put him on the phone."

Lorain looked at Nicholas. "Mom, I don't think this is a good time to talk to Nicholas . . ." Lorain's words trailed off once Nicholas signaled for her to go ahead and give him the phone. "It's my mom," Lorain warned in a whisper.

"I know." Nicholas nodded as he reached out for the phone. He just adored Eleanor. He thought she was classy, sophisticated, and more unpredictable than a firecracker with a short wick. Maybe talking to her was what he needed to up his mood. "If it isn't the lovely Eleanor," he greeted into the phone receiver.

"If it isn't my future son-in-law," Eleanor shot back.

"Well, uh—"

"I know both you and Lorain could just strangle me. I haven't really congratulated either one of you on the engagement. But I'm sure, considering the circumstance, you both can forgive me. Besides, I'm sure neither one of you really got to bask in the idea of actually being engaged; not with what happened to the boys and all." Eleanor sighed. "Of all days for it to have happened, it was on the day Lorain finally put that ring on her finger and came up to your job to make things official."

Nicholas's heart dropped, and his eyes shot over to Lorain's hand. He didn't know what Eleanor was talking about, because on the hand he was looking at, the ring finger was still vacant of his engagement ring.

"I was too happy to oblige when Lorain asked if the twins could stay with me that day while she came up to your job to make the engagement official. I can only imagine the look in your eyes when you saw that ring on her finger. My God, the Lord sure is able. I mean, I never thought my baby girl would settle down, would find a man worthy to be her husband." Eleanor then made clear, "Now, I'm not saying you aren't a worthy catch, Nicholas. You are a fine young man indeed. Any woman is a blessed woman to be able to call herself your wife. But my Lorain has been through so much. She deserves it, she really does. She deserves the best, and you, Nicholas, are truly the best son-in-law a mother could ask for her daughter. The way you've just stood by her side is so admirable and . . ." Eleanor was so overcome with emotion that she couldn't even get her words out. "Look, I need to go get myself together. Tell Lorain I'll call her back."

"Oh, I'll tell her all right," Nicholas assured Eleanor while glaring at Lorain.

"Bye, dear."

"Bye-bye, Miss Eleanor." Still looking at Lorain, Nicholas ended the call and handed her the phone.

Lorain took the phone with hesitation and was about to put it back to her ear.

"She said she'll call you back." Nicholas shot her a cold stare.

"What . . . What is it?" Lorain fumbled hanging the phone up because she was too concerned with why Nicholas was staring at her that way. What in the world could her mother have possibly said to bring about this reaction from him? She'd find out soon, but would it be soon enough?

# Chapter Twenty-one

"I'm glad you changed your mind and decided to trust me on this," Unique's attorney said as they stood side-by-side in the courtroom. "I really believe God is going to work in your favor on this one, Unique. I'm not a churchgoing woman, but I know God when I see Him. And believe you me, honey, He's showed up in this courtroom aplenty of times. And if He did it for some of the heathens I've had to deal with," Unique's attorney looked her square in the eyes and meant every word she was about to say, "I know He will do it for you, woman of God."

The court hearing hadn't even gotten started and already Unique was emotional. She was scared and nervous. She prayed she was doing the right thing. She had been so adamant about taking a plea, but that one thing her attorney said to her changed her mind instantly. *"And you call yourself a Christian."*

Yes, Unique did call herself a Christian, and as a Christian, she was supposed to have faith in

God. Taking a plea, in her case, would have been almost like lying. She wasn't a liar. She was a Christian . . . with faith.

"You okay?" her attorney asked her.

"Yes, it's just that from where I come from, from where I've been, I've been called a lot of things. Not once, though, not ever have I been called a woman of God, and by someone who doesn't really know me."

"Humph. That's sad," her attorney shrugged. "If any person can look at you and not see God, then they must be blind. Look how well you're holding up. With all you've been through, that is nothing but God."

"I don't know about all that. I mean, you should have seen the way I was carrying on the other day after I talked to my sister on the phone. God wasn't anywhere to be found up in that mess. I could feel the Holy Spirit leave my body and run for cover," Unique joked, wiping a tear before it fell.

"Well, what's that thing about people falling short of the glory?" Unique's attorney reminded her.

"Oh yeah. Thanks for reminding me about that." Unique shook her head. "It's funny, I call myself a Christian, but yet, here you are the one who keeps having to remind me of it."

Her attorney smiled. "Trust me, Unique, by the time this case is over, I'm sure I'm going to be a full-fledged believer."

"All rise!" a voice ricocheting across the courtroom said, interrupting Unique and her attorney's conversation. "The Honorable Judge Peaks has now entered the courtroom." The bailiff continued his spiel before turning the court over to the judge after saying, "Court, you may be seated."

"Mrs. Martinez," the judge looked directly at Unique's attorney, "as you know, your client is being charged with several counts. But I see that you have petitioned the court to separate her charges concerning drug possession with those concerning the death of her children."

"Yes, Judge Peaks," Mrs. Jawan Martinez stood and said. Her medium-length, locked hair reminded Unique of Sister Deborah's from church before she cut all her hair off.

They were in the tiniest and neatest little locks Unique had ever seen. They weren't the traditional locks referred to by some as dread-locks. Unique could tell they were Sisterlocks because they were exactly like Sister Deborah's had been. With her brown skin, dark brown eyes, and not to mention her hair, it was obvious that even though her last name was Hispanic, she was not. Her husband was though. Unique, never one to bite her tongue, had come right out and asked her attorney, "What's a sista doing with a name like Martinez? Is that your real name, or do you use it to trick people so that they don't think you are just some janky black attorney?"

Thank goodness Unique's lawyer had a sense of humor and had not taken offense to her blunt statement. She just let out a chuckle and shook her head at Unique, informing her that her husband was Puerto Rican. Right now, though, as she stood before the judge, Unique's attorney was in serious mode.

"Well, Mrs. Martinez, I also see that you've agreed to allow the same judge to hear both cases."

"Yes, that is correct, Your Honor," Jawan confirmed. "I trust you to be a fair judge, and you will not hold anything against the defendant from one case to the other."

"Mrs. Martinez, you didn't have to indirectly remind me of my instructions and duties as a judge." The judge scanned over some paperwork that rested before her.

"Yes, Your Honor. Sorry, Your Honor."

"I see from the notes of the defense attorney before you that Ms. Gray wished to waive her rights to a jury. Is that still the case?"

"It is, Your Honor. Once again, Judge Peaks, I trust that you will—"

"Once again, Mrs. Martinez, don't push it."

Jawan slightly lowered her head. "Thank you, Your Honor."

Rustling the papers into a nice, neat pile, Judge Peaks spoke. "And this morning, is your client ready to enter a plea concerning her charges for drug possession?"

"Yes, she is, Your Honor."

"And what might that be?"

Jawan looked at Unique, signaling with her eyes for Unique to enter her plea.

"Not guilty!" Unique said. "Not guilty, Your Honor."

Judge Peaks stared at Unique. This made Unique feel as though she were being judged right then and there. It was as if the judge were making a split-second decision about Unique based on that very moment; how she looked, what she said, etc.

"Okay, and so it is entered," the judge replied. "I'll have my bailiff check my calendar and the court docket and get this on the calendar."

"Thank you, Your Honor," Jawan said.

"And now, for the charges of child endangerment and involuntary manslaughter," the judge continued.

There was a gasp in the courtroom. It sounded like someone trying to hold back tears. Unique and her attorney looked behind them to see Lorain trying to maintain her composure.

The judge also noticed too. She shook her head at Lorain as if warning her that she'd put her out of the courtroom before she'd let her have a breakdown in it. Judge Peaks was known to show very little emotion and didn't want that of someone else influencing her own.

Fortunately, Unique's pastor and a couple of other New Day Temple of Faith church members were there to comfort Lorain and help calm her down. Unique didn't see Eleanor, her biological grandmother. She figured that she was needed to stay home and sit with the twins.

*The twins,* Unique thought about them, and rightfully so, considering her mind, her heart, body, and soul had been so consumed with the loss of her boys, that she never thought about checking on them—asking about them—not even once. The boys had been her life though. No one could blame her.

"What does your client plead on those charges, Mrs. Martinez?" Judge Peaks asked.

Jawan turned and looked at Unique. Unique returned the action. For about five seconds the two women just stood there staring at each other. Finally, Jawan nodded for Unique to go ahead and enter her plea.

"Mrs. Martinez, what does your client plead on the charges of child endangerment and involuntary manslaughter?" the judge repeated with an agitated tone.

"No contest," Unique pleaded, still looking at her attorney. She needed yet more confirmation from her attorney that for now, pleading no contest was the wisest thing to do. Her attorney had assured her this was the right thing to do pending the outcome of the drug charges.

Unique had feared entering such a plea. She felt that people would automatically assume there was a chance she was responsible. If not, why not just plead "not guilty"? But she'd prayed on it, and it felt right in her spirit. She hadn't talked to any of her family about the plea because she didn't want their opinions to persuade her one way or the other. This was too serious of a matter. The only advice she needed right now was that of God and her lawyer, and thus far, everything her lawyer had suggested lined up with what God put in Unique's spirit. Her family would just have to trust her on this, and she, no matter what it looked like, would have to keep trusting in God.

# Chapter Twenty-two

"So how did things go in court?" Eleanor asked as she and Lorain packed up the twins' things so Lorain could take them home.

"Not like I expected," Lorain replied.

"Is that good or bad?" Eleanor was concerned. She'd only known Unique to be her granddaughter for almost two years, but she loved her like she'd always been a part of her life. She didn't want to see anyone, especially her blood, in such a predicament.

"I don't know. I mean, she pleaded not guilty for the drug charges, but then when she had to enter a plea for the charges about the boys, she entered no contest."

"What the . . . no contest," Eleanor spat, hands on hips and a scrunched-up face.

"I know, right?"

"Heck, she might as well have gone ahead and pleaded guilty. What's this no contest stuff? Either she did or she didn't do it." Eleanor shook her head. "My God, what is the jury going to think about that?"

"Well, she's waiving her rights to a jury trial as well."

"Holy!" Eleanor threw down the baby blanket she was folding. "What kind of lawyer did the church go out and get to represent the poor girl? She might be better off defending herself."

"Jawan Martinez is supposedly one of the best. We just have to hope that there is a method to this madness, that she knows exactly what she's doing."

"Let's do more than hope. Let's pray, and with a little faith behind it."

"Yeah, that's really all we can do." Lorain looked so weak and hopeless, as if she was just going to break down and fall over at any minute.

"Oh, baby." Eleanor took her daughter into her arms. "It's going to be all right, sugar. We just have to trust in the Lord."

"I know, Ma, it's just that . . . When God brought Unique back into my life, I had no idea it would be only for a season."

"Hush your mouth. You're acting like the judge done already convicted her, locked her up, and threw away the key. This thing is just getting started, which means we have plenty of time to pray, fast, and hold steadfast that God is going to show up and show out in this situation. That His will will be done."

"That's just it, I don't want to pray about God's will. I don't care about God's will. I want my daughter out of jail whether it's His will or not." Lorain broke down crying as the twins sat buckled in their little pumpkin seats that doubled as car seats once secured in the base.

"I understand, because I'd probably feel the same way had that been you." Eleanor patted Lorain's back.

"I'm trying to be there for Unique, but my babies need me too." Lorain pulled herself away from her mother, and then wiped her tears. "Then, of course, there's this thing with Nicholas."

"Oh my." Eleanor put her hand to her mouth. "I can't apologize enough for blabbing my big mouth off to him. It's just that you never told me you didn't get a chance to let him know you were going to marry him. I'd just assumed . . ." Eleanor's words trailed off. "Well, I guess that's what they mean when they say you should never assume anything."

"It's not your fault, Ma. I've been stringing that man along long enough. It served me right that he'd demand his ring back from me and leave me standing in my living room looking like a stupid fool. Because I am a stupid fool."

"You are not. Now, enough is enough." Eleanor was putting her foot down. "God says that you are fearfully and wonderfully made. Marvelous are His works. Now if the twins come home from school one day with something they made you in art class, they give it to you, but then you turn around and talk about how stupid looking it is—how do you think it would make the twins feel?"

Lorain looked down at the girls, who were now starting to doze off. She shrugged. "I don't know. Not so good, I guess."

"It would tear up their heart, that's what it would do. Something they made and you sit there and talk about it so negatively." Eleanor took her hands and gently turned Lorain's face to face hers. "Well, that's exactly how God feels when you talk about something He created, and baby, He created you." Eleanor paused for a moment. "You went to the hospital to see Nicholas that day with good intentions. No one could have ever imagined something like this would have happened. But in all honesty—and I'm only saying this because you are my child and I want to see you happy—what is going on right now with Unique doesn't have anything to do with you marrying Nicholas. And I'm sure that's what is truly angering him."

"I want to say you're right, Mom, because most of the time you are."

"Most of the time?" Eleanor said with a furrowed eyebrow.

Lorain cracked a light smile, and then got serious again. "Okay, pretty much all of the time. But there's just too much going on right now. When I become Nicholas's wife, I don't want to have issues, and right now, that's all I have."

"Oh well, in that case, I'm wasting my breath. You should have told me that in the jump." Eleanor wiped her hands clean, which confused Lorain. Why was her mother giving up on the situation so easily? What had she said to make her do that?

"What? Why do you say that?" Lorain asked.

"Because if you're looking to go into a marriage and not have issues, then you've got another think coming. A marriage without issues doesn't exist; therefore, you and them twins better get mighty close, because those two are all you're going to have for the rest of your life. Sure, you have me, but even though it's hard to tell with how good I look, I'm getting up there in age. I won't be around forever. But not to worry, you'll have your kids. You won't have a husband, but you'll have kids."

"Hold up. I didn't say all that. I'm not saying that I'm never going to get married—"

"That's exactly what you said," Eleanor interrupted, "because like I said, a marriage without issues does not exist. So if that's the excuse you want to use for not marrying Nicholas, so be it."

"God, now you're sounding like him." Lorain was frustrated. "I'm not making excuses."

"Sure, you are. But eventually you'll run out. And maybe when you do, Nicholas will still be hanging around waiting for you. I mean, it's not like there aren't other women out there who'd want to pursue a well educated doctor who gives God all the honor and the glory. Oh no. In two or three years when you come around, maybe when you don't have any more issues, he'll still be sitting there waiting for you."

Lorain thought for a minute. "Hmmm. Do you really think so, Ma?"

"Nope," Eleanor said. "Not at all, but obviously you do."

Lorain cut her eyes at her mother who waltzed off to go gather the rest of the twins' things. This moment alone gave Lorain time to really think about whether she should just let things die down between her and Nicholas or if she should go after him. What seemed like an obvious decision wasn't. Here Unique had just come back into her life, and now she had the twins in her life as well. Unique was going through such a tragic situation that Lorain knew she needed to be there for her daughter. If not, Korica would be. Lorain couldn't let that happen. She just couldn't. So her decision had been made. She looked down at the twins and said, "Well, girls, it looks like it's just me and you . . . forever."

# Chapter Twenty-three

"If I have to get rid of my tats, then I guess I just won't be joining the dance ministry," Kiki said as she and Unique sat in their tiny cell.

Unique couldn't help but burst out laughing. Why? Because that is the same thing she'd said when someone at New Day had mentioned to her about joining the dance ministry. And now, as she sat there trying to minister to Kiki, she couldn't believe her cell mate had said the exact same thing.

Still chuckling, Unique replied, "But girl, after watching you just dance to that slow jam like you were telling a story, I can only imagine if you were telling a story for the Lord. You'd have everybody up in the church catching the Holy Ghost."

Not just five minutes ago Kiki had been listening to the radio. When one of her favorite slow jams came on, she began to move and sway like a ballerina.

"You flow like a butterfly," Unique had complimented. "When you get out of here, you should come visit my church and see about joining the dance ministry." Unique had eyeballed the thin white girl with blond hair that was French braided down her back. Although thin, she had slightly muscular arms. Not the Venus and Serena Williams kind, though. More like the Madonna kind. Her long legs did straight and perfect kicks. Her body twisted in ways Unique didn't even know a body could twist.

"Dance? In a church?" Kiki had replied.

"Yes, girl. I know; I thought the same thing when I first started going to church, and they introduced the dance ministry. I was like, 'Word? Oh, I'm gonna like it here. I didn't know the Lord be gettin' crunked.'" Both women laughed. "But no, for real, it wasn't even that kind of dance that people do at parties and clubs. It was . . . it was . . ." Unique searched for words to describe it, but she fell short. "You'd just have to see it, and you'd have to see it done right. Because some folks just get out there to entertain. But, honey, when you get someone out there whose mind is set on ministering the Word of God through dance . . . let me tell you . . ."

Kiki had been hanging on to Unique's every word. Kiki had thought about how much church sure had changed since her mother would drag her there on Easter Sunday when she was a little girl. They would have never allowed any dance in the old Baptist church she'd gone to. But then again, if times are changing like that, then, who knows? That old Baptist church on the hill could have the best dance ministry in the country for all she knew. But she wouldn't know. She didn't want to know. She was in prison. To Kiki, she might as well have had the word "sinner" stamped on her forehead. So church was no place for a sinner like her . . . was it?

"You can't just go out there and dance though," Unique had told her. "Just like with any other type of dance, there is some training involved. There is practice. They even have rules."

"Rules? Like what?" Kiki wasn't one to follow rules, or laws, obviously.

"Well, not actually rules, more like bylaws." Unique had sat back and recalled what some of the bylaws were she'd been told when she looked into being on the New Day dance ministry. "There are certain garments you have to wear to dance in. You can't wear jewelry while you dance . . . or makeup. And you can't have loud colored polish on your nails. If you do wear polish or rings, though, you can cover them with gloves, but other than that . . ."

"And what is the deal with makeup? Wouldn't you want to look pretty out there on the dance floor?" Kiki had questioned.

"If you were dancing for the world, maybe. But when dancing for the Lord, you'd rather look like Jesus than look pretty."

Unique could tell by the way Kiki scrunched up her face that she didn't get it, so she tried to explain it the way it had been explained to her. "A praise dancer, which is what the dancers are referred to, has to humble him or herself when she goes to minister. It's not about them. It's not about whether they look cute. Jesus didn't look cute hanging on the cross. And when the praise dancer is telling that story about Christ through song, the audience needs to see Christ in that dancer, and they shouldn't have to see it through layers of makeup or long, multicolored acrylic nails. That's a distraction.

"Instead of looking at the dancer's eyes and finding the emotion of the song in facial expressions, all you see is how cute her dual eye makeup looks, or how perfectly lined her lips are. You start making mental notes to ask her where she bought the makeup from. Your mind gets diverted from the Christ in the dancer and the message she's trying to relay. Same with jewelry. You don't want the audience to see the bling-bling in your ears or on your wrist or neck. The only light you want to cast is the light of Jesus. It's just about humbling yourself—going out there naked before the Lord, giving Him yourself plain and simple, just as you are."

"What if you go out and get your nose pierced or something? They expect you to take that out every time you dance?"

"Piercings . . . And tattoos can't show either."

That's when Kiki made the comment that had Unique laughing and reminiscing in the first place. "If I have to get rid of my tats, then I guess I just won't be joining the dance ministry."

"That's exactly what I said," Unique laughed. "But if you already have tattoos, you just make sure you try to cover them up as best you can.

"One day this dance ministry from a women's shelter came and ministered at our church. One of the women had a tattoo on her neck. To this day, I can't tell you what song they ministered to, how they danced, or anything. I was much too distracted and focused on that tattoo on her neck."

"But what was she supposed to do about that?"

"They have turtleneck bodysuits you can wear under your garments."

Kiki shrugged. "Yeah, I guess that does make sense. But still, that's too many rules. Why can't a sista just go to church?"

Unique gave Kiki the once-over. "Sista?"

"Yeah, mama. White girls can be sistas too. I thought you knew." Kiki twisted her neck and snapped her fingers.

"Oh, I know. Our pastor is white, but I say she's more like a chameleon. She can transform into being like whomever the person is she's trying to minister to. If she's ministering to a black person, a white person, an Asian, a Latino, or whatever, it's like she knows how to relate to their world. She's kind of like Apostle Paul."

"Paul? Apostrophe? Who's that?"

Unique stifled her laugh and just smiled and shook her head. "How about I introduce you to him after lunch?" Unique had been given a Bible by the prison minister. She was going to read to Kiki about Paul from it.

"He's in here?" Kiki's eyes lit up as she looked around the cell.

"Silly, let's just go eat lunch. I'll show you later." Unique got up, and she and Kiki prepared to go eat. "But even if he were in here, what would you do with a man? After all, you did say you had a girlfriend." Unique shot her a knowing look.

"Girl, please. Man, woman—I can handle either/or." Kiki chuckled. "I guess I'm like Apostrophe Paul too."

Unique rolled her eyes up in her head. "Girl, come on before you get struck by lightning before I can even get you saved."

# Chapter Twenty-four

Initially, Lorain was going to work straight through lunch. She'd only been back to work a few days since taking off after the boys' death. She'd been promoted six months ago. The promotion included additional duties than what she was used to, so her workload had almost doubled. Her pay didn't double, but the workload did. Still, she was grateful for the pay increase that she had received. It came in handy raising two kids.

Hunger ended up creeping up on her in a mighty way. When her boss came into her office to update her on some things, Lorain could barely hear what he was saying over her growling belly. She was so embarrassed. Evidently, though, she was more hungry than embarrassed. After apologizing every few seconds to her boss for the loud interrupting rumble, her boss finally left her office and she realized she wouldn't accomplish much working through lunch as starved as she was. She wouldn't accomplish much for the entire rest of the day if she didn't get something in her stomach.

Deciding she had a taste for the Olive Garden, but not the time to sit down and actually eat her meal there, she decided to order carryout from the Italian eatery. Within a half hour after her boss had left her office, Lorain was up at the Olive Garden picking up her order.

"It will be just five more minutes," the hostess told Lorain when she arrived at the restaurant.

"No problem," Lorain replied. There was a bench to sit on and wait, but Lorain stood instead. She didn't want to sit and get too comfortable, giving the appearance that she was okay with the wait. She decided to stand. With her arms folded, she stood as the hostess escorted a couple of patrons to a table. Lorain observed the décor of the place. She'd never taken the time to do that before. It was beautiful. By just looking around the place, really taking it in, one might have thought they actually were in a garden smack in the middle of Italy. Within moments though, Lorain noticed something that made her heart drop to her stomach. No longer feeling as though she were in a garden in Italy, she felt like she was in the Garden of Eden, like Eve, about to do something she might regret. But she couldn't help it as a sheet of steam rose up in her body.

Lorain blinked her eyes at the vision her eyes were glued to. No way did this familiar side profile belong to the person she thought it did. And if that was the person's face, who did the pair of legs on the opposite side of the table belong to?

"Your order is ready," the hostess told Lorain, extending the carryout bag to her.

The steaming aroma rising from the bag made Lorain's belly growl its loudest yet. That wasn't the only thing that was about to get loud. That wasn't the only thing that was steaming.

Not taking her eyes off of her subject for a single moment, Lorain passed right by the woman while saying, "Just one moment, please."

She proceeded to walk over to the table where her eyes had been fixated on for the last few moments. The closer she got, the more she was convinced that she was right on the money; that this familiar-looking person was *exactly* who she thought it was.

"Nicholas?" Lorain said once she was at an angle where there was no doubt it was him. That angle just happened to be right smack in front of him.

"Well, hello—" He went to stand.

"No, sit." She held her hand out, stopping him. She looked over at the woman sitting across from him. "Oh, so she gets lunch at the Olive Garden, and all I ever got was hospital cafeteria food?" Lorain spat out of pure jealousy. It was jealousy, and she knew it was jealousy. She knew that emotion was not of God. Right about now, though, she wasn't trying to be about her Father's business. She was about giving Nicholas *the* business.

Still recognizing the fact that she was on her lunch break, Lorain didn't have time to dance around the situation; the situation being that she was appalled to see Nicholas out with another woman just days after their breakup.

"Excuse me?" Nicholas appeared baffled. This insulted Lorain even more, because she thought Nicholas was about to pretend he didn't even know who she was in front of this other woman.

"Oh, you're excused all right. Excused and dismissed!" Lorain spat. She folded her arms across her chest, and then stood there waiting to see what Dr. McHottie had to say for himself.

"Look, Lorain, I think you might be confused about what's going on here." Nicholas looked at the woman dining with him and smiled. "This is—"

Lorain cut him off. She didn't care who this woman was. Well, she cared, but she didn't want to know. She didn't want to know who this woman was that he'd just smiled at differently than he'd ever smiled at her. He smiled at her so knowingly. Like he knew her well, and she knew him. Like they knew each other better than any two people possibly could. Someone who Lorain felt Nicholas knew far better than he had known her.

"No need for introductions," Lorain spat. "I'm sure the chances are slim to none that I'll ever come into contact with her again anyway." Lorain only nodded toward the woman. She didn't want to just look at her; she wanted to look at her *real* good. She wanted to give her the once-over to see just how beautiful the woman was who'd captured Nicholas's eyes in a matter of days. The last thing she wanted to do, though, was have visions of that woman in her head the rest of her days as she perhaps wondered about what could have—should have—been between her and Nicholas. She shook her head. No no no! She was not going to look in that woman's direction.

Staring Nicholas down as if her eyes were shooting daggers, Lorain had no problem with looking at him. "Anyway, I won't keep you,

Doctor. I'm not even sure why I came over here in the first place. I guess just shocked that you'd be entertaining the likes of another woman only days after breaking it off with the woman who you'd proposed to—several times."

Finally, the other woman gave some sign of life as she jerked her head toward Nicholas. "Nicky, you proposed to her? Why didn't you tell me?"

In the first instant, Lorain was all giggly inside. She'd gotten a reaction out of the broad. She figured Nicholas hadn't told her he was fresh out of a serious relationship. But then something the woman had just said put a halt to Lorain's celebration.

*Nicky*, Lorain repeated in her head. Already this woman had given him a pet name? Something told Lorain that Nicholas and this woman knew each other beyond a mere few days since their breakup. A hot, scalding lightbulb went off in Lorain's head. Could Nicholas have been seeing this woman on the side? Did he have her waiting in the wings all along just in case Lorain never came around and married him?

Now Lorain was more furious than jealous. "Yeah, *Nicky*, why didn't you tell her?" Lorain questioned. "Why didn't you tell her you practically begged me a million times to be your wife? You told me you could see yourself being with me forever. You told me that . . ." Lorain pointed an accusing finger at Nicholas as she went on and on and on, tears building up with every word she spoke.

It felt as if Lorain had gone on forever, running down a list of everything Nicholas had ever said to her pertaining to her being his wife. The entire time Nicholas just sat there looking at Lorain unfazed.

"Are you finished?" Nicholas asked calmly.

Swallowing tears and humiliation for acting out in a public place like that, the only words Lorain had left to say were, "Yes, . . . Yes, I am." She'd said it as though she'd just received an award for her performance; with confidence and grace. On the inside, though, she wanted to crawl up under a rock and die.

"Good," Nicholas stood, "then Lorain, I'd like you to meet my sister, Sherrie." He looked at the woman sitting across from him. "Sherrie, this is Lorain, the woman I've been dying for you to meet." There was definitely a little sarcasm and humor with Nicholas's last statement.

"Shh, Shh, Sherrie?" Lorain stuttered. "Sherrie, as in the sister-who-is-always-out-of-town-on-business-with-her-job Sherrie?"

"That would be me." Sherrie extended her hand and smiled.

It was then that Lorain recognized her from the family portrait that hung above Nicholas's parents' fireplace. Lorain had been to his parents' house for dinner a couple of times to meet his family. Usually, everyone was in attendance at one time or another. It had been his sister Sherrie who had never been able to make it due to her work schedule. She was out of town more than she was in, which is why she'd opted to still live at home with her parents versus buy a home or pay rent on a place she'd never get to enjoy.

"Oh my God. Oh my God." Lorain covered her hand with her mouth. Humiliation didn't begin to explain how she felt. She stared down at Sherrie's extended hand. Too ashamed and too embarrassed at this being how their first meeting turned out, she ran off, leaving Sherrie's hand hanging, Nicholas's face hanging, and the hostess hanging on to her food.

# Chapter Twenty-five

"It's not mine! It's not mine!" Kiki shouted as the guards hauled her out of the cafeteria kicking and screaming.

"Oh yeah?" a guard spat back. "Then how come we found it under your mattress?" The guard shook her head. "And I thought you were smarter than that. You've been here long enough to know that you can't keep nothing away from us. And you know what this means, don't you? Solitary," the guard answered before Kiki even had time to digest what was being said to her, let alone digest the food she'd just eaten.

"It ain't my knife," Kiki declared with conviction.

"Oh, so whose is it then, your roommate's?" The guard looked over at Unique who was sitting dumbfounded at the scene going down before her. "What would she need with a blade? Ain't no babies in here to kill."

The other two assisting guards chuckled at the comment their comrade had made.

"Then again, though, guess she could need it for protection." The guard shrugged. "But it was found under your mattress. So unless the ghetto princess wants to claim it, you're going down for it."

Unique had just eaten lunch with Kiki and was just as shocked as Kiki when the guards came and scooped her up. But what really shocked Unique were the very next words that Kiki said.

"It's hers. She needed it for protection." Kiki looked at Unique with desperation in her eyes. "Tell 'em the truth, Unique. Tell 'em it's yours."

Unique looked at Kiki like she had lost her mind. She liked the girl and all. Kiki had taken up for her and had her back a couple of times since she'd been locked up, but Unique wasn't about to do no time in the hole for her.

"But it's not mine," Unique said. She looked at Kiki as if asking her why she was insisting she admit to something like that.

"You needed it for protection, so you copped it." It was as if Kiki was feeding Unique lines. And she truly expected for Unique to chew them up and swallow them.

Unique shook her head. She was choking on just the thought of fessing up to the ownership of contraband. Especially when it would have been a lie. "But . . ." Unique's words trailed off. This was all happening too fast. Life was happening too fast. Unique didn't know what to do. She didn't know what to say. She felt tormented as she watched the guards drag Kiki farther and farther away from her.

"Unique, just tell them the truth. Trust me. You have to tell them the truth. You needed it for *protection*." Kiki stressed the word protection. Again, Kiki was pleading desperately with her eyes.

Frozen, Unique couldn't force any words out. Be it the truth or a lie, every letter in the alphabet was stuck in her throat. Then out of nowhere, like it was the voice of someone else rising up out of her, she yelled out, "Wait!"

Just as the guards were about to disappear with Kiki in tow, they stopped upon hearing Unique call out.

The guard who had been doing all the talking began to grin. "Don't tell me ol' girl's got a conscious. She's actually going to take one for the team." Releasing Kiki with confidence that her counterparts had a good hold on her, the guard strutted toward Unique. Once she was all up in Unique's face, practically nose to nose, she said, "Well, are you claiming the contraband we found in your and your celly's cell? Is it you, or is it her we are going to drag off to the hole?"

With her heart rate the speed of the fastest car in a NASCAR race, sweat began to pop up on Unique's forehead. It reminded her of how New Day's church mother, Mother Doreen, would perspire at the sign of any discord. Well, this scenario went beyond discord if Unique did say so herself.

"Look, we don't have all day. Are you going to fess up or not? Who's taking the rap?"

Unique tightened her lips—on purpose—so that she didn't have to say what she knew Kiki wanted her to say; what she didn't want to say. But something inside of her just kept tugging at her to do it. Just do it. Just do it. Just say it already!

And within seconds, before Unique realized it herself, her hands were extended in front of her, assuming the position to be cuffed. She'd said it, and the words she'd said were about to land her in solitary confinement.

"Well, this one's got some heart," the guard laughed, looking back at the other two guards, who reluctantly released Kiki, then turned their actions toward Unique.

As the guards cuffed Unique, she tried her best to show that she had heart. Her jaws tightened, she poked out her chest, and she held her head high as she was escorted out of the cafeteria. Upon passing Kiki, she didn't even look her way. Why should she have? There was no turning back at this point.

It was when Unique found herself in a room the size of a closet that she let her emotions erupt. This nightmare was only getting worse. One minute, just when she felt the hand of God was upon her, the next minute she felt as if the devil's foot was stomping her. She was in hell. This had to be hell. Why was God making her live hell on earth? Was it because of the lie she and Lorain were living when it came to the twins? Because she'd denied the twins, had God taken her boys?

Was this her punishment for having all those babies out of wedlock in the first place? For sleeping with every man who told her she was pretty? And for, on occasion, sleeping with one of her babies' daddies just so she could get a little extra ends from him toward child support? Maybe she didn't deserve her boys, such angels. Maybe that's why God sent them back to heaven.

"But I thought you forgave me," Unique began to cry as she sat on the paper-thin mattress that lay across the floor. The mattress took up pretty much half of the room. "If you forgave me for all those sins, God, then why? Why am I here? I don't understand. I don't understand." Unique began to heave as the tears flowed more forcefully. Everything in her wanted to curse God, but she just couldn't. She wouldn't. She refused to curse God. She had to remain faithful. She had to trust God. Besides, who else in there could she trust?

# Chapter Twenty-six

"Lorain, wait! Lorain, will you wait up please?"

Although Lorain could hear Nicholas calling for her as she made her way through the Olive Garden parking lot, she refused to stop. No way could she face him after the way she'd just showed her butt. If there had ever been a chance in God's creation that they might get back together some day, she'd just completely blown that.

"Lorain, please—baby, wait."

Arriving at her car and fumbling for her keys, Lorain felt like those women in movies that were being chased and couldn't get away fast enough. Just when she'd managed to get her remote situated in her hand in order to unlock the car, she dropped the keys. Definitely a scene straight out of a movie.

"Here, let me get that for you," Nicholas said as he bent down to pick up Lorain's keys.

"No, I've got it," Lorain insisted, bending down, only to clank her head against Nicholas's. "Ouch!" Lorain grabbed her head.

"Yikes," Nicholas followed suit, grabbing his own head. "I knew you had a hard head, but dang." Nicholas squinted his eyes and clinched his teeth. He looked up at Lorain whose eyes were watering. "Gee, it really hurt you that bad, huh?"

Lorain nodded her head. "Yes, it hurts . . . really bad." She began to cry a mini pond.

It was obvious to Nicholas that it wasn't the head collision that was hurting her so badly. "Come here." He opened his arms, signaling for her to rest her head against his chest.

"No, I can't." This time she shook her head.

"Come here, woman," Nicholas ordered.

Lorain began taking small steps toward Nicholas until she stood face to face with him. Without saying a word, he took her by the back of her head and gently pulled it to his chest.

"It hurts," Lorain began to cry. "It really does hurt. Just the loss, and I mean, I've lost everything. The boys, Unique." She paused. "You." She looked up at Nicholas with red, wet eyes. "I have lost you, haven't I?"

Nicholas sighed and pulled her head back against his chest. "I don't know, have you? I mean, you know what I want, Lorain. I've made it clear that I want you. Why you don't want me, I have no idea."

"But I do want you," Lorain was quick to say. "And I want to give myself to you, all of me. I know that's not something I can do right now though. Nicholas, you know what I'm going through. And I have Victoria and Heaven I have to take care of."

"But that's all the more reason why you should want me to be there for you. For the twins' sake." Nicholas pulled away from Lorain and spoke intensely. "Every day in America, 4,184 babies are born to unmarried mothers. That's according to State of America's Children 2008 Report. Over 40 percent of our children grow up in a home without a father. God only knows how much the numbers might have increased since then." Nicolas rested his hands on each side of Lorain's face. "Baby, I don't want you and the girls to be a part of that study. I want you to be in that 60 percent where a father is present in the child's life. Not just a father, a father figure, or a boyfriend, but a husband. Marry me, Lorain. Stop playing with me, woman, and marry me in the name of Jesus. I mean, my God, woman, I love you, my family loves you, I love your family, and I think your family loves me."

"Umm, I'm not sure about all that."

A frown covered Nicholas's face. "What? Your momma don't like me?"

"Oh no, it's not that. Eleanor loves you as if you were her own son," Lorain assured him. "It's *your* family I'm worried about." Lorain nodded toward the restaurant.

"Oh, Sherrie? Please, she thought the way you acted in there was the show of a black woman truly in love. I think her exact words were, 'Bruh, only a woman who really loves you would act like such a fool in public.'" Nicholas couldn't help but chuckle.

"Thanks a lot," Lorain pouted.

"Seriously. Like Big told Carrie in that movie *Sex and the City*," Nicholas took his index finger and his middle finger and pointed them at his eyes, and then to Lorain's. "It's just me and you."

"Yeah, but didn't Big leave Carrie at the altar? And what in the world were you doing watching *Sex and the City*? I thought that was a chick flick."

Nicholas cleared his throat. "Uh, well, uh, one of the nurses told me about it. Yeah, that's right." He played down the fact that *Sex and the City* was a guilty pleasure of his after seeing a few episodes in the hospital staff lounge.

"Yeah, right," Lorain laughed. "Anyway, they'll be no anybody leaving anyone at the altar when we get married, that's for sure."

"Sooo, are you saying what I think you're saying?"

Lorain closed her eyes, took a deep breath, and then exhaled. She opened her eyes, looked Nicholas straight in his, and said, "I'm saying it, Doctor Nicholas Wright. I'm saying that I want nothing more than to be your wife."

Nicholas could hardly believe his ears. "So let me get this straight. Viola Lorain Watson, you agree to marry me, Nicholas Leon Wright?"

"Yes," Lorain smiled. "Yes yes yes!" she shouted. Before she could even attempt to contain herself, Lorain flung her arms around Nicholas's neck. "I love you, Nicholas. I'm so sorry if I ever made you doubt my love for you. But I love you, I love you, I love you, and I can't wait to walk down that aisle and let the entire world know."

"And I can't wait to let Momma know. She's going to be so happy."

Both Nicholas and Lorain looked over to see Sherrie standing behind Nicholas. She had tears in her eyes.

"My brother finally found true love, and a woman of God, at that. I'm so happy for you."

Sherrie spread her arms out wide and began walking toward the newly engaged couple.

Nicholas opened his arms wide, prepared to envelop his little sister in his arms. He was surprised when she strolled right past him and embraced Lorain instead.

"Welcome to the family, sis," Sherrie said to Lorain. "Girl, we gon' tag team him and get him into heaven yet."

"Oh no, you don't." Nicholas shook his head and held up his arms. "Don't you go influencing my wife already, even before she's my wife. Lorain knows how I am about this church and God thing, and she respects that. That's one of the things I love about her. She doesn't preach to me or Bible bash me. So don't go putting ideas in her head."

"Yeah, well, you can say that now, but in the end, us sisters, especially us sisters in Christ, always stick together." Sherrie winked at Lorain.

Smiling back, Lorain did what she knew needed to be done. "Look, Sherrie, I'm so sorry for the way I acted in there. That is absolutely not the way I wanted to make my first impression on you."

"Girl, don't apologize. You got cool points for that. I like the fight in you. My brother needs a woman like that in his life, someone who is bold and ain't afraid to step up when need be."

Sherrie left Lorain's side and walked over to Nicholas. "'Cause this man's got a calling on his life. And you know how women can be when they see that a man has a special gift; a calling. I'm not talking about his being a doctor. Lord knows that alone brings out the gold diggers. I'm talking about that calling on his life to preach God's Word."

"Oh, now, come on, sis. Not now with all that prophetic prophesy stuff," Nicholas begged.

"Okay, okay," Sherrie put her hands up in defeat. "I'll let it go," she shot her brother a stern look, "for now." She then walked back over to Lorain. "So, how's it feel about to become the wife of a doctor?" Sherrie asked, then in a whisper said, "and even more so, how's it feel about to become the wife of a future preacher? Because face it, my dear, whether my brother over there wants to acknowledge it or not, he *will* preach the Word. Which means, you, sister-in-law, better get your hat collection in order and your matching shoe game on lock. What kind of first lady would you be if you didn't?"

# Chapter Twenty-seven

Unique had no idea how much time might have passed while she was in solitary confinement. She tried to keep track of the days by counting her meals. Eventually she lost count of those too. All she knew was that she was glad to finally be out of that hellhole. She never imagined the day she'd say it, but she was glad to be heading back to her jail cell.

"Home sweet home," one of the two guards who escorted her back to her cell said as he uncuffed Unique.

Unique massaged her wrists, glad the cuffs that she'd pleaded with the guards—to no avail—to loosen were finally removed. She walked into her cell. The first thing she noticed was that Kiki wasn't in there. Unique had no idea where she could be, but she did have a thing or two to say to her once she did return.

Climbing on the top bunk, Unique lay down, placed her hands behind her head, and just stared up as if she were gazing into God's eyes.

*Why?* That's still the only question she had for God. Still, she had no answer.

Hours passed, and not only had Unique opted to skip dinner, but Kiki had yet to return to the cell. Finally, Unique got down from the bunk and stood by the doorway. She waited for a cordial face to pass by before she posed the question, "Where's Kiki?"

When it came to being in jail for harming a child, Unique definitely only had a friend in Jesus. She may not have had any friends in that place, but Kiki did. The woman she stopped to ask about Kiki's whereabouts was a woman Unique had seen Kiki sort of being friendly with on an occasion or two.

"Where's Kiki?" the woman repeated as if Unique had some nerve even just asking. "She's where you should have been—in the infirmary. But no, she had to mess around and let you be all safe and sound in the hole while she got her brains nearly beat out." The woman got in close to Unique. Unique could smell the Benson and Hedges menthol on her breath. "It should have been you. It was supposed to be you. Kiki was supposed to be out of the way, letting what business needed to be handled get handled. So while you were away on vacation at Disneyland, she's been fighting for her life."

It only took a few seconds at the very least for Unique to put two and two together. She figured out what had actually gone down; why Kiki had insisted she take the rap for the knife. It had all been a setup; a setup to get Unique alone in the cell so that harm could be done to her. But instead of letting that go down, Kiki intervened. All this time, Unique thought she'd been covering up for Kiki, taking the fall for her, when all the while Kiki had actually taken the fall for Unique.

"Oh my God," Unique said after coming to the realization of it all. "She did all that for me?"

"Yeah, I guess she did." The woman shook her head. "And why, I'll never know." She looked Unique up and down. "Because you ain't that hot." She shrugged. "But I guess you must have some good stuff to make her go up against the L Crew," the woman said before walking away.

Now things were becoming clearer. From what the woman had just said, it sounded as if Kiki knew all about the setup. Maybe she had even been in on the setup at first. Who knew? Unique was just glad that she'd had a change of heart. But why?

There was that question again. Frustrated, Unique retreated back to her bed. She was fed up. There were too many why questions but not enough answers.

"God," Unique whispered as a tear fell from her eye, "why won't you answer me?"

The next morning, Unique was starved after skipping dinner the night before. Morning chow couldn't have come soon enough. When Unique saw the guard coming to get her, she became more than just a little excited.

"Gray, visit," the guard called out.

"Visit? Right now?" The disappointment in Unique's tone was evident. "But it's breakfast time."

"Oh yeah, that's right," the guard said. "I could have them fix you a tray, put it to the side, then we'll microwave it and bring it to your room after your visit."

"Really? Would you do that for me? I'd really appreciate it." Unique was so relieved.

"No, I wouldn't do that. Where do you think you are? The Embassy Suites? This is a jail, not a hotel. There's no room service here, Cookie. The only time you get that is when you're on death row about to get needles stuck in your veins." Letting out a wicked laugh the guard then added, "So, I guess soon enough you'll get that room service. No way are the courts gonna let a mother responsible for the death of not one, not two, but all three of her children, get to live."

"Yeah, well, I guess you don't know the God I serve," was Unique's comeback.

The guard laughed as she scanned the cell. "From where I'm looking, it seems like God don't know you. Now enough of the chitchat. Do you want to see your attorney, or do you want to go join your colleagues for a nice breakfast prepared by your own personal chef, Booger-eating Betty?"

"Ugh." Unique rolled her eyes. "Just take me to my visitor, please."

"You got it. I'd have the concierge call for a car, but that might take too long." The guard refused to let up on the sarcasm.

A few minutes later, Unique was sitting down at a table meeting with her attorney. She'd been sitting across from Jawan who had been staring at her while sitting there quietly with a stupid grin on her face.

"Well, are you going to tell me why you're sitting there looking like that Cheshire cat, or should I just assume you and your husband were both a little late getting to the office this morning, if you know what I mean?" Unique said. "I mean, you're lit up like a pipe at a crack house." Unique thought for a minute. "I suppose in my case I should have come up with a better analogy."

"Unique, Unique, Unique," was all Jawan managed to get out.

"That's my name, don't wear it out."

"Girl, girl, girl." Jawan did everything but squeal.

"What is it?" Unique demanded to know.

"Okay, okay, let me regain my composure, pinch myself, and make sure all of this is real." Jawan began to scan the case file that was in front of her. She'd look at the file, then look up at Unique, look down at the file, then at Unique again. This went on to the point where Unique thought that she herself was going to bust.

"Will you just tell me what's going on already?" Unique shouted. She stood up abruptly, causing her chair to slam against the floor. This prompted the guards to enter the room.

"Okay, I will, just relax and lower your voice, OK?" Jawan said to Unique. She then turned to the guard. "It's okay. Everything is good."

Once the guard was satisfied that everything was okay, he left the room.

"I've got good news," Jawan said. "A friend of mine on the force shared a little information with me." Jawan leaned in and began to whisper. "Apparently that crack house that was busted, the one your son's father worked out of, the one you were visiting trying to get child support . . ."

Unique sat back down. "Yeah, I know the crack house already. Come on, would ya?" Unique was full of anxiety.

"Well, apparently, that house had been under investigation and surveillance for months before it was ever raided."

Unique didn't see where that was such great news. "Yeah, and . . . So what? I don't think anyone could dispute it's a crack house."

"This investigation included staking out, undercovers going in and buying drugs . . ."

"Yeah, and . . ." Unique waved her hands as if trying to hurry Jawan along.

"This investigation also included pictures, a little wiretapping, you know, the basics."

"Yeah, well?"

"Are you kidding me? What do you mean, 'Yeah, well?'" Jawan said, still smiling as she held the key to all her excitement behind those white teeth of hers. "Unique, not in one of those pictures, not one of those drug transactions, and not one phone wiretap do you exist. There is not one shred of evidence or any sign of you ever being at that house with the exception of that day of the bust."

"Okay . . ." It was starting to sink in to Unique where Jawan was going with this.

"Those cops know darn well you are no crack dealer or user. They're just trying to get you to roll over and give them any information you might have. You're a token, Unique. Once the judge gets a whiff of this mess, she'll throw out those drug charges like dog poop."

"Okay, you're right, that is great news," Unique agreed. "That takes care of the drug charges, but what about the charges involving my sons' deaths?"

Jawan's eyes watered as she tried hard to contain her emotions. "Unique, if I didn't believe it before, I believe it now. There is a God, and He loves you, girlfriend, because last night when surfing the Internet, I came across something that I know was nobody but God who sent me there."

"The Internet?" Unique questioned.

"Yes. I scour the Internet lots of times when researching my cases. You'd be surprised what these fools will stick on YouTube, Facebook, and all those other social network sites that just let you put your business all out there." Jawan's smile, just when Unique thought it couldn't get any wider, did. "Thank God for YouTube!"

"So what was it you found on YouTube?" Unique was literally on the edge of her seat by now.

"Why don't you see for yourself?" Grinning from ear to ear, Jawan pulled out her myTouch slide phone and connected to the Internet. Once online, she went straight to YouTube, punched in a few words, and then held the phone up for Unique's viewing.

Watching the small screen, at first Unique didn't know what was taking place, but then soon enough, it all came together. "Oh my God." She placed her hand over her mouth as her eyes stayed glued to the screen. "Oh my God," she kept saying. When the video was finally over, she looked at her attorney and asked, "So what exactly does this mean for me now?"

Leaning in and not giving a care in the world that a lone tear had escaped from her eye, Jawan balled her hands around Unique's and said, "What it means, my friend, is that you are about to be a free woman."

# Chapter Twenty-eight

"Now that dress is definitely the one," Eleanor said as Lorain came out of the bridal shop dressing room.

"You don't think it's too much, do you?" Lorain asked her mother with a worried expression on her face. She then turned and looked at the Cinderella-like gown in the mirror. There were pearls, rhinestones, layers of sheer netting, and a detachable train that was to die for. "I mean, I don't want it to be about the dress, the reception, or the cake, for that matter. I just want it to be all about Nicholas and me committing ourselves to each other for the rest of our lives."

"I get all that, but baby, you still want to look beautiful walking down the aisle. You don't want that man thinking he's marrying a ragamuffin do you? You coming down the aisle in some dress you could have easily worn to a cocktail party? I said it when I saw it hanging up, and now I'm saying it as I watch my baby girl wearing it," Eleanor pointed adamantly. "That right there is the one."

"You really think so?" Lorain turned her back to the mirror, and then looked over her shoulder.

"I know so," Eleanor confirmed. "Like I said, you don't want that man seeing you walking down the aisle looking like some ragamuffin."

"Ma, had you seen the way I acted last week at that restaurant, ragamuffin would be a come up."

Eleanor chuckled just imagining Lorain acting out at the Olive Garden. "So you really showed out that bad, huh?" Eleanor asked.

Regretfully, Lorain nodded. "And then some."

"Well, it worked. You got your man back, and my grandbabies right here are about to officially have a daddy." Eleanor bent over and pinched each of her granddaughters' cheeks. The twins sat in their double stroller admiring the fashion show Lorain was putting on.

"Yes, indeed." Lorain admired her little girls. "Mommy got us a man!"

"And me a son-in-law," Eleanor's voice cracked. "I'm so happy for you, Lorain."

"Ma, don't start up in here. I've only been officially engaged for a week. Save it for the actual wedding."

"Oh, allow a mother her emotions, would ya?" Eleanor sniffed and wiped her eyes. "Anyway, what date are you two talking about?"

"We were thinking next spring," Lorain answered.

"Oh my. That only gives us less than nine months. See, that's exactly why you should have said yes when the man asked you to marry him the first time. We'd already have the wedding out of the way by now."

"It's better late than never, Ma. And at least I finally did wake up."

"Yeah, I suppose." Eleanor thought for a minute. "Have you told Unique about it yet?"

"No. I would have if I could have." Lorain's entire demeanor went frumpy as she headed back to the dressing room to remove the gown.

"Don't you dare. Girl, you better get your behind back here and tell me why you just went from a rose to a wilted carnation."

"I didn't want to tell you, but Unique was in solitary confinement for the last week. She wasn't allowed any visitors."

"What?" Eleanor stood to her feet. "Oh, dear Lord. Solitary confinement? You mean, the hole?"

Lorain nodded.

"Oh, Jesus!" Eleanor was in complete drama mode. "My grandbaby done shanked somebody, and they done put her in the hole with water and bread to eat and one square of toilet paper to wipe her behind with."

"Mama, if you don't stop it this minute," Lorain said in embarrassment, rushing over to Eleanor to calm her down.

"Is everything okay?" the clerk who'd been assisting Lorain earlier walked over and asked.

"Yes, everything is fine." Lorain stood in an attempt to distract the woman's attention from her mother. "And I'm definitely going to take this dress."

"Oh, okay, wonderful." It had worked, as the clerk's concerned expression turned into an all-out grin when dollar signs flashed in her eyes at just the thought of the commission that would be involved.

"But is it okay if I just put the money down and we do the fitting and all that stuff another day?" Lorain asked.

"Oh, sure. By all means. Just meet me over at the counter to get all your paperwork started." The clerk rushed off, forgetting all about the poor, old, elderly woman clutching her chest.

"My grandbaby," Eleanor whined.

"Mother, I promise you if you don't stop, you are going to get to see firsthand how I acted up in the Olive Garden," Lorain warned. "It's not

like that. Unique didn't shank anybody." Next
Lorain mumbled under her breath, "Not yet
anyway."

"What do you mean?"

"They found some kind of blade, knife, or
something in her cell. That's all. She didn't cut
anybody with it." Once again, Lorain spoke
under her breath. "They confiscated it before she
could do all that."

"Mary, Mother of God," Eleanor said.

"But she's out now, so you can cut all that out.
She got out yesterday. I haven't made it up there
yet to see her though."

All of a sudden Eleanor got serious with attitude. "She's out? Well, why the heck didn't you
just say that in the first place?"

"Look, let me go get out of this dress and we'll
talk about it over something to eat."

"Oooh yeah, child, because my sugar acting up.
I need to eat."

Lorain sucked her teeth. "Ma, you have never
had issues with your sugar a day in your life."

"Girl, I know, but you know that's the excuse
some of us black folks use in order to eat every
three to four hours like we a newborn baby or
something."

Lorain burst out laughing. "Eleanor, you are
too much," Lorain said to her mother before

opening the dressing room door, preparing to go inside.

"Lorain," Eleanor called out, stopping Lorain in her tracks to turn around to face her. "You are too much too . . . more than enough. I couldn't have asked for a more perfect daughter."

"Oh, Mommy," Lorain replied, getting emotional. She hadn't called her mother Mommy since she was a little girl. She wondered if the only time she'd ever hear it herself was once the twins were able to say it.

# Chapter Twenty-nine

"Where on earth did you hear about this hole-in-the-wall?" Eleanor asked Lorain as they walked inside the little soul food joint.

"Unique and I ate here once. This is where she brought me for Mother's Day last year."

Eleanor looked around the shack with her nose turned up in the air. "If this is where your child brought you for Mother's Day, then she's exactly where she needs to be; locked up!"

"Mother! Don't you think you've cut the fool enough today?" Lorain shook her head. "Guess I got it honest."

"Y'all can sit anywhere," a young girl yelled out after noticing the two women with the baby stroller standing by the door. "Someone will be over to serve you."

"Thank you," Lorain replied, then pushed the stroller over to a booth. She sat down and got nice and comfy in the booth. She was going to get the twins' high chairs, but then decided she'd just let them stay in their stroller since they were half-asleep. She'd feed them in their stroller if need be. A few seconds passed by when she looked up and saw that Eleanor was still standing. "What's wrong, Ma? Sit down."

"Not until you run over to that dollar store next door and grab me some Fabuloso and some Clorox wipes. I ain't about to sit down in this place. No telling what I'm liable to take back home with me. You know bed bugs are hard to get rid of."

"You are not going to get bed bugs on this wooden bench. Sit down, Mama."

Eleanor gave the bench a once-over. "Termites, then. They just as hard to get rid of too!"

Restraining herself from saying another word, Lorain simply shot Eleanor the look of death, and within seconds, Eleanor was easing down in the seat. A few seconds after that, the women were flipping through the menu of soul food combo meals. Next, they were giving the waitress their orders of barbeque ribs, macaroni and cheese, greens, corn muffins, potato salad, fried okra, fried catfish, cabbage, and baked beans. And when their food arrived at the table, Eleanor forgot all about how awful and unsanitary the place looked as she dove in headfirst to what tasted like a five-star meal.

"You talk about some good cooking." Eleanor sat back and exhaled heartily. She'd practically eaten every morsel on her plate.

Lorain looked up at her mother and immediately started to giggle.

"What? What's so funny?" Eleanor began to wipe her face. That's when she realized she had barbeque sauce all over her face. It was stuck down in her fingernails and everything.

"You thought this place was nasty?" Lorain spat. "*That's* nasty." She was referring to Eleanor's sauce-covered appearance.

"I guess I ate my words about this place, huh?"

"Literally," Lorain remarked.

"Let me go get cleaned up." Eleanor scooted up out of the booth. "Do you know where the restroom is around here?"

"Over there," Lorain nodded toward the entrance.

"Lord Jesus, if I'm not back in five minutes, call those people who come clean up them people's houses on that show *Hoarders*."

"Get, Ma!" Lorain playfully shooed Eleanor along. She then looked down at the babies. Victoria was sound asleep while Heaven was bright eyed after sleeping through the entire meal. "That Grandma of yours is crazy, yes, she is. That Grandma is something else."

"Yeah, your grandma is something else."

Lorain clinched her teeth, and then looked up only to see the woman who owned the voice that was mockingly cooing behind her.

"Oh yeah, that's right. She's not your grandma, now, is she? No, she's playing the role of mommy," Korica taunted.

"As a matter of fact, I was referring to my mother, the baby's grandmother."

"Correction, the baby's *great*-grandmother." Korica rolled her eyes up in her head. "Oh, forget it. I can't keep up with the game of charades you're playing with my daughter and *her* babies."

"Excuse me, but I'm not playing any games with Unique. And unless you've forgotten, she's my daughter too."

"Really now? So when's the last time you've been to visit your daughter?"

"You know as well as I know that Unique has been in solitary."

"Then you too must know she's been out since yesterday."

"Of course, she called me."

"So, you've talked to her?"

"Well, uh, no, I didn't actually get to talk to her. Portions of those recordings were on my voice mail. I knew it was her trying to call me collect. She just couldn't get through."

"Oh, so you haven't talked to her?"

Korica was trying her best to make Lorain feel like an inadequate mother, and it was working. "Actually, I plan on going to see her tomorrow."

"What a coincidence. So do I. And thank goodness I went up there to see her today, or otherwise, I wouldn't have even known about the emergency hearing tomorrow."

"What? Huh? What emergency hearing?"

Korica stood there, running her tongue across her teeth as if contemplating whether to share the information she knew with Lorain.

"Look, Korica, if something is going on with my daughter, then I deserve to know."

"Well, I beg to differ. But it's not about me. Surely, and only the Lord knows why, Unique would want you there tomorrow." Still, Korica paused.

"So will you please tell me, then, what's going on?"

"That attorney chick of Unique's done dug up some dirt that she feels 100 percent is going to get Unique freed."

"What? Are you serious?" Lorain was elated. "What is it? What is it she dug up?"

"Some videos and pictures and stuff. I could hardly understand what Unique was saying between all that crying and praising she was doing while trying to explain it to me. I figure

I'll just hear it in plain English tomorrow. The hearing is at nine in the morning. If all goes well, she'll be out tomorrow. That's why I'm here; to get her favorite meal." Korica smiled. "She said, 'Mommy, I don't care what time it is when I get out of this place. I want some Captain Souls.' Since this place don't open for business until four in the afternoon, I figure I better come in here while they're open just in case she gets home before they open up again for business."

"This is, this is wonderful news," Lorain rejoiced. "Thank you so much for sharing it with me, Korica."

"Yeah, yeah," she said nonchalantly, then turned her attention toward the twins. "Oooh, child, you look just like your mommy," she said to Heaven, since she was wide awake while Victoria slept. She cut her eyes at Lorain, and then clarified, "Your *real* mommy, that is."

"Okay, look, Korica, thanks for coming over and letting me know what was going on with Unique. I appreciate it. Have a good one."

Korica twisted her lips. "My, my, my. I guess I know when I'm not wanted." Shooting Lorain an evil glare she added, "I can name someone else who probably knows what it feels like not to be wanted too."

That was a low blow to Lorain that she managed to let go.

"But I guess the irony of it all is that somebody wants you." Once again, Korica was addressing Heaven. "So I'm just going to leave you here with your . . . your . . . mommy." Korica acted as if she wanted to choke on the word "mommy." "Yep, I'll leave you with Mommy Lorain . . . for now anyway." That last comment was laced with a threatening tone.

"And just what is *that* supposed to mean? *For now?*" Lorain was quick to ask.

"Just what it sounded like," Korica answered through clinched teeth. "You think you had a bulletproof plan? To come back into Unique's life, the child you left for dead, and take the only kids she's got now? Well, the game has changed, baby. Things are different. With the boys gone, it might look as though Unique's got an empty nest, but I guarantee you that if I have anything to do with it—if it's the last thing I ever do—it won't be like that for long."

Lorain gasped at what Korica might be insinuating. Instinctively, she reached down and grabbed Heaven's hand as if it would be the last time she ever touched her. If Unique did get out of jail tomorrow, and Korica had her way, it just might be.

# Chapter Thirty

"Let me get this right." Judge Peaks stared down at the paperwork Unique's attorney had presented to the court. "This woman has been locked up for months under the pretence that she was a drug dealer operating at said property in which was raided by the Columbus City Police Department?"

Jawan nodded to confirm the judge's statement. "Yes, Your Honor."

"All the while the police department has been in possession of months' worth of investigation materials such as . . . ." The judge paused to flip through the contents of the folder before her. "Pictures, records of drug transactions, the persons conducting the transactions, aliases, street names, recordings of telephone conversations, cell phone records, and so on?"

Once again, Jawan nodded. "That is correct, Your Honor."

The judge shook her head. "And even right here in the courtroom, only the defense is acknowledging the existence of this evidence." She gave the prosecution a stern glare. "You are even too ashamed to confirm it, aren't you?"

The prosecuting attorney, who'd had his head down the entire time, finally spoke up. "Well, Your Honor, I apologize for thinking you were presenting a rhetorical question. I didn't realize the need to make verbal confirmation."

Judge Peaks removed her reading glasses she'd slipped on in order to read the file. "Don't you dare get fresh with me, young man. You didn't confirm it because you, just like I am right now, are ashamed to know that you were sitting on information that could have had this woman out of jail a long time ago. You were sitting on information that could have possibly allowed her to attend the funeral of her children."

"Speaking of which, Your Honor," the female prosecutor who was assisting the gentleman being chastised by the judge interrupted, raising her hand. She stood. "The State wishes to drop the charges against Ms. Gray in reference to the death of her children as well."

There was a sigh of relief coming from every corner of the room. Unique gasped, holding in the shout she really wanted to release.

"You wish to drop the charges?" the judge repeated. "This is kind of like the employee who knows he's about to get a pink slip. He quits before he can be fired."

Both prosecutors looked at each other, and then looked down again.

"Well, Frick and Frack," Judge Peaks continued over the light chuckles in the courtroom, "let me just entertain your request by asking why you want to drop the charges. Would it happen to have anything to do with that video clip on YouTube titled . . ." Once again the judge looked through her files, "Baby Daddy Betta Have My Money"?

Again, there were light chuckles throughout the courtroom.

"Order in my courtroom," the judge declared, banging her gavel twice. She then glared at the prosecution. "Well, don't just stand there, answer me. Or wait a minute—let me guess. You thought that too was a rhetorical question."

The male prosecutor swallowed. "No, ma'am. No, Your Honor. I believe that video clip that some youth recorded of the defendant arguing with her baby's father about child support pretty much confirms the defendant's story about exactly why she was at the house at the time of the raid."

"And is it safe to say that at that time, and only that time, do you have proof of Ms. Gray ever being at that residence?"

"Yes, Your Honor," the prosecutor answered. "It's, uh, very safe to say that."

"And, Judge, if I might," Jawan interrupted, pulling a piece of paper from her file. "We have a sworn affidavit from the defendant's deceased son's father regarding how it came about that Ms. Gray was even in possession of the drugs in the first place."

"I have seen that statement, Mrs. Martinez," the judge told her. "And I have been informed that the defendant signed such statement under his own free will. No plea bargains or deals are pending based upon his confession of the drugs being that of his own."

"That is correct, Your Honor," Jawan confirmed.

The judge looked back at the prosecution. "Looks like you no longer have a case against this woman on any of the charges."

"Uh, yes, it does look that way," the male prosecutor replied.

Leaning in and staring down at both prosecutors, the judge spoke firmly. "Look, I don't know if it's due to your lack of experience, laziness to fully research your case and all that is involved, sloppy work, or just being a good old-fashioned shyster, but as an officer of the court and a believer in our system and the Columbus Police Department, I'm going to pray it's not the latter. But anyway, an injustice has been done against the defendant." The judge looked at Unique who wanted to explode with happiness. She had to settle for the tears of joy that were flowing down her face.

"And, Ms. Gray, on behalf of the court, the police department, and the state of Ohio, I apologize. Each and every case and each and every charge is hereto dismissed."

Unique couldn't hold it in any longer. When the gavel hit the judge's desk, a yelp came out of her mouth as she nearly collapsed into Jawan's arms. "Thank you. Thank you so much. I don't know what I would have done without you and without God Almighty Himself. Thank you for taking my case, Mrs. Martinez. Thank you, thank you, thank you."

"It's all right, honey. You're going home. You're going home."

Unique pulled herself away from Jawan and gathered her composure.

"Congratulations," Unique heard from several different voices.

Turning, Unique saw Korica, Lorain, her pastor, and a couple other members of New

Day. Her sister Renee, who she hadn't spoken to since their falling out on the phone, was even there in the courtroom to support her. A couple of her other siblings were there as well.

"Thank you. Thank you all for coming," Unique said, overjoyed, tears still flowing from her eyes. "Mommy, did you get that meal I wanted?" she asked Korica.

"It's at my house waiting for you in the fridge," Korica replied, wiping her own tears of joy,

Lorain hoped to God no one noticed the jealous twitch her lips were giving off.

"Come on, Unique." Jawan pulled Unique away from the crowd. "Unlike in movies, when charges get dismissed, you don't always just get to walk out of the courtroom, not when you've been in jail anyway. You have to get processed out."

"How long is all that going to take?" Korica asked with an attitude. "We've got a celebration dinner to attend."

"I'm not sure. I'll get your contact information from Unique and let you know. But I do know that none of you should wait around."

"Well, I've waited on my baby to come home this long, what's a couple more hours?" Korica said. "Come on, y'all," she said to her other adult children and exited the courtroom, but not without having a brief stare down with Lorain and brushing by her, slightly nudging Lorain's shoulder.

"I'll see everybody when I get out," Unique said as Jawan pulled her along.

"See you, Unique," Lorain waved. The expression on her face looked torn. It looked as though she was glad that Unique was being released, but at the same time, disappointed, scared, perhaps even fearful. All she could think about was Unique getting out, missing her boys, and wanting the girls as replacements to fill the nest.

Once Unique had been led out of the courtroom by both Jawan and a guard, she let out one big and worthy, "Hallelujah to the blood of the lamb!"

Jawan couldn't help but smile. "What did I tell you, girlfriend?"

"You told me not to give up," Unique answered. "And I'm so glad I didn't. But what I'm even more glad of is that God didn't give up on me, and neither did His chosen vessel, you."

"It was an honor. And once things get back to normal, I'd like to discuss you perhaps filing a—"

"Unique Emerald Gray," a police officer said as he walked up on Unique. "Are you Unique Emerald Gray?"

"This is my client, Unique Emerald Gray," Jawan spoke for Unique. "What seems to be the problem?"

Ignoring Jawan's question, the police officer simply looked at Unique and said, "Unique Emerald Gray, you are under arrest for violation of the Ohio State Penal Code in which prohibits the possession of contraband in an Ohio prison. You have the right to remain silent. Anything you say can and will . . ."

After that, Unique clocked out of what the officer was saying to her. She became as limp as a wet noodle as she cried out at the top of her lungs, "Whhhhhhyyyyy? Why, God, why?"

It was that same question she'd been asking God for the past few months. Still, there was no answer.

# Chapter Thirty-one

"What do you mean she's not coming home? That she's been arrested?" Lorain couldn't believe what Unique's attorney was telling her from the other end of the phone. "But I was just there. I saw the judge say she was free to go."

"What you heard the judge say," Jawan explained, "was that the current charges against her had been dropped. This is a new charge, the one involving the incident that caused her to be put in solitary confinement."

"Do you mean that knife or whatever it was they found?"

"Yeah, that one got by me." It was clear in Jawan's tone that she felt as though she'd failed Unique after all. "I wasn't prepared for it. Considering all that the State put her through, I had no idea they would add salt to the wound by pulling something like this."

"She must be devastated."

"Devastated is not the word."

"When can I see her?"

"I'm still waiting to see her. I'm at the jail now. I'm going to get to the bottom of things. I promise you that."

"I know you will. You haven't let us down yet."

"Yeah, well, I feel like I have. I let this one get by me," Jawan repeated, shaking her head in dismay. "Unique doesn't deserve this. She just doesn't."

"I know. But we'll keep praying on our end that God shows her favor and she gets to come home to us soon."

"Prayer works. That much we know. The system might not always work, but prayer does."

"Thank you, Mrs. Martinez. I'll be waiting to hear from you." Lorain ended the call and just stood there dumbfounded.

"I put the flowers in water so that they won't be wilted by the time we get to the gravesite," Eleanor said as she exited the kitchen of her home carrying a vase full of flowers.

On the way home from court, Lorain had stopped off at Floweroma to pick up some flowers to place on the boys' graves. Korica might have had her favorite meal over there ready for her, but Lorain knew the first thing Unique would want to do was to visit her boys' graves.

That meal would have to wait. Lorain was going to get first dibs on Unique.

Lorain felt guilty that at a time like this she was competing with the woman who raised Unique. Playing tit for tat wasn't her style, but somehow she knew she couldn't sleep on Korica and anything she might have had up her sleeve. Lorain was no fool. She knew Korica had a much stronger influence over Unique than she did. After all, Unique grew up with the woman. Lorain couldn't compete with just three years of being in Unique's life with how much time Korica had put in. But she'd be darned if she didn't try her best, no matter how unchristian-like things might get. That would have to be something Lorain faced and dealt with later. Right now, all that mattered were her daughters—all three of them.

"What are you looking all pitiful for?" Eleanor asked as she set the flowers on the table. "Your daughter is about to come home from a jail she had no business being in. I'd think you'd be ecstatic."

"She's not coming home," Lorain mumbled, shaking her head while staring at her cell phone that was still in her hand.

"What?" Surely Eleanor had not heard her daughter correctly.

"She's not coming home, Ma," Lorain repeated, looking up from the phone and into Eleanor's eyes. "They've arrested her."

"Fo' . . . For what?" Eleanor was so beside herself, she had to sit down at the dining-room table before toppling over.

"For that incident that happened in jail with the knife. You know, when they sent her to the hole."

Eleanor closed her eyes and rested her face in her hands. "This is a nightmare. I can't believe it." She looked back up at Lorain. "Are you going to go see her? Go ahead. I'll stay here with the girls. Besides, they're sleeping good right now. Unique needs you. I'm sure she's going crazy if the good Lord ain't keeping her mind."

"I can't. The attorney said something about they have to reprocess her. I don't know." Lorain went over to the couch and flopped down.

Standing, Eleanor asked her, "So what are you going to do? Just sit there and wait?"

"What else can we do besides wait on God, Ma? You want me to go bust her out or something?"

"Waiting on God," Eleanor said mockingly. "You Christians are always using that as an excuse to do absolutely nothing!"

"Pardon me?" Lorain said, twisting her neck to get a good look at her mother, making sure Eleanor hadn't lost her head or something. "It's not an excuse to do nothing. And what do you mean by 'You Christians'? You're a Christian too."

"Yeah, but not *that* kind. Not the kind a lot of you who are sitting up in the church are. Humph, I bet that other mother ain't sitting around waiting on God. Bet she's going down to that jailhouse right now and throwing her weight around as a mother and going to see about that baby."

That did it for Lorain. Her blood had never boiled or risen so high in her entire life. "How dare you." Lorain stood up from the couch. "How dare you question my concerns as a mother to Unique. I love her, and God knows I do. Heck, I thought my own mother knew that I loved her too. I would never just leave her there for dead. What kind of mother would . . ." Lorain's words trailed off as what she was saying really sank into her head. Once upon a time she had left Unique for dead. Literally. Tears spilled out of her eyes at just the thought. "You're right, Ma. You're right. I've done her wrong since the day she was born. I threw her in that dumpster, and then went back to school and sat there and did nothing, just like I did a minute ago. I guess a leopard never changes its spots." Feeling weak, Lorain fell back to the couch.

"Oh, baby, I'm sorry." Eleanor rushed over to Lorain's side. "I didn't mean it. I didn't. I know you love Unique and want nothing but the best for her. I guess I'm just so angry at this entire situation. It's such a letdown. One minute you run in here talking about she's free and is about to come home. The next minute you're telling me she's not. I know it's not your fault, and there's nothing you can do about it. I'm sorry I took my anger and disappointment out on you."

"No, Mom, you're right. I bet that heffa Korica is trotting down there using that ghetto mentality of an attitude to get exactly what she wants, which is her daughter." Lorain quickly regained her composure, sitting upright on the sofa. "And I'm sure she'd use it to get her granddaughters too." That last thing Lorain said more so to herself than Eleanor.

"Huh, what do you mean?" The comment had gone straight over Eleanor's head.

"What? Huh? Oh, nothing," Lorain said as she stood up and scrambled for her purse and keys. "Look, Ma, I gotta go."

"Go where?"

"To the jail," Lorain answered her mother as she rushed toward the door.

"But you said they won't let you see Unique," Eleanor called out just as Lorain hit the doorway. "I don't mean for you to go down there and get yourself in trouble trying to see Unique." Eleanor had a worried look on her face.

"Oh, don't worry, Mom," Lorain said right before exiting the house. "It's not Unique I'm going to see."

# Chapter Thirty-two

"How are you holding up?" Jawan asked Unique as she sat across from her in the visiting room.

Unique didn't reply. She just sat there looking as though the world had come to an end.

"I'm going to look into having the charges against you reduced. I wanted to have them dropped completely, but my colleagues, after reviewing the case file, feel that would be a waste of time since you admitted, with witnesses, to owning the contraband. So, I want to treat it as though we have only one silver bullet and need to hit the State right in the heart with it."

Jawan tried to sound positive, but none of that mattered. She might as well have been talking to the walls. Unique wouldn't even look at her to acknowledge her, let alone respond.

"I was thinking we create some sort of time line of you're being here and the harassment you've been subjected to. I know at one time you told me about death threats, being spit on, other inmates threatening bodily harm to you, etc. . . . . It's a long shot, but we could prove that you feared for your life. We could use the fact that almost everyone knows the rumor of what happens to those incarcerated for harming a child. We could say it's the State's fault for having you wrongfully jailed for so long. We could also—"

"Let it go." Finally, there was some sign of life from Unique. It was as if she hadn't even blinked since being brought into the room. Now, though, she had spoken.

Jawan almost couldn't believe her ears. "What?"

"I said, let it go. This is useless. It's hopeless. Heck, I'm useless and hopeless." Unique looked at Jawan dead in the eyes. "I'm a useless and hopeless case, Mrs. Martinez. I'm sorry to have wasted your time. I know you did most of this pro bono, but I promise you that as soon as I get out of here," Unique looked around, "*if* I ever get out of here, I'm going to pay you back for every minute of your time."

"Unique, please. We've been down this road before, and I'm not going to put on my party hat and blow a horn to help you celebrate at your pity party. Get over yourself already," Jawan snapped. "Besides, you couldn't afford to pay me what I'm worth."

Jawan flipped through Unique's case file. "What is it you did before getting locked up? Got a welfare check, did a little catering, pushed cosmetics on the side? Heck, you might as well have been selling dope. At least dope boys are consistent. At least they hustle. At least they put in real work. Some of those thugs don't sleep for days so that their kids can eat. What did you do? You were satisfied with nothing, or should I say, satisfied with a little bit. So is that what your boys' lives were worth? A little bit? A monthly check, a commission for a tube of lip gloss here and there, and the proceeds from a pan of wing dings and meatballs? Was that enough? Is that how this is all going to end?"

Because Unique sat there with tears spilling from her eyes and still not reacting to Jawan's words, Jawan kept pushing. "You mean to tell me you don't want to continue the fight, continue the struggle because your boys aren't here anymore? The heck with a legacy. The heck with them to be able to look down from heaven and say, 'Mommy made it!' No, they get to look down and see what a quitter you are. How you didn't fight for them even after their death."

"Ahhhhhggggghhhh!" was the only sound that filled the room as Unique launched at Jawan's throat like a pit bull. But Jawan was quick and swift. She moved just in the nick of time to see Unique splat on the floor like a fly that had just been swatted. With handcuffs and all, Unique got up and tried to get to Jawan.

With her hands on the table, balancing, bobbing, and weaving from one direction to the next, Jawan kept taunting. She couldn't help but wonder where the guards were now that she really might need them. Perhaps they'd cried wolf one too many times and now the guards were used to Jawan and Unique's visits getting a little loud. "Oh, so you mad now. It took you getting mad to put up a fight. Well then, maybe you should have gotten mad when your boys were alive. Maybe you should have gotten mad enough at all them babies' daddies to make they sorry behinds help you raise them boys so that you could have your own place. So that they could have their own rooms and not live in somebody's basement. *That's* when you should have gotten mad."

"Ahhhhhggggghhhh." Unique kept charging but was unable to get her hands on Jawan. It wasn't for a lack of trying, though.

"You wanna fight me, huh? Fight the system. Fight your way out of here. Help me to help you.

Take that anger and use it to fuel your desire to get out of here. What if your boys were here? What if they were alive? Is this where you would want to be? In here while they were out there?" She pointed to the door. "Fight, Unique, fight!"

"I'm tired of fighting!" Unique screamed. "I'm tired. I'm so tired." Tears and wetness flowed from Unique's eyes and her nose as she leaned over the table, using the last little bit of strength she had to balance.

"All right, that's enough," a guard said entering the room, glaring Jawan down. "I was down the hall talking to my partner and could hear you guys. The party's over." He walked over to Unique. "Come on, Ms. Gray. Your visit is over too." This was the first time a guard had ever been sympathetic toward Unique since she'd been there. "You ought to be lucky we don't report you to the bar for your actions," the guard spat at Jawan as she escorted Unique out of the room.

Jawan wasn't fazed by the guard or what she thought about her tactics. All she knew was that she had to do something—anything—to make Unique want to fight. Otherwise, she'd die in that place. Not physically and literally rot in jail and die. But mentally and spiritually, she would die. Jawan dealt with people all the time who went into jail one way; full of life and alive, but at some point, they just died—just gave up on life. In spite of what Unique felt by not having her boys in her life anymore, she still had a lot to live for. If only she could see it.

# Chapter Thirty-three

Lorain didn't know whether Unique's attorney had called her first with the news about Unique not being released, or if she'd called Korica first. What she did know was that either way it went, she probably had only called the women seconds apart. And Eleanor was right. Although Lorain didn't have her MO down to a science, she knew Korica wasn't one to lie down and just let things be. She wasn't one to wait on anybody or anything.

No sooner than she'd gotten the phone call, Lorain knew Korica would be marching up to that jail to see about Unique. Lorain would be right behind her—or right in front of her—however it panned out. She just wanted to catch her while she could.

Ever since Lorain had gotten over the guilt of giving birth to and abandoning Unique, she'd not let it haunt her. She'd forgiven herself, Unique had forgiven her, and more important,

God had forgiven her. And if God's words were true, which she believed them to be, once she'd repented and He'd forgiven her, it was cast into the sea of forgetfulness. God would not hold it against her; therefore, she would not hold it against herself. But lately, guilt and shame had been trying to dog-paddle its way up in the deep waters.

Lorain knew another woman had raised her child. And although Unique hadn't been raised in the church, hadn't been raised with more than enough, Lorain was still grateful. She really had planned on thanking the woman who'd nurtured her baby girl all those years. But she had no idea that the woman would bring out the emotions in her that she had. Lorain didn't want to thank Korica. She wanted to wring her neck.

As Lorain spotted Korica coming out of the building as she was going in, she prayed things wouldn't come to that.

*Lord, please orchestrate my every word,* Lorain prayed silently. *Touch Korica's heart to receive the words that I am about to speak to her. In Jesus' name.*

"Well, well, well, if it isn't Momma Number Two. A day late and an hour short, just like always," Korica spat as one of her daughters walked behind her. "If you're here trying to see

Unique, you can forget it. They ain't letting her have any visitors."

"I know. Her attorney told me when she called to give me the bad news."

"Humph, then like me, you decided to come up here anyway and try to strong-arm your way in, huh?" Korica looked Lorain up and down like she was trash that needed to be taken out. "You didn't come across as the aggressive type. I might have misjudged you. Guess you and me do have a couple things in common."

"We do, and those things in common are what I came here to talk about," Lorain said.

"Didn't you just hear me? They ain't letting nobody in to see her."

"I meant I want to talk about those things with you. I kind of figured you'd be on the first thing smokin' trying to get to Unique. So, in all actuality, I came up here to catch you. I think you and I need to talk." Lorain looked over at the girl that was standing behind Korica. It was her way of suggesting the two women speak alone.

"Oh, this here is Tahja," Korica said, nodding to the girl behind her. "This is one of my other daughters." She looked over her shoulder at Tahja. "Baby, why don't you go get the car? Let me talk to Unique's—" She paused. "Let me talk to Lorain here."

"Okay, Mom," Tahja agreed, walking off. "Nice meeting you, Miss Lorain."

Lorain smiled and nodded at the cordial daughter. She was soft spoken and had a very mannerly and pleasant tone. For the life of her, Lorain couldn't see Korica having raised someone of that character. She knew that wasn't saying much about her daughter. But who was she kidding? Unique was a hot mess who said what she wanted to say, when she wanted to say it. But she'd gotten better over the years. One deliverance at a time is how Lorain saw it.

"Okay, so shoot, what's on your mind, Momma Number Two?" Korica asked, hands on hips.

"First off, I'd appreciate it if you'd stop referring to me as Momma Number Two. I'm Unique's mother, plain and simple."

"Oh, Missy, you and I both know it ain't that cut-and-dried. As a matter of fact, just who else knows? Do them church people know the real deal yet?"

"Not that it should concern you any, but like I said before, they know that Unique is my daughter."

Korica shook a finger at Lorain like she was a small child who had just done something wrong. "Now, now, now, you know what I'm talking about. Do they know the *entire* story yet, about how you threw Unique away, the twins really being your grandbabies, and all that good stuff?"

Lorain swallowed. She was caught off guard by Korica's line of questioning. She was the one supposed to be leading this conversation. This was not what she'd intended on talking about. And since it wasn't what she'd come to talk about, she remained silent on that issue.

"Uh-huh, I see. You only gave *half* a testimony, huh? What's all that mess about one person's testimony helping somebody else, setting someone else free, helping somebody else to get delivered? And here you go only giving *half* a testimony. Tsk-tsk-tsk." Korica shook her head. "Guess that makes you only half a Christian," Korica chuckled.

That did it for Lorain. She had every intention of being cordial and talking to this woman like she had sense, but she'd said the ultimate no-no; that thing a person just doesn't say to a Christian. A person does not question the status of a Christian . . . and get away with it.

"Looky here." Lorain put all of her weight on her right leg, put one hand on her hip, pointed a finger in Korica's face, and got to snapping her neck. Who was the so-called ghetto one now? "I came here to talk to you woman-to-woman, not be belittled and have my Christianity questioned.

And for the record, I'm not half a Christian. I am a full-fledged member of the body of Christ. You, on the other hand, are nothing but the devil's advocate here to kill, steal, and destroy what I have with my daughter."

Lorain was seething with anger as she continued. "So you took care of Unique after her foster mother dumped her. You helped scam the government. Whoop-de-do, thank you." Lorain gave off a sarcastic hand clap. "But—if I've said it once, I'm saying it again—I carried her in my womb for nine months. Her veins pump the same blood as mine. Biologically and legally, I'm her mother."

"Biologically, maybe, but not legally." Korica stood there with a smug look on her face, one that Lorain couldn't wait to knock right off her face. She wouldn't do it with her hands though. She'd do it with her words.

"Oh, I guess Unique didn't tell you then." Finally, Lorain had one up on Korica. It was obvious that Unique hadn't shared with Korica how she and Lorain had gone and taken a DNA test, then had her birth certificate amended. "My name is listed on her birth certificate as her mother."

"Ha, yeah, right," Korica laughed. "I have a copy of Unique's birth certificate, and nobody is listed as her mother or father. It states she was abandoned by a Jane Doe. How you think I was able to get her in school and stuff?" Korica chuckled. "Jane Doe, I guess that would be you. Hmmm, guess you are on the birth certificate then."

Talk about cruisin' for a bruisin'; Korica was walking on razor's edge with Lorain.

"The certificate was amended," Lorain taunted right back.

"The only amendment is the one in which a name was added to her birth certificate, replacing the name Baby Doe with Unique Emerald Gray."

It was like a game of Ping-Pong as the two women went back and forth.

"Not so. Unique and I had it amended again after the DNA testing. I'm now officially listed as her mother."

Korica's jaw tightened, and her eyes turned bloodshot red. And all that happened right before she called Lorain the B-word. "You, stinkin' filthy, low-down, B-word," is what she actually called her.

"I'll be that, but you, like I said, are the devil."

"So, I'm the devil. I'll take that, but when you see me, you *know* you looking at the devil. I don't try to hide my horns like you. A Christian sitting up in church crying out 'Holy, holy,' when you ain't nothing but a ho, ho."

"Tut, I know you ain't calling me a ho, Miss I-Got-More-Baby-Daddies-Than-P.-Diddy-Has-Names."

"Yeah, but I claim mine. I takes care of mine. That's what a *real* woman does. And you don't see me lying around with some man." Korica looked at Lorain suspiciously and with her nose turned upward. "Yeah, I know about that so-called doctor you've been dating. Got him running in and out of your house. What kind of example are you setting for Victoria and Heaven? Me, I don't have no man. My focus is my kids, even now that they're grown. So do you see now? That's the difference between you and me, boo. I'm a *real* chick who takes care of hers. While a ho like you just spreads and dumps her baby for any ol' body to take care of."

"That's not what happened," Lorain shot back.

"Does it really matter what happened? I mean, really, does it? All that matters is that you ran off, got into church, and been hiding behind the cross. Now you want to come back into my daughter's life and play momma. Well, think again. Because I'm the one who has been momma in your absence, and I'm the one who is going to stay momma in your presence—no matter what some piece of paper says. Don't fool with me."

"No, you don't fool with me," Lorain shot back in a threatening tone.

"Or what? What you gon' do? Remember, *I'm* the one with an influence on Unique. I'm the one she's obligated to, and don't you *ever* forget it."

"Oh, I won't, and I'm sure you won't let me, but let me tell you something that you shouldn't forget; Unique is my daughter, my flesh and blood and—"

"I don't give a darn about the flesh and blood thing. It takes more than just having the same DNA to be a parent. I'm her mother! Me!" Korica poked herself in her own chest. "And I'm not going to let you take her from me. I'm not. You swooped up Heaven and Victoria like an eagle, but you will not take Unique too." Korica took a minute to calm down. "Look, this is getting us nowhere. How about we just make a little deal?"

"Me, make a deal with the devil? I don't think so." Lorain crossed her arms and looked off to the side.

"Will you just listen?" Korica requested in somewhat of a normal tone. "Look, you've already got the twins. You're attached to them. They know you as their mommy. Leave me Unique. She's mine. She's been mine. I don't care if she is a grown woman, she's mine. So I'll tell you what. You just fade out, and I'll help Unique to get over her loss of the boys, you know, so she won't try to fill the empty void with something like, you know, wanting Heaven and Victoria back." It was clear that Korica was making an underlying threat.

"You really are the devil," Lorain replied, "and I don't make deals with the devil." On that note, Lorain turned and walked away, thanking God she'd had the strength to restrain herself from putting her hands on that woman.

"All right," Korica yelled at Lorain's back. "Have it your way, but the day you're packing up Heaven and Victoria's things and trading them back over to Unique, don't say I didn't warn you."

Lorain turned sharply on her heels to face Korica. "And the day that happens will be over my dead body," and before Lorain walked away she added, "or yours."

# Chapter Thirty-four

Unique swung her balled fist, landing a perfect shot. Her feet danced like she was the greatest. She floated like she was a butterfly. *Pow*, an uppercut. That had to have stung like a bee. Blow after blow, shot after shot, Unique fought those invisible evil spirits and principalities. She punched the air as she shadowboxed. She envisioned taking out every single beast that had tried to rear its ugly head up against her. She was sending unwelcome spirits to the pits of hell where they belonged with every blow.

"Humph. Take that." And she talked smack while doing it. "Um, tsss, tsss, humph." She fought like she was fighting for her life. Let her tell it, she *was* fighting for her life. All she kept hearing were Jawan's words: *"Fight. Fight, Unique."* So that's exactly what she planned to do. That's exactly what she was doing now.

She wasn't going to give up, so all those voices

that were telling her she deserved to be in jail, all those voices that were telling her she wasn't nothing, all those voices that kept telling her that nobody wanted her, that she would never amount to anything—they had to go.

At first, hearing Jawan say all those negative and hurtful things to her made her angry. Then that anger turned into determination. By the time that guard had escorted her away from her visit with Jawan, she realized why her attorney had said all those things to her. It took saying those things to make Unique angry enough to want to take some heads off. Initially, it was Jawan's head she wanted to take off, but she realized it was that multiheaded beast she needed to go to work on. She would fight him and whatever else the devil brought, and whatever else God let the devil bring.

God loved Unique; that much she knew. She knew that some things the devil did to her were through the permission of God. Even then, she knew God wouldn't allow the devil to do to her any more than she could bear. But some things that sneaky rascal was doing under his own authority and not God's. And the last time Unique checked, the devil had no authority over her life. It was to her that God had granted authority over the devil. It was fine time she started walking in that authority in Jesus' name.

"And take that, and that too," Unique raved. "You thought you was gon' take me out, devil? For real? Well, I've got something for you." Unique wacked, kicked, and punched the air.

"If you ask me, you're the one they need to take to the infirmary," Unique heard someone say. "Drug you up and put one of those white jackets on you. Yeah, that ought to do it."

"Kiki!" Unique exclaimed, putting an end to her bout with the devil and running toward her cell mate with her arms open to embrace her.

"Whoa whoa whoa!" Kiki held her arms up to block Unique from touching her. "Let a chick heal completely before you go trying to love on her," Kiki said. "Besides, I thought you didn't get down like that."

Unique sucked her teeth. "Girl, they might have knocked the sense out of you, but not your sense of humor," she joked. "Anyway, what are you doing out? You still look a little banged up to me."

"Humph, you think I look jacked up? You should see the other broad's fist. It's *really* tore up."

"This is not funny, Kiki." Unique gently

touched Kiki's bandaged forehead.

"Aaahhht, aaahhht, don't touch." Kiki slowly made her way over to her bed and sat down as if she had the bones of a ninety-year-old woman.

"They got you pretty good, huh?" Unique asked, sitting down next to her. She looked down at the sling Kiki's arm was in.

"It's not as bad as it looks. I could have been out of the infirmary days ago. There was just this hot nurse I was trying to holler at."

Unique twisted her lips.

"Sike, naw. I'm just kidding." Kiki slowly went to lie down. Unique moved out of the way to help her, and then sat back down next to her. "Anyway, the question is what are you doing here? Word around the joint was that you were getting out of this place."

Unique sighed. "I was. The judge dropped all those charges against me, but then they hit me with a charge for that weapon they found under your mattress."

"Oh yeah. I'm sorry about all that. It's just that if you hadn't said it was yours, this right here," Kiki ran her hand down her bruised body, "it could have been you, only worse."

"I kind of figured all that out," Unique told her. "By the way, thank you for all that."

"Don't thank me. It's because of that whole

situation that you're still in here. If I had never agreed to let them put that thing under—" Kiki stopped speaking, then looked at Unique regretfully.

"It's all in the past." Unique assumed Kiki was about to fess up to her part in the entire scheme.

"But still, I knew about the setup and what they were going to do to you. I was the one who was supposed to go to solitary while they got at you. I wasn't supposed to be in here when it all went down so that your blood wouldn't be on my hands, and so that they couldn't do anything to try to get me to snitch or charge me with anything."

"What were they going to do to me?" Unique asked Kiki.

Kiki looked at Unique as if to say, "You don't want to know."

"Never mind. Anyway, I'm just glad you're okay."

"Me, too. I just wish it all didn't come back to bite you in the tail like this."

"I know, especially since the knife really wasn't mine. But I'm sure me telling them won't do any good."

Kiki didn't reply. She just lay there as if something had come across her mind and she was in deep thought about it.

"What? What are you thinking about?"

"Nothing. It ain't nothing. Look, I been out of commission for a while. I'm about to go check out the scene. I'll catch you later."

"You need me to help you? To come with you?"

"Oh, no no no. I'm good," Kiki was quick to say. With the help of Unique, she got up out of the bed and exited the cell.

Unique watched her walk away before saying to herself, "That girl is up to something, and it's probably no good."

"Gray! Let's go!" a guard yelled, waking Unique up. "You got an hour to get packed up or you stay with us."

"Huh, what?" Unique yawned, wiping her eyes.

Just then, two more guards entered the cell. They woke Kiki up, demanding she come with them.

"Hey, where are you taking her?" Unique questioned. "And where am I going?"

"She's going to solitary," one of the guards answered, "and you, you're going home."

Unique couldn't believe her ears. This had to be a dream, because all she was used to were nightmares.

"Home?" Unique had to make sure she'd heard correctly.

"It seems that way," the guard replied, and then looked at Kiki. "Guess the warden bought your story. He put in a word to the State and voilà, this one's free." He was referring to Unique. "Just like you wanted, I'm sure. But somebody's got to pay. Not only are you going to solitary for possession of that knife, but as you agreed, they're tacking more time on your sentence."

"Yeah, I know, I know. Let's just do this." Kiki got out of the bed and walked over toward the guards, surrendering herself.

"Kiki, what have you done? What did you tell them?"

Kiki looked at Unique as if she had two heads. "What do you mean what did I tell them? I told 'em the truth. What else sets a person free? You are free now, right?" Kiki chuckled. "Guess it does work after all."

"Kiki, my God. I can never repay you for this," Unique said as her heart filled with joy.

"You already have, in more ways than one."

"God's going to bless you for this."

"Now that's where you're wrong," Kiki told her. "God blessed me for this long before I ever did it.

I'm not waiting on Him to pay me back for some good deed. I'm the one paying Him back for what He's already done for me."

Unique had a shocked expression on her face. She wasn't used to Kiki talking about God like this.

"What happened to you while you were away?" Unique asked. "Maybe they really did do a number upside your head."

"No, Unique, it was you who did a number upside my head." Kiki had a serious look on her face as she took a couple of steps back toward Unique. "I watched you day after day, week after week, sit up in this joint, and through it all, you held on to your faith and trust in God. I'd hear you up there praying at night sometimes, reminding God about how His Word says He's not supposed to forsake you and all that stuff. At first I used to put my pillow over my head so I didn't have to hear all that jibber-jabber stuff. But then I started listening. After you'd get finished praying, I'd look up to heaven and say, 'Yeah, ditto, God, what she just said.'"

Unique laughed.

"Anyway, I see that mess worked. It's like all that stuff in the Bible is really true. At least the parts you've told me about and the parts I've read."

"The parts you've read? Girl, I ain't never seen you read a Bible. You don't even own a Bible."

"You think?" Kiki winked and patted her sling, signaling that that is where she was keeping her Bible. "I guess I was covered in so much blood after my beat down they thought I was going to die. They had the old chappy come pray for me. He gave me a Bible. Heck, I ain't have nothing else to do while I was laid up. I figured I might as well crack it open. And you know what? I'm glad I did. It's a pretty good book. So good, that like any good book, I couldn't help skipping to the end to find out what happened. And you know what? We win."

Unique smiled. "Yes, Kiki, yes, we do win. But you don't have to wait until the end. You can start winning right here, now, on earth."

"Word?" Kiki asked.

"Do you believe what I've told you and what you've read about Jesus Christ? Do you believe that He was the Son of God and that He died on the cross for the remission of your sins?"

Kiki nodded.

"Do you believe that He rose again and dwells in heaven?"

Kiki nodded while closing her eyes, envisioning Jesus floating up to heaven and doves flying around to welcome Him back home. "I do. I really do," Kiki said.

"Then repeat after me." Unique proceeded to say the sinner's prayer and the prayer of salvation, instructing Kiki to repeat after her. In less than a minute, Kiki had dedicated her life to Christ. Kiki was saved. Unique rejoiced, throwing her arms around Kiki. "Welcome to the family, sister in Christ."

"Okay, all right, already," one of the guards said. "We've let this go on long enough." He snatched Kiki by the arm. "Let's go."

"Okay, I'm coming," Kiki replied, walking back over to the guards as they began to escort her out of the cell. "See you around, Esther," Kiki said over her shoulder as she walked away.

"Esther?" Unique said, puzzled.

"Yeah, you're my Esther anyway, for I know you were born for such a time as this." Kiki winked and was led away.

"Fifty minutes now," The guard shouted to Unique. "You've got fifty minutes to get packed if you want to be a free woman."

Unique smiled. "Oh, I'm already a free woman," she told the guard with a huge smile on her face. "I'm a free woman indeed."

# Chapter Thirty-five

"Come on, let's get married. Why should we wait? We've been waiting forever it seems. Let's just go get our license, head down to the courthouse, or even elope somewhere like my mom did when she got married." Lorain was adamant about her and Nicholas not waiting another day to tie the knot.

Nicholas chuckled as the two walked the hospital grounds. The cool, crisp breeze was a sign that fall was on the way. "Girl, do you know my momma would kill me if I ran off and got married and didn't give her the opportunity to turn this thing into the biggest shindig ever? Trust me, as a daughter-in-law, she'd never let you live it down."

Lorain knew Nicholas had a point. Eleanor would be fit to be tied as well if she didn't get to have her say in the preparations of planning her only daughter's wedding.

"I've got it." Lorain snapped her fingers. "The two of us can just go ahead and get married on our own, but then we can still have our big reception as planned."

Nicholas thought for a minute. "Ummm, not the same as having you walk down the aisle and say 'I do' in the family church."

"The family church?" Lorain snapped. "I thought we were going to get married at New Day."

"Oh, I just assumed since I have an extended family and a church family that could fill a football field, and since my church is bigger, we'd have it there."

"But, but, it's not even your church, not really. I belong to New Day. I'm an official member on the books. Don't you think we should get married at the church at least one of us belongs to, even if that means we have to trim the invite list down?"

"Well, actually, I guess with so much going on I forgot to tell you." Nicholas stopped walking and Lorain followed suit. "When you and I went through our little breakup, I realized something was missing; something besides you. And I knew that if my life was ever going to be whole, it was going to take more than me just getting a wife. I was going to have to know and learn how to keep a wife. Life itself is hard work when it's just me to worry about." Nicholas started walking again, and so did Lorain. "I knew marriage would be hard work as well. And even though I've never confessed and dedicated my life to God, I know I didn't get where I am without Him. So just imagine how much better, and maybe easier, things could have been had I accepted Christ into my life and was under the complete direction of the Holy Spirit."

Lorain nodded. She'd felt the same way many a time. She frequently imagined how different so many things in her life might have turned out had she placed God in her life earlier.

"All that's in the past. I'm thankful and grateful for how far He's brought me in life. But regardless, I know I can't get to where I'm trying to go without Him," Nicholas reasoned, "without accepting Him completely—all of Him.

"So, during altar call at my family's church, I did it. I went down that aisle without hesitation and confessed who I know Jesus to be, and I dedicated my life to Him. Not because my family wanted me to, not because it was the right thing to do, but because I owed it to Him. He gave me my life, literally, so I owe Him mine."

"Nicholas, that is, that is absolutely wonderful." Lorain was completely overjoyed inside.

God was doing this thing, and He was doing it big. The concern in the back of her mind Lorain once had about marrying a man who hadn't dedicated his life to Christ as she had done was no longer a worry. "Why didn't you tell me?"

Nicholas started walking again. "Like, I said, so much has been going on. Not only did I get saved, but I joined the church as well."

"Really?" Lorain was happy, but disappointed that he hadn't joined New Day all the same.

"Yeah. I know I've had my concerns in the past about the size of the church and church folk mentality, but I'm learning that it's not about me and what I'm comfortable with. It's about Jesus."

"Amen to that," Lorain agreed. "I'm just so happy that you're a saved man of God. What else can a wife ask for in a husband?"

"I'm glad I'm saved too. As a matter of fact, that's why Sherrie and I were having lunch that day at the Olive Garden. She was kind of giving me the scoop on what to expect now that I'm saved."

"Oh my, and I interrupted that, huh?"

Nicholas laughed. "Yeah, well, no worries. She finished it up via Skype from over in Japan."

"Japan?"

"Yeah, I thought I told you her job sent her there for two months."

"No, you didn't. I guess there are a lot of things you didn't tell me." Lorain sounded disappointed. Here it was they weren't even married yet, and already there was an issue with communication.

"Which reminds me, with Sherrie over in Japan, there's no way we can get married. All my immediate family has to be there, whether it be a courthouse or a cathedral."

Lorain sighed. It felt like a no-win battle, but she wasn't about to give up. "Come, on, Nicholas, just think; we'll be husband and wife. We won't have to wait months to do husband and wife things." She winked and shrugged her shoulder. "And besides, now the twins wouldn't see you just coming and going. You'd be like a real daddy in their lives. You said yourself that over 40 percent of our children grow up in a home without a father. Why should Victoria and Heaven have to live another day as a statistic?" Lorain was going on and on, spilling off one reason after the next why she and Nicholas should forego the big wedding they had planned for next spring and just do it now on a whim.

"Hold up." Once again, Nicholas stopped walking and shot Lorain a peculiar look. "Why is it that just weeks ago I couldn't get you to marry me to save my life, and now, all of a sudden, you want to have a shotgun wedding?" He smirked.

"You're not pregnant and trying to set a brotha up, are you?"

"No, silly. Cut it out." Lorain playfully nudged Nicholas in the shoulder. "It's just that I realize what I've been missing and how we could have long been married now enjoying each other as man and wife. And it's all my fault." Lorain was really starting to get worked up as her voice began to crack.

"Oh, baby, come here." Nicholas pulled Lorain into his arms. "Does this really mean that much to you?"

Lorain nodded her head.

"Then, I don't know. Let me think about it. Let me pray on it, okay?"

"Really? You would do that for me?" Lorain perked up.

"I mean, the least I can do is just consider it," he shrugged. "I mean, if it really means that much to you."

"It does, Nicholas. It really does," Lorain assured him, throwing her arms around his neck. He had no idea just how much it really meant.

# Chapter Thirty-six

"You are free, Ms. Gray," the judge said, "and this time, we mean it." The judge winked while banging her gavel. "Court adjourned."

"Is this really happening this time?" Unique turned and asked Jawan.

"You packed your stuff up before you even came to court, didn't you?" Jawan asked as Unique replied with a nod. "That was one of the stipulations I made; that this time, you get processed and don't even have to go back there, not after the devastation it caused the last time. Speaking of which . . ." Jawan dug through her briefcase until she pulled out a business card and handed it to Unique. "Here, take this. It's a friend of mine, a civil attorney. Give her a call once you get situated. I've enlightened her on your situation."

Unique accepted the card, although she was puzzled about why Jawan would want her to contact an attorney. The case was over. Unique never wanted to have to hire another attorney or see another courtroom again as long as she lived. "Thank you, Mrs. Martinez."

"Call me Jawan," she insisted.

"Thank you, Jawan, for everything. I mean, I still don't understand why you did all you did for me." Unique looked down and shook her head while staring at the card.

"Hey, because us single, young mothers trying to raise all these babies alone have to stick together."

Unique looked up at Jawan with a perplexed expression on her face. "But you're not a single mother. You're married."

"Yeah, but I'm an alumni. I didn't always have that fine husband of mine helping me raise my kids."

Unique was shocked to be learning this information about her attorney. All this time she'd pictured Jawan married with kids, never having to struggle a day in her life; never having to beg and do obscene things for child support. "Your kids are not your husband's?"

"Well, yeah, they are now. He adopted them. The youngest of the children is his and mine together, but the other four—"

"Four? You have five kids altogether?" Unique couldn't hide her shock if she wanted to, or that tongue of hers. "And I thought I was bad."

Jawan poked out her lips at Unique.

"Oh, I'm sorry. I didn't mean for that to come out like that," Unique apologized.

"But, yeah, girl, I started spittin' 'em out when I was fifteen," Jawan confessed.

"Wow, fifteen."

"Yep, and had one every year thereafter like I didn't have nothing better else to do. And like I didn't have any sense on top of that."

"That sounds like me."

Jawan turned and grabbed Unique by the shoulders and got real serious. "I know it sounds like you. It is you. I am you and thousands of other young girls out there. I'm that chick who got called the ho, the whore, the baby maker; even by my own mother and father."

"But at least you had two parents in the home." Most girls Unique knew who grew up in that type of predicament came from single-parent homes.

"Girl, not only did I have two parents in the home, but my daddy was a minister. Okayyy?" Jawan, for the first time ever, was in sista-girl-friend mode with Unique. She knew this was the kind of talk Unique could relate to. And she wanted nothing more right now than to get Unique to be able to relate to her. "My family was fit to be tied when I turned up pregnant. Even tried to talk me into having an abortion a couple of times."

"Not your father, with him being a Christian and all."

"Humph, he was sailing the ship. Didn't want me embarrassing the family and destroying his ministry. I refused to abort my babies though. When I refused to get those abortions, my mother and father tried to instill fear in me. They told me how much it would hurt delivering the baby, how much it would ruin my life, how I wouldn't amount to anything, how me and my kids were going to live in lack for the rest of our lives, and how my children would repeat the cycle."

Unique nodded at those all too familiar words. "I hear you. That's how it is with my family. We're all in the cycle, and we can't get out. It's hard to picture yourself doing something with your life when society tells you you're nothing but a welfare mom freeloading off of taxpayers. And then when you look around and see the women in your family living the same life, you really start to feel there is nothing else out there for you." Unique began to tear up. "It's just this cycle, this curse that you get caught up in and you can't get out."

"That's not true. You *can* get out, Unique. Look at me," Jawan said. "I did everything everybody told me I couldn't do. Heck, I didn't even want to go to college, let alone go to law school and become a lawyer. But because nobody thought I could do it, I wanted to do it just to prove to them otherwise. Of course, eventually, law became my passion. I guess you could say it became my ministry, because it gives me the opportunity to share myself and my story with so many people, people like you, Unique. All of this that happened to you, baby girl, it wasn't even about you. It wasn't even about me. It was about that one thing, that something, that work God wanted to do in somebody. But all I know is that I've definitely reaped a benefit. I got to share my story with you, which I don't do with just anybody now," Jawan made clear.

"And it seems as though each time I'm led to share my story," Jawan continued, "it's like therapy. It's like this release. It's this reminder to let me know that I made it, but at the same time, to never forget where I came from. Because if I forget, then how can I tell it? How can I ever be an encouragement for that single mom out there struggling, thinking she's nothing, nobody, and is never going to be anything?"

Jawan shook Unique gently by the shoulders. "Join me, Unique. Be a part of the story. Let your story be an encouragement to save the next one, and then the next one, so that they may be an encouragement too, if you know what I mean."

Jawan stood straight up. "Look, I don't care what anybody says about Fantasia's song, 'Baby Mama.' There are plenty of times when I look back and feel too that it should be a badge of honor. But not until that baby mama does something with herself should she receive the badge of honor. Not until that baby mama gets off welfare. Not until that baby mama stops shacking up with men that are not her husband and having babies knowing they are going to be born in lack. Not until that baby mama has a degree under her belt, a job with career-oriented goals. Not until that baby mama and not some rapper chick becomes her children's role model. Not until then should being a baby mama be a badge of honor."

"Not until that baby mama is being who she wants her kids to be," Unique finished.

"Exactly." Jawan thought for a minute. "Hey, isn't that a holiday now or something?"

Unique nodded, but then a tear fell from her eyes. "I hear you, Jawan, and I agree, but I'm not a mama anymore," Unique reminded her attorney.

"Oh yes, you are. Those are your boys, and they will always live in you. So what you gon' do, Unique? You gon' get out of here and go back to doing the same ol' same ol'? Or are you going to fight? Are you going to fight to be everything somebody told you that you couldn't be?"

"I'ma keep fighting," Unique promised.

"That's my girl," Jawan said, once again preparing to leave. "I know you can do it. I did it. With the help of God, I did it. And I know on every beat of every last one of my children's heart that if God did it for me, then . . ." Jawan couldn't even finish her last words she was so emotional.

"I know, I know," Unique said. "If God did it for you, then He can do it for me."

Jawan shook her head. "No, God *will* do it for you. He will, Unique. He will." Just then, Jawan's phone vibrated. "It's the office. I've gotta go. They are having a meeting to go over some things about the firm's new partner." A huge grin spread across her face. "Yours truly."

"What? Are you serious? You made partner?"

"Not bad for a former baby mama, huh?"

"Not bad at all," Unique smiled.

"Anyway, I think it's safe to leave you this time, but if once they get you in the back and decide to arrest you for something else, you know who to call," Jawan winked. "But seriously, you take care of yourself, girl." Jawan gathered her things, and then turned to head out of the courtroom. "And, Unique?"

"Yes," Unique replied before the guard escorted her away.

"Keep fighting. In the end, you win."

Unique smiled and nodded as she walked out of the courtroom with the guard. She knew she had to keep fighting because the fight was far from being over. The fight wasn't over until life was over, and she still had a long life to live. So as long as she was breathing, she was prepared to fight until victory was won.

# Chapter Thirty-seven

When Unique was released from jail, there was not a single family member or friend waiting for her and that's just how she wanted it to be. She'd asked Jawan not call anyone and let them know what was going on. She just needed a minute; some time to gather her thoughts. She didn't need any of the infamous "Me Time." She needed some "God Time."

While in jail, she'd been praying up a storm, but she'd been doing all the talking. Not once had she stopped talking to God long enough to hear whether He had anything to say about her situation. She'd asked him "why" more times than she could count. All the while she thought He wasn't answering, she simply wasn't giving Him time to answer before she started yapping off again. But on this day, she would give God all the time He needed with her.

It was early Wednesday afternoon. Unique knew nothing was ever scheduled at the church on Wednesdays due to Bible Study. More than likely only Pastor and the church secretary would be there, with the exception of any persons Pastor might have set up counseling appointments with. Still, Unique really didn't want to go to the church either. She knew she could hear God from anywhere. So with the seventy-three dollars she had in her pocket that was left over on her books from jail, Unique went and got a room at the Red Roof Inn. After catching the bus there, she checked into a room, closed the door behind her, and went and took a long, hot shower. Wearing makeshift pajamas she made out of three towels, Unique lay on the bed. She didn't turn on the television or anything; just lay on the bed feeling clean and refreshed.

"Well, God, I'm all yours," she said, looking up at the ceiling. "Tell me where to go and I'll go. Tell me what to do and I'll do it." And then she closed her eyes and waited. She waited until God spoke. By the next morning, she knew exactly what she needed to do.

"Unique! Oh my God, girl! What are you doing here? I just talked to Mama, and she said she was on her way up to see you." Unique's sister, Renee, was talking ninety miles per hour.

"I'm out. They let me out," Unique informed her of the obvious.

After a brief moment of awkward silence, Renee pulled Unique in and gave her a hug. "I'm sorry about everything, sis. I'm sorry about everything I said on the phone that day, and I'm even more sorry for holding a grudge and not being there for you and coming to visit you and—"

"It's okay. Everything is okay now," Unique assured her. "Look, I, uh, was just wondering if I could still stay here for about a month or so."

"You can stay as long as you need to," Renee said, releasing Unique from the embrace.

"No, just about a month—two months at the longest. I just spent the morning filling out apartment applications at a couple of places that go by your income. I'm going to show them copies of my last couple years of tax returns that show the money I made from catering and Mary Kay and stuff."

"But what are you going to do to make money to keep the rent paid?"

"Well, now that the boys are g . . ." Unique had to take a moment to remind herself to be strong; to be strong in the Lord. "Now that the boys are gone, I have more time to dedicate to my Mary Kay business. I really am good at it, Renee."

"I know you are, li'l sis. You're good at everything you do. If you ask me, you could run your own catering business instead of working with that lady from your church."

"Yeah, well, speaking of which, I gave her a call too. She's going to give me a chance to really prove myself and perhaps consider taking me on as a partner in the future. So I'm going to be doing that and my Mary Kay."

"Girl, get the . . . Are you serious? You've managed to line all this up and you ain't been out of jail but a minute?"

"Sis, this is stuff that I should have long been doing. It shouldn't have taken all this to get me to do what I needed to be doing in order to live a prosperous life."

"But you were a single mother doing the best you could."

Unique chuckled. "You know what I've come to realize? That there is a fine line between doing the best you can, and doing all you can. And, sis, it's about time I start doing all I can. You feel me?"

Renee nodded. "As a matter of fact, I do feel you. Heck, I think I might even try to do some thangs on the side. Maybe a little bit of that entrepreneurial spirit on you will rub off on me, you never know."

"Yep, you never know. But right now, I guess I better start making phone calls to let everybody know that I'm out and that I'm okay." Unique thought for a minute. "I wonder if Mama still has that food from Captain Souls."

"I'm sure she does," Renee laughed. "Well, I wish I had known you were coming home today. The kids are all in that free program over at the community rec center, and I have to go to work here in a little bit."

"Oh, it's all good. I'm going to go downstairs, make my phone calls to the family, and then pull out my customer contact list from all my past Mary Kay sells and start communicating with them."

"Aren't you going to rest first?"

"Girl, I've been resting all my life, calling myself 'waiting on God.' Now it's time for me to work." And with that said, Unique headed to her room in the basement to begin the start of her new life.

# Chapter Thirty-eight

"I can't believe I let you talk me into this," Nicholas said as he and Lorain flew on the plane back from Las Vegas. "My mama is going to kill me when she finds out." He looked down at Lorain. "And I'm not so sure this is the best way to start off your mother-in-law/daughter-in-law relationship."

"I'll deal with Momma Wright later. Right now, I'm just focused on me and my new husband." Lorain cuddled up against Nicholas's arm as she held baby Victoria in her own arms. Heaven sat in the extra window seat on the other side of Nicholas. Although both girls were under the age of two and could have flown for free if they were to remain on the adults' laps the entire trip, the couple had opted to purchase a third seat for more comfort.

"Did you tell anybody what we were up to?"

"Just Pastor, Unique, and my mom." Lorain thought for a moment. "Who else is there for me to tell? The only people that really mattered were right here anyway." She kissed Victoria on the top of her head as she slept.

"How did Miss Eleanor take it?"

Lorain began to mock her mother. "You had me wasting all my time trying on those ugly dresses and picking out them ugly wedding colors. It was probably gon' be an ugly wedding anyway. And if you two ever decide to have kids of your own, the baby is probably gon' even turn out to be ugly. 'Cause God don't like ugly. And what you two did, depriving me and Mrs. Wright to marry off our babies, was just plain ugly."

Nicholas laughed. "Then what did she say?"

"Nothing. She just burst out in tears, told me how happy she was for me, and said to kiss her ugly son-in-law for her." This time Lorain chuckled. "I promised her we'd make it up to her and that she and your mother could still do plenty of planning for the reception, which I'm still going to go ahead with and wear that gown I originally picked out. We'll still have our groomsmen, maid of honor, and all that good stuff."

"You do know that we are going to have to have the mother of all mother receptions to get back on our family's good side."

"Yeah, I know. And Unique, well, you know her. She's so nonchalant about things; she was happy for us too. She was just leaving a catering affair about to go work a Mary Kay party when I called her. The first thing out of her mouth was that I had to let her do the makeup for the entire bridal party."

"Well, that leaves us men out."

"Oh no, she's got something for you men too; skin care treatment, a facial, or something. She's going to make sure you men are glowing for the wedding pics."

"A facial or something? Oh, heck to the naw," Nicholas rejected.

"Oh, come on. It will be fun. As a matter of fact, Unique knows this lady who owns a little studio in Reynoldsburg called R Studio. She's going to let Unique rent it out next week to host a coed Mary Kay Mixer."

"A coed Mary Kay Mixer? What the heck has Unique come up with?"

"I'm telling you, there is absolutely no stopping her. She's inviting couples and singles to introduce her products to. She's going to be doing free facials and makeovers. Her and Sister Tamarra are even going to cater it, so that the catering business will be promoted too."

"Wow. She came out of that life's trial and hit the ground running, didn't she?"

"She did. I hardly talk to her any more. She's always on the move. But I'm glad she's staying busy. It keeps her mind off of . . ." Lorain paused and thought about what she was about to say. "It keeps her mind off of her loss of the boys, you know."

"Yeah, I know." Nicholas yawned and leaned his seat back the little bit it would go. He then closed his eyes.

Lorain let out a soft sigh of relief. She'd almost said something that she didn't want anybody to know was on her mind. Yes, she was glad that Unique was keeping busy and therefore not dwelling on the boys' deaths. But what she was most grateful for was that not once had she said or done anything to insinuate that she was even thinking about taking the twins away from Lorain.

Lorain loved Unique. She loved her dearly, but she had grown tremendously attached to Victoria and Heaven. It was as if the girls had grown in Lorain's own belly. She never once looked at the twins as her granddaughters, but instead, as mini versions of the baby she threw away so many years ago. This was her second chance to prove to herself that she could be a mother. That she could do the right thing and raise a healthy, prosperous, God-fearing child.

She was not about to let anyone or anything come between that self-imposed challenge.

As much as she loved Unique, she wouldn't even allow her to. If it came down to it, Unique wouldn't be the only one walking through life with determination and the spirit to fight. Lorain would fight. She would fight to the end, even her own daughter. But as she lay her head back and joined her new husband and her baby daughters for a nap, she said a silent prayer that it would never come down to that.

# Chapter Thirty-nine

"This was a wonderful idea. I'm so proud of you," Lorain said to Unique as she popped a forkful of macaroni and cheese in her mouth. That was the catering business's signature dish.

"Thank you. To God be the glory," Unique replied as she looked around the studio and admired all the guests having a ball. There were over two hundred guests. Unique had it set up where she could do and instruct a facial class every half hour, twenty guests at a time. So far, she'd done two sessions and had made more product sales than she could have ever imagined. She'd even booked two catering affairs for Tamarra's business. Tamarra assured her that any gigs she booked, she could work to make the money.

Unique had never been so proud of herself in her life. If only her boys were alive to see it, enjoy it, and reap from it. But even though they couldn't, in her heart, she was still doing it all for them.

"Baby, you need to take some credit too," Eleanor added as she strolled Heaven and Victoria over to where Unique and Lorain were standing. "You put a lot of thought and work into your dreams, honey. And it looks as though they are all coming true."

"Thank you, Granny Eleanor," Unique replied, using the name the boys had referred to their great-grandmother as.

"Well, well, looky here." Korica approached the group. "It's about, what, four generations here?" She shot Lorain a glance. "Or is it three? I get confused."

"Mommy, you made it." Unique hugged Korica.

"I wouldn't miss my daughter's special event for nothing in the world." Korica's eyes stayed fixed on Lorain as she and Unique released each other from the embrace. "How's it going?" She now turned her attention to Unique.

"Fantastic," Unique replied. She looked down at her watch. "But I've got to go, Mommy. It's time for my next session." She looked over at Lorain. "Why don't you tell her how everything's going? You two have never really gotten to talk or to know each other."

"Oh, baby, we've talked more than you know," Korica said to Unique. "Haven't we, Momma Number . . . Momma Lorain?"

"Uh, uh, well, yes, we have," Lorain swallowed.

Korica looked down at the twins in their double stroller. "Oh, look how big those li'l mamas are getting. And they looks just like the boys. Don't they, 'Nique?" Korica nudged Unique.

"Yes, I guess they do." Unique stared down at the twins as if looking at them for the first time. A sweep of guilt even looked to have swept over her face. It didn't stay for a long visit or anything like that, but it'd definitely made a cameo, one that Lorain noticed.

Since getting out of jail, Unique had dedicated most of her time seeking God, getting her business in order, and visiting the boys' graves weekly. But in all honesty, she hadn't really spent much time with the twins, or even thinking about them, for that matter. The boys and striving to do right by their legacy had been her motivation to keep pressing on. The boys had been all she knew in life. They'd always been her focus. Dead or alive, they still were.

Needless to say, Lorain couldn't have been any happier about that. Out of sight—out of mind was how she saw it. And even when Unique did call Lorain up and wanted to get together when she had a minute to spare, it was Lorain who always made up some excuse why they couldn't get together. Even at church, Lorain made sure she got to church so early that Victoria and Heaven were some of the first kids in children's church. And right after benediction, she was the first parent to claim their children and be out the door.

This was a selfish act, Lorain knew that much. She knew she wasn't acting like a Christian and trusting God the way she should. But for the time being, she felt it's what she had to do. She didn't want to risk Unique having a "moment" with the twins, and then realizing she wanted them back. She didn't want Unique feeling as though she needed to replace her loss of the boys with the girls. And every day Lorain repented for it, but the next day, she woke up thinking about it and went to bed thinking about how to strategically keep Unique from bonding with Victoria and Heaven. As manipulative as Korica was, Lorain, deep down inside, wasn't any better. That's something she'd have to live with, justifying it by her love for the twins.

"When you get your new apartment, since it has two bedrooms, maybe you can get the twins some nights," Korica suggested to Unique. "You know, give Lorain here a break."

"I thought you said you were getting two bedrooms because you were going to make one your office," Lorain shot back across Korica's face and right into Unique's ears.

"Yeah, uh, I guess I did say that." Unique was still gazing down at the twin girls, observing how she could see some characteristics from each of her boys in the little girls.

Lorain sniffed the air. "Uh-oh. I think somebody has a stinky boo-boo." She sniffed again. "Mom, why don't you go change the girls?"

"I just came back from changing them," Eleanor replied. "One of 'em probably just broke wind or something."

"No, I know the difference between gas and an all-out explosion," Lorain begged to differ. "And that's an explosion."

"Hmmm," Eleanor said. She then looked up at everyone. "Y'all gon' have to excuse me while I go see what these babies done did." Eleanor sniffed. "Although I don't smell a—"

"Mother, please." Lorain tried to remain calm, but she was getting agitated. "Can you just take the twins and go change them for me, please? I'd do it, but I'm eating this food, and I want it to stay down." Lorain took another bite of the macaroni.

"All right, okay." Eleanor gave in and excused herself. She then headed for the bathroom with the twins in tow.

"Well, uh, I guess I better go on to my next session," Unique said after watching Eleanor stroll the girls away until they were out of sight.

"Yeah, you don't want to keep the people waiting or lose out on any money," Lorain egged her on.

"Okay, so I'll catch up with you two later," Unique said as she walked toward the room in which the facials were being held.

Once Unique was out of sight, Korica turned to Lorain and asked, "So is that how you gon' do this? Rush her off somewhere to try to keep her from realizing that she's far more connected to those babies than you are, and that she should be the one raising them?"

"I have no idea what you're talking about." Lorain twisted her lips, rolled her eyes, and jerked her body in the opposite direction of Korica.

As surely as Lorain had just turned away from Korica, Korica put her hand on Lorain's arm and jerked her back around. "Don't try to play me. Many have tried, and as it turned out, they ended up playing themselves."

"I know one thing. You better get your hands up off of me," Lorain spat.

Korica removed her hand from Lorain's arm. "You ain't tough. You can stand here and try to sound tough and try to act tough all you want, but I know the real. I know you're scared. You are scared out of your mind that this little world you've created with Victoria and Heaven is all going to come tumbling down."

"What's your deal?" Lorain snapped. "I mean, I don't get it. You act like I stole the twins from Unique. You act like they are never going to know who Unique really is in their life. Unique and I discussed all of that before we ever even made the agreement."

"Oh, so I guess now I'm not the only one who makes agreements when it comes to a child."

Korica had Lorain on that one. Lorain had kept drilling the fact that Korica would have never even ended up with Unique had it not been for the agreement she'd made with the foster mother who was supposed to be caring for Unique. In many ways, Lorain had done the same thing, made the same type of agreement with Unique in order to raise the girls.

Initially Lorain was going to legally adopt the girls. At one point, though, they considered Unique perhaps taking the girls back to raise them once she got in a position to do so. So instead of doing a full adoption, Lorain basically took temporary custody of the twins. She was their legal guardian. This way she was responsible for them financially. She didn't want that burden to be placed on Unique; otherwise, it would defeat the purpose of Lorain raising the twins in the first place. This left the door open for Lorain and Unique to do a multitude of things when it came to raising the girls and shifting custody. In hindsight, Lorain wished she'd nailed the door shut. She had no idea she'd grow so connected to the girls. Even if Unique ever did decide she wanted to raise the girls herself, Lorain knew she'd still be able to see the twins. But that wasn't enough for Lorain. Not now.

"Look, I'm not going to stand here and do this with you." Lorain began to walk off.

"Oh yeah, that's right. Keep running, keep running scared," Korica teased her. "It's okay that you're scared, because guess what?" Korica sneered. "You *should* be."

Lorain stopped in her tracks and marched back over to Korica. Through clinched teeth she said, "I'm not scared, especially of you."

"Oh really?" Korica said as she bounced her head up and down. "Well, I've got a little secret for you. You should be."

# Chapter Forty

"Where's Granny Eleanor?" Unique asked Lorain after coming out of her session.

"Oh, uh, I, uh, accidentally spilled some of my punch on Heaven when I was trying to give her a sip. It got all over her clothes," Lorain stammered. "Mom just went ahead and took both the girls home so she could get Heaven cleaned up and change her clothes. They were both tired anyway."

"Oh, I bet they were." Korica approached Unique and Lorain carrying a cup of punch.

"Mommy, when are you coming in for your session?" Unique asked Korica.

"So what you trying to say? That I don't already look good?" Korica spat.

"No, Mommy, I'm not saying that at all," Unique smiled. "Mary Kay isn't just to make you beautiful; it's to enhance and maintain your beauty."

"Oh, okay, in that case, sign me up for the next one."

"Great, I'll go put your name down on the list before it fills up," Unique said.

"Why don't you put Lorain down too?" Korica suggested. "It would be fun, you and your two moms getting makeovers." Korica gave off the best fake chuckle she could.

"I've already had my facial and makeup application," Lorain bragged, patting her face.

"Oh, sorry, I couldn't tell," Korica said, taking a sip of her punch, and then rolling her eyes.

"Mommy!" Unique said. She then looked at Lorain. "Sorry, but at least you see I got it honest." Unique playfully rolled her eyes at Korica, and then proceeded to go sign her up for the next session.

"Surprise!" Lorain heard a voice say from behind her, and then she felt the palm of a hand cover each of her eyes.

"Who is this?" Lorain asked, pulling the hands off of her face, and then turning around. "Nicholas. My goodness. What are you doing here? I thought you had to work at the hospital." Lorain put her arms around Nicholas. She closed her eyes. He was a welcomed guest, that was for sure. He was her protector, and hopefully, he could protect her from the gripping claws of Korica.

"Oh my, I had no idea you'd be this happy to see me," Nicholas said, peeling Lorain's hands from his neck. "How is everything going?"

"Everything is going just fine now that you are here."

"Ahem, ahem," Korica cleared her throat.

Both Nicholas and Lorain turned their attention her way.

"Oh, excuse me," Nicholas apologized to Korica. "I know how gross PDA can be. But see, I just missed my new, beautiful wife. So, you'll have to forgive me until this newlywed bliss wears off."

"Oh, so you're the lucky fella," Korica said to Nicholas, and then looked at Lorain, "if you want to call it that."

Lightweight offended by the insult Korica had just hurled at his wife, Nicholas took a step toward Korica. "I'm sorry, I don't think we've met." He extended his hand.

"Oh, forgive me. I'm Korica, Unique's mother," Korica introduced herself.

Relaxing himself a little more Nicholas said, "Oooh, Korica. It's nice to meet you." He shook her hand. "I'm Nicholas," he looked over his shoulder at Lorain. "Lorain's husband, and I guess you can now say Unique's stepfather."

"I guess we can say that now, can't we?" Korica shot a wicked knowing smile at Lorain before gulping down the last of her punch. "Oooh wee, that was delicious."

"I, uh, can grab you another if you'd like," Nicholas offered, and then looked at Lorain. "Honey, can I grab you something as well?"

"Oh no, I'm good," Lorain declined.

"You sure?" Korica asked. "After you accidentally spilled yours all over the baby, I'm sure you must be parched." Again, she gave Lorain a knowing look.

"I said I'm good," Lorain glared back. "But, uh, let me go get the punch." She looked at Nicholas. "I'll get you some too, honey, and you go sign up for one of Unique's sessions."

"Do I have to? Can't you just order up a bunch of stuff for the two of us?" Nicholas whined.

"Honey, we've already had this talk. Now go on and support her," Lorain scolded.

"Oh, all right," Nicholas pouted as Lorain left to fetch the punch. Nicholas was about to walk off to go sign up for a session until Korica spoke.

"So, how's married life treating you thus far?" Korica asked him.

"Better than I could have ever dreamed," Nicholas answered.

"Yeah, Unique told me how you two ran off and got married on a whim."

"Well, not exactly on a whim," Nicholas corrected. "We already had plans to marry next spring. It's just that we decided, why wait." He shrugged. "So we just did it."

"And let me guess. I bet it was all Lorain's idea to not prolong the wedding." Korica was using that all too familiar knowing tone.

"Well, you know, she presented the idea, but eventually I agreed."

"Well, that was definitely a good move on her part. That's definitely something the courts would take into consideration," Korica said.

"Courts? What are you talking about?" Nicholas's curiosity was piqued, and that's right where Korica wanted it.

She opened her mouth to speak, but then gave a pause on purpose. "No, I better not say anything."

"No, please, say it," Nicholas pressed.

"Well, Lorain and I were talking, and she was a little worried about perhaps Unique wanting to take the twins back from her, you know, to fill the void of the loss of the boys," Korica informed him. "I told her she shouldn't worry, but she got all worked up about her not really being in any better of a situation than Unique. I mean, by her being single too and all."

Nicholas's brown complexion was now a shade of red.

"I'm sorry. It's obvious she hasn't discussed this with you," Korica said. "Please don't tell her I shared this with you. As Unique's mothers, she and I need to get along, and I don't want to throw a monkey wrench in that by speaking on something I perhaps shouldn't have."

"Oh, don't worry. I won't say anything," Nicholas assured her.

"Thank you. Thank you so much. Well, I'm in the next session, so I better get going." Korica began to walk off, feeling delighted that even though she'd yet to have caused a wedge between Lorain and Unique, she'd just done a fine job of at least planting a splinter in Lorain and Nicholas's marriage. It was a start anyway. And maybe some day she'd get to finish . . . just maybe.

As Korica moseyed on to her session, Nicholas was left standing there with a million and one thoughts running through his head. A few seconds later, his thoughts were interrupted by Lorain's voice.

"Here you go. This is Unique's special blend of punch," Lorain said to Nicholas, carrying two cups of the beverage. She looked around. "Where's Korica?"

"Oh, she had to go to her session," Nicholas replied.

"Oh well, I guess I'll be having punch after all. Here." Lorain handed Nicholas a cup of punch while she held the other one.

Nicholas went to take a sip of his punch.

"Wait a minute. Let's toast," Lorain suggested. "To love, marriage, and parenthood." Lorain held up her cup. A few seconds went by and her cup still remained in the air. "Nicholas?" she said after another moment passed, and she was still left hanging.

There were a million things running through Nicholas's head right now. He didn't know how to feel about the information Korica had just shared with him. He didn't know if it mattered that Lorain might have convinced him to move up their marriage for her own selfish reasons. Life was good right now, and he didn't want any of that to change. But something told him if he was to bring it up to Lorain, so much would, in fact, change. But there would always be this nagging feeling inside of him wanting to know the truth. At this second, he didn't know which to give in to.

"Nicholas, what are you going to do?" Lorain asked him, and a good question it was. "Are you going to toast, or are you going to leave me hanging?"

Nicholas looked up into Lorain's eyes, and at that moment, he knew what he had to do.

"To love, marriage, and parenthood," he said, lifting his cup. "May we live happily ever after," he added before they tapped cups.

"Yes," Lorain agreed. "May we live happily ever after."

# Chapter Forty-one

"I do hope you all enjoyed that word today from God," the pastor of New Day Temple of Faith said.

"Amen," some congregation members replied as a sign that they had.

"It was delicious," another called out.

"I just want to give a special thanks for all the family and friends who came out to celebrate this year's Family and Friends Day here at New Day Temple of Faith," the pastor said. "But I want to thank, even more so, those of you who invited friends, family, and some complete strangers to come out and fellowship with us."

Unique looked over at her homegirl, Joelle, who was sitting next to her. She was glad that this year Joelle had finally decided to come out and visit New Day for Family and Friends Day.

"I know how hard it is for some of us to pick up the phone and invite someone to church," the pastor continued. "It's not as easy as it was to pick up the phone, back when we were in the world, and invite folks to the club."

"Oh, you still preaching, Pastor," someone said.

"Naw, naw, I'm done preaching for today. I just want to talk to you now. Is it okay if I just talk to you?"

"Talk to us, Pastor," some beckoned.

"See, I was one who could call up a girlfriend or a cousin in a minute and say . . ." Pastor put her hand to her ear and mouth to symbolize a phone. ". . . Girl, you want to meet me at the club? . . . Oh, don't worry about not having no money, I'll pay your way . . . Girl, please, you know I'll buy you a drink." Pastor looked at the congregation. "And if we got real lucky, we could find some guy to not only buy the drinks, but maybe to even go home with."

"Amen," both Unique and Joelle said, looking at each other and giving a high five. The two of them had called each other on more occasions than they could remember and said some of those exact words.

"You get all dressed up to go out to the club," Pastor said. "And I don't know about y'all, but when I was going out, when I was in the world, I gave the devil my best. I'd fidget over what to wear for hours sometimes, because I wanted to look my coolest. If I was gon' sin, then I was gon' look good while doing it. If I were going to hell, I'd look so good that the paparazzi would follow me there, cameras just a-flashin'." Pastor began striking poses and a couple members stood to their feet clapping. "I'm talking name brand see-through shirts with a designer bra on underneath, miniskirt, and thigh-high boots that I bounced a check to buy."

Laughter erupted throughout the congregation.

"Oh yeah, some of us did it up in the world, didn't we?" Pastor asked.

"Yes, we did," some answered.

"But now we won't even iron the raggedy jeans we throw on for Sunday church service."

"Ouch, Pastor," someone shouted.

"Oh, my bad. I didn't mean to step on your toes." Pastor began tiptoeing across the pulpit.

Members of the congregation laughed, at both her actions and her use of slang. It was always funny in the church when pastors used slang. But it was even more laughable for some reason when it was a white pastor, such as New Day's pastor, using slang. New Day's congregation, now almost over 90 percent black, didn't see color when it came to their pastor though. All they saw was a vessel God was using to deliver His Word. Color, race, sex, and creed mattered not. God could use whomever He wanted, whenever He wanted, and however He wanted. Selah.

Pastor looked around at some of the faces. "Don't go getting offended up in here, because I'm not talking about you. I'm talking about me right now," the pastor said. "Can I talk about it? Can I talk about myself real quick?"

"Talk about it, Pastor," a woman said as she stood up and shooed her hand at the pastor.

"See, because I'ma tell the truth and shame the devil. When I was in the world, I gave the devil my very best. But then when I started getting into church, giving God my best was a whole nother story."

"Aw, shoot, Pastor. What's your story?" someone called out.

"Like I said," Pastor replied, "I'd spend hours picking out clothes to go to the club, but would get up and throw on anything to go to the Lord's house. But thank God I know to do better now."

"We hear you, Pastor," someone spoke while someone else hollered out, "I know better now."

"Remember, though, don't get offended, I'm not talking about you. I'm talking about me right now."

"You're talking about me too, Pastor," someone wasn't ashamed to say. "That used to be me."

"It used to be me too," Pastor reminded everyone, "but thank God I know better now." The pastor almost went into a hoop as she continued with, "I know better now, because now I don't call up my girlfriends and cousins talkin' 'bout 'Meet me at the club, it's going down.'"

By now, half the congregation was on their feet at Pastor's play on the hook to a once-popular hip-hop song.

"Now I get on the phone and say, 'Meet me at the church, it's going down!'" Pastor could feel the hoop coming on as she tried to contain herself. Typically, she wasn't a hooping pastor, but for some reason, the Spirit that was running through her wasn't the typical spirit. Today wasn't church as usual.

"You know you preaching now, Pastor. You know you preaching," a gentleman said, wiping a tear from his eye from laughing so hard at his own truth that Pastor was speaking.

The pastor continued. "Now I get on the phone and say 'Don't worry about money, because there is no cover charge. The price has already been paid!'" Pastor shouted.

Now everyone was on their feet; New Day members, friends, family, and visitors alike.

"And guess what? If you come on communion Sunday, drinks are on the house!"

The church exploded with praise.

"And you don't have to go write a bad check for the perfect outfit, because we have a one-size-fits-all outfit waiting on you called the armor of God."

"Glory!" a woman shouted and fell to her knees.

"And if you're still worried about what to wear, do what I used to do until I learned better from the mothers at the church. Wear those raggedy, wrinkled jeans. In other words, come as you are. Jesus will give you a makeover. Not a Mary Kay cosmetics makeover like our Sister Unique here does so well." Pastor winked at Unique who had tears running down her cheeks. "But a spiritual makeover. You'll look so good that by the time my God is done with you, when you try to step foot back out there into the world, folks aren't even going to know who you are. Folks aren't even going to recognize you. 'Who are you?' they are going to ask. 'We don't recognize you. You don't belong here.'"

"Yes, God! Yes!" Unique cried out.

"And you'll walk out of here with a man all right. A man that will comfort you." The pastor wrapped her arms around herself and began rubbing her own arms. "He'll protect you. He'll provide for you. He'll give you all your heart's desires that line up with the goodness of the Word of God. He'll teach you and guide you and direct your path. He will never leave you nor forsake you. He's an extension of God, and He goes by the name of Holy Spirit."

"Hallelujah," people shouted out. A couple even broke out into a spiritual dance.

"Glory!" others cried out.

Crying out, praises and worshipping took place for the next few minutes before everyone's spirit settled down.

"You wanna go to that club or that pub where everybody knows your name?" the pastor asked, referring to the theme song from the old sit-com *Cheers*. "Well, come on up in here, because even though everybody might not know your name . . ." She pointed up to the heavens. ". . . He knows your name. He knows your name!" Pastor repeated and the church was in a complete holy uproar. It took a few minutes for the shouts and praises to die down before Pastor could continue.

"But I ain't gon' preach to y'all. I'm done preaching," Pastor said as members began to laugh, knowing good and doggone well that Pastor had just preached her butt off. "But seriously, I do want to thank all who participated in Family and Friends Day. God bless you. God bless you all."

"Humph, I guess your pastor tooolllld me," Joelle said in a singsong voice.

"She told quite a few of us," Unique replied. "That word just wasn't for you."

"That was crazy, though, because it was like she'd read my mind for all these years regarding how I felt about coming to church." Joelle shot Unique an accusing look. "That is, unless you been talking about me behind my back to your pastor."

Unique smacked her lips. "Child, please. That wasn't nothing but the Holy Ghost giving her those words to say. I haven't been talking about—"

"Hey, isn't that your other mother and the girls?" Joelle nodded toward the church exit doors after cutting off Unique.

Unique turned to look just in time to see Lorain getting ready to exit the church. "Mama Lorain!" Unique called out. "Mama Lorain!"

Lorain just kept it moving, although Unique was sure she'd heard her. She had to have heard her; everyone else seemed to have. Even the lady that was exiting the church in front of Lorain turned around to see who was doing all that yelling.

*Humph, maybe she didn't hear me,* Unique surmised. "Oh well, I guess she couldn't hear me, being so focused on the twins and all," Unique reasoned, still not 100 percent sure, but not finding it something she needed to make a big deal out of.

"Yeah, I guess not," Joelle shrugged.

"No worries, though. I'll catch up with her. There's something I need to talk to her about anyway."

Joelle noticed the expression on her friend's face. "It must be serious."

Unique sighed. "Believe me, it is."

# Chapter Forty-two

It was early Saturday morning. Nicholas had been at the ER since the evening before. He was pulling a double shift. Lorain, along with the twins, had been sound asleep. At least Lorain hoped the babies were still asleep after whoever was at the door had continuously hit the doorbell.

"This better be the FedEx man with my million-dollar check." Lorain stomped to the door, tying her robe around her waist. When she looked out the peephole, her heart nearly dropped. It was Unique. Why was she here this early in the morning? She hadn't even called. It must have been urgent. What could have been so urgent that Unique just had to rush over first thing in the morning without even calling? What could it have concerned?

Lorain looked toward the twins' bedroom up the staircase in fear. Could this be it? Could this be the day Unique decided that she couldn't wait not another minute? That she wanted her girls back, and she wanted them right now? Had Korica finally gotten to Unique?

Although Korica hadn't been a problem for Lorain since Unique's Mary Kay and catering event, Lorain knew she couldn't sleep on Korica and what she was capable of doing. She was vengeful and spiteful. Somebody like that never let go of a grudge until they were delivered from it. If Lorain was so lucky, maybe some of Unique's Christianity would rub off on Korica first, convicting her for the misery and fears she'd been instilling in Lorain. Such as right now—Lorain feared just opening up her front door.

Once upon a time, Lorain's heart would have dropped for good reasons had Unique been standing outside her door. She had welcomed Unique's visits as a chance for the two of them to bond as mother and daughter, something Lorain never imagined she'd be able to do. But God had made it all possible. God had made so much possible. Those little girls upstairs were proof of that. She was getting to be the mother she never got to be with Unique. But one black cloud still remained over her otherwise sunny picnic. That black cloud was the fact that Unique was the biological mother of Heaven and Victoria. She was a cloud that could open up and rain down on their picnic any day. Was today the day?

Lorain didn't want to find out. She didn't want to open that door. A part of her wanted to tiptoe back to her bedroom and pretend as though she'd slept right through the ringing of the doorbell. It was believable. She could say she'd had a long night up with the girls and was exhausted. After all, her little stunt of pretending not to hear Unique's shouts out to her in church last Sunday had worked. Pretending not to have heard her phone ringing after looking down at the caller ID all week had worked. Pretending not to have gotten Unique's messages all week, therefore, not calling her back had worked. Pretending not to hear the doorbell could work equally as well. Lorain knew, though, that if Unique rang that bell one more time, the twins would more than likely wake up and start fussing. With double the noise of the average toddler being woken up out of their sleep, Unique would hear them and know something was up.

"Oh, I hate to admit it," Lorain said to herself, "but maybe Korica is right. Maybe it's fine time I stop running scared." And on that note, she decided to open up the door.

"I'm sorry if I woke you," Unique apologized after Lorain opened up the door. "I know it's early. I've been meaning to talk to you. I tried to catch up with you last Sunday at church. I've called you a few times and left a couple of messages." There could have been a question mark at the end of Unique's statement, because the look on her face was asking Lorain whether she'd gotten her messages or not. Unique assumed she hadn't since she hadn't returned not one of them.

"Oh yeah, I, uh, have been meaning to call you back. I've just been so busy this week packing to move into the new house. Nick is still packing things up at his old apartment. The twins had a doctor's appointment this week, and on top of all that, we're trying to plan a reception. It's just—"

"Yeah, I know. You don't have to tell me. I've been packing up my stuff at my sister's to move into my new place too."

"Oh yeah, that's right. You got approved for one of those apartments you filled out an application for a while back."

"Yeah, through the grace of God. They didn't do a credit check or anything."

Lorain paused for a minute. "So, uh, how many bedrooms did you end up getting?"

"It's a two-bedroom," Unique answered.

Lorain would have felt better had Unique said she'd gotten a one-bedroom. That way she'd know beyond a shadow of a doubt that Unique had no intentions of trying to move the girls in with her.

"I'm turning one of the bedrooms into an office/spa-like boutique room. I'm going to schedule facials and consultations in the room. I have so many wonderful decorating ideas. When people walk into the room, I want them to forget all about the fact that they are in an apartment. I want them to feel like they're in a little salon somewhere. You know what I mean?"

"Yes, yes, I do," Lorain smiled. She was glad to hear Unique's plans for that second room, but still, as long as there was a second room, she still had options. "I'm so proud of you." Lorain pulled Unique in for a hug. Realizing Unique was still standing outside, Lorain felt embarrassed. "Oh my, what am I thinking? Come on in here."

"Thanks," Unique said as she entered Lorain's condo.

Lorain noticed Unique looking around.

"Uh, I know it's a bit of a mess right now, but like I said, I'm still packing."

"Oh no, you're okay. I was just wondering where the girls were."

Why did Lorain want to tell her that the girls were over Eleanor's? But she didn't. "They're asleep."

"Oh." Unique appeared to be a little disappointed.

"Is something wrong? You said you've been wanting to talk to me about something." Lorain swallowed hard. "Does it have something to do with the girls?"

Unique shook her head while looking at Lorain. "No."

Lorain exhaled.

"It has *everything* to do with the girls," Unique continued.

Lorain had barely gotten a chance to breathe in again before Unique cut her breath off. It was time; the time was now. That dreaded talk she knew Unique would be wanting to have with her was finally here.

"I know we had an agreement," Unique started, "and I know that all a person has in this world is their word. The last thing I ever want to do is to go back on my word." Unique paused and looked down at the floor.

"Wha . . . What is it?" Lorain asked, trying hard to keep her voice intact and her tear ducts dry.

"I know we agreed that you'd raise the girls. We agreed that I'd still be able to get them and eventually they'd know who I really was to them."

"Uh-huh," was all Lorain could get out. She knew that if she spoke, she'd break down.

"Well, things have changed," Unique said, now looking at Lorain again.

Lorain cupped her hands as if she was about to pray and rested them on her lips. She closed her eyes, to not only keep the tears that were threatening to fall from actually doing so, but to brace herself for the words she knew Unique was about to say.

"I hope you don't get mad at me," Unique continued, "and I hope you don't think I'm a bad mother, but I was hoping that maybe the girls could . . . could . . . that we could terminate the temporary custody agreement."

Lorain exhaled, and a gasp flew out of her mouth that she tried to catch with her hands. "You don't want me to have temporary custody of the girls anymore? Is that what you're saying?" Lorain wanted to be very clear.

"That's exactly what I'm saying," Unique told her as she quickly wiped a falling tear from her eye. "I want to change it to a permanent custody agreement. I want you and Nicholas to adopt the girls, legally."

Lorain put her hand over her heart. "Wha . . . What? What did you say?"

"Please don't think that I'm a bad mother. I know with the boys gone I should want to and I should be able to take the girls and raise them myself. But, I'm still healing. I still hurt a lot. I still cry a lot. Some days the fight is simply getting out of bed. But Jesus," Unique said, raising a finger. "Because of Jesus, I feel like going on. I just don't think I'm strong enough to drag those little girls along for the ride. You know what I mean? I struggled with my boys. I don't want to put my girls through that same thing. I can't. I won't. So please say you'll do this for me. Please," Unique cried.

"Yes, yes, I'll do it," Lorain said. She walked over and squeezed Unique tightly. "We'll do it. Nick and I will do it." She hated the pain her daughter was going through. She hated that she'd been so selfish that she hadn't been there for Unique like she should have been. But obviously, it had all worked out. It was all going to work out for both Unique and Lorain.

"So you don't think I'm being selfish?" Unique asked, pulling away from Lorain. "I just want what's best for them. And I believe without a shadow of a doubt that you are what's best for the girls; you and Nick."

"Thank you, sweetie. And, no, I don't think you're being selfish. This is the most selfless thing any woman could ever do for her children."

"So you don't mind raising the girls?"

"God, no, I don't mind. I don't mind at all."

"What about Nick?"

"Oh, please; this will be the best wedding present anyone could give him. He loves Victoria and Heaven."

"And I can tell they love him too," Unique smiled, "just as much as the boys did."

"Yes, they do," Lorain agreed.

"Then it's all settled," Unique said, regaining her composure. "I've talked to my caseworker, and she's going to make a couple referrals so that we can get the ball rolling on the custody matter, adoption, or whatever they call it."

"Don't worry about all that now. We'll work it out."

"Okay," Unique agreed. "Well, I'll let you get back to sleep."

"All right, then," Lorain said, escorting Unique to the door as quickly as she could. She realized, once again, how selfish she was being—how selfish she had been ever since Unique had gotten out of jail and Korica had planted that ugly seed in her subconscious. Now that she felt more secure than ever that the girls would be and would remain a permanent fixture in her life, it was time for Lorain to now be selfless. She had to now trust God's ways and not try to help things along with her own ways. So she stopped and asked Unique, "You want to go peek in on the girls before you leave?"

Unique thought for a minute. "Yeah, that would be nice. I'd like that. I just didn't want to wake them."

"If they didn't wake up from all that doorbell ringing, they surely aren't going to wake up just from you looking at them."

"Oh yeah, sorry about ringing your bell all loud that early in the morning. It's just that I needed to come over here and say what I had to say before I lost my courage."

"Yeah, I know," Lorain said as she led Unique to Victoria and Heaven's nursery. Lorain slowly opened the door and stepped aside in order to allow Unique to enter the room.

"They are sleeping like logs," Unique whispered. "They must have had a long night."

"They did. They were having so much fun up playing with each other last night that I gave them an extra hour. They're worn out."

Just then, one of the twins squirmed and began making a sucking motion with her lips. Both women giggled.

"Okay, well, let me go before I wake them up. Besides, I have a catering gig and a consultation today," Unique said.

"You do have a busy day indeed," Lorain agreed. "But thanks for coming by, and Unique?"

"Yes?" Unique replied.

"Thank you." She nodded to the twins.

"No. Thank you."

Lorain smiled and allowed Unique to exit the nursery first. Then she closed the door behind them knowing that this time, the door was definitely nailed shut.

# Readers' Group
# Guide Questions

1. Do you feel Nicholas should have told Lorain about her grandsons through his prayer, or should he have told her some other way?

2. Lorain judged Unique by her own emotions and demeanor when she first saw Unique in jail. Do you feel juries have done the same to defendants in the past?

3. Have you ever stepped out of your holiness and had someone say to you, "And you call yourself a Christian?" How did that make you feel?

4. Unique had focused so much on the death of her sons that she never even thought to ask about the twins, who were alive and well. How do you feel about that?

5. Unique led Kiki to Christ. It was alluded to that Kiki lived a homosexual life. Do you feel homosexuals can be saved Christians?

6. Lorain wanted to hurry up and marry Nicholas because she didn't want Korica to use her being a single woman dating men against her in a fight to take the twins from her. Do you feel Lorain was wrong for this, or do you feel that since she and Nicholas had plans to marry anyway, it didn't matter?

7. How do you feel about Lorain purposely keeping Unique away from Victoria and Heaven?

8. At Unique's mixer event, do you think Lorain might have spilled the punch on the baby on purpose just so Eleanor would have to take the twins home?

9. Do you think Nicholas should be angry at what Korica told him at Unique's mixer event? Do you think he should ultimately confront Lorain about it?

10. Who do you feel is to blame for the deaths of the three boys? Why?

# About the Author

BLESSED selling author, E.N. Joy, is the writer behind the five-book series, "New Day Divas," coined the "Soap Opera In Print." Formerly writing secular works under the names Joylynn M. Jossel and JOY, this award-winning author has been sharing her literary expertise on conference panels in her hometown of Columbus, Ohio, as well as cities across the country.

After thirteen years of being a paralegal in the insurance industry, Joy finally divorced her career and married her mistress and her passion: writing. In 2000, Joy formed her own publishing company, End of the Rainbow Projects, where she published her own works until landing a book deal with a major publisher. Under End of the Rainbow, Joy has published *New York Times* and *Essence*® Magazine Bestselling authors in the "Sinners Series," which includes, *Even Sinners Have Souls*, *Even Sinners Have Souls Too* and *Even Sinners Still Have Souls*.

In 2004, Joy branched off into the business of literary consulting in which she provides one-on-one consultations and literary services such as ghost writing, editing, professional read-throughs, write-behinds, etc. . . . Her clients consist of first-time authors, *Essence* Magazine bestselling authors, *New York Times* bestselling authors, and entertainers.

Not forsaking her love of poetry in which she has published two works of poetry titled *Please Tell Me If The Grass Is Greener* and *World On My Shoulders*, Joy plans to turn her focus back to the genre one day. "But my spirit has moved in another direction," Joy says. Needless to say, she no longer pens street lit (in which two of her titles, *If I Ruled the World* and *Dollar Bill*, made the *Essence*® Magazine bestsellers list. *Dollar Bill* appeared in *Newsweek* and has also been translated into Japanese). She no longer pens erotica or adult contemporary fiction either, in which one of her titles earned her the Borders bestselling African American Romance Award at the Romance Writers of America National Conference. Instead, under the name E. N. Joy, she pens Christian fiction, and under the name N. Joy, she pens children's and young adult titles. Joy's children's story, *The Secret Olivia Told Me*, received the American Library Association

Coretta Scott King Honor. Book club rights have also been purchased by Scholastic Books, and the book is on tour at Scholastic Book Fairs in schools across the country. Elementary and middle school children have fallen in love with reading and creative writing as a result of the readings and workshops Joy performs in schools nationwide.

Currently, Joy is the executive editor for Urban Christian. When she's not adding her two cents to other authors' works, she's diligently working on her own. Joy's "New Day Divas" series took the literary world by storm, which incited her to continue some of the characters' stories by writing the "Still Divas" series. Joy has always been certain that her Divas project was the one that was going to afford her with the title of *New York Times* Bestselling Author. But she's always been satisfied with the title of BLESSED selling author.

# Be Who You Want Your Kids To Be

June 1 of every year is being declared as "Be Who You Want Your Kids To Be Day." Parents and guardians around the world, please commit to being just that by filling out the commitment form below and signing it. Let's celebrate around the world the positive changes we want to see in our kids by starting with ourselves. Let's be our own kid's role model.

*Today, I, as a parent/guardian, commit to doing, saying, typing, texting, wearing, listening to, watching, and thinking only things I would want my kids to. I will not do, say, type, text, wear, listen to (this includes music, gossip, rumors, etc. . . .), watch, or think things that I would not want my kids to. Today, I am going to be who I want my kids to be. Today, my kids will see me love, smile, read, help a complete stranger, and turn the other cheek. Today, my kids will see me be who I want them to be.*

Name _____

Date _____